THE DEATH CLOCK

THE DEATH CLOCK

William B. Keller

To order additional copies of this book, contact:
Xlibris Corporation
1-888-795-4274
www.Xlibris.com
Orders@Xlibris.com
65986

THE DEATH CLOCK

William B. Keller

To order additional copies of this book, contact:
Xlibris Corporation
1-888-795-4274
www.Xlibris.com
Orders@Xlibris.com
65986

This book is dedicated to Jill, Will, and Abby.

ONE

Lois Henderson was a Midwest farmer's daughter, raised on two hundred acres of prime crop growing land near Kenton, Ohio. She was taught to expect the simple existence of hard work and Sunday worship with a good husband and six kids. Lois blindly accepted her future until Leroy Wilcox took her to the drive in movies on her sixteenth birthday. Leroy was a senior and first string fullback on the football team. When she drove him half out of his mind with passion during the first twenty minutes of Easy Rider she knew that Lois Henderson could do better than a farmer and six kids.

Ohio State University opened a door to the world she had only dreamed about since her father wasn't around to check the time when she got home and her mother wasn't dragging her off to church twice a week. Her freshman year found her in bed with every decent looking guy within sight, but the wildness finally wore off and she became more selective.

The study of the inside of the human body did not interest her nearly as much as the outside. Lois registered for the course in anti-aging because rumor had it that no one got below a C. One look at Brad Richardson, the professor of the course, made Lois an instant fan of research gerontologists. She read several books on the subject before making her move. Something urged her to go very slowly with this one, and for some reason she wanted him more than any man she had ever seen.

Indian Summer cooperated with a warm day in October. Lois wore skintight slacks with a light blue cotton shirt pulled tightly over her large breasts. The warm day eliminated the need for a jacket, which would have hidden some of her splendor as she waited on the top step of the biology building. She had studied his daily routine and knew he would soon be emerging from the building at the end of a class. He had tried to avoid staring at her earlier during his lecture on stress and aging, and Lois had noted with pleasure that she was distracting his concentration. She stood with her hands clasped behind her back.

"Excuse me Dr. Richardson," she called out as he hurried out the door. "My name is Lois Henderson, I'm in your gerontology class this fall."

He paused with an easy smile and quickly extended his hand, obviously struggling to keep his eyes from moving below her neck. "Yes, Miss Henderson.

I recognize you from the class." He was quickly losing the battle as his eyes kept lowering. "It is my pleasure to meet you."

"May I walk with you and ask some questions?"

He put his hand lightly on her back and guided them off the top step. "Surely, I'll answer anything I can."

"How long have you been into aging research?" Lois mentally kicked herself. She sounded like an afternoon talk show host. Everything she said must be just right to land this one.

"Nine years." They had reached the last step and Brad automatically turned toward the lab. His pace was exactly two miles per hour, perfect for releasing any tension created while instructing the class. "How long have you had an interest Miss Henderson?"

"Just since I started your class," she said truthfully. "And please, call me Lois."

He glanced at her as he paused to pick up a discarded candy wrapper to throw into a trash can and resumed his stroll. "I'm Brad."

Lois beamed her best farmer's daughter innocent grin. "Your study is based on the pituitary gland isn't it?"

"That's right. The pituitary controls the endocrine system. Something goes completely wrong at about twenty-five years of age and a major malfunction begins. I believe the pituitary produces age causing substances and the endocrine system dutifully regulates the body functions into old age. That's the whole thing, very simply of course."

"What about Death's Dominion?"

"My goodness, you have been studying. That theory is not scheduled in my lectures until the end of the quarter."

Lois shrugged. "Well, I guess we do all have an interest in this don't we. After all, four or five hundred years of quality life would sure beat eighty."

"Yes it would" he answered with a smile. "By the way, as a sneak preview, I don't think the Death's Dominion theory holds too much promise." Brad stopped and gestured to a small building almost hidden behind the main campus bookstore. "Here's my lab." He hesitated briefly and then quickly said, "Come on inside and we'll talk more about it. If you have the time," he added.

"I'd love to Dr. Ri . . . , I mean Brad." She knew he was hooked; all she had to do was be careful. She gathered her thoughts as he led the way down the narrow sidewalk. This would not be the time to say something stupid and break his mood. He was obviously enjoying talking to someone interested in his study.

"Death's Dominion just doesn't make sense," he said as he shook a key ring in an attempt to dislodge an overcrowded key from the tangled clump in his hand. "Ah, here it is." The door stuck slightly, forcing Brad to push against it with an open palm before it gave way reluctantly and permitted them to enter. "Come in. My office is in the back. Go make yourself at home and I'll get us some herb tea."

Lois walked into a hospital white laboratory complete with every piece of modern equipment imaginable. She moved past the small kitchen where Brad was heating water for their tea, walking through an opening that led her into a room lined with heavy steel cages. In the back of the lab was a small area that she recognized as an operating room. Surgical equipment sat quietly waiting to be brought to life by skilled hands.

She moved around the room, looking into the cases. Most contained various members of the rodent family while others contained dogs, cats and monkeys. Six cages were labeled 'testing group' and numbered with a red pencil. They contained a dog, two cats, two mice and a small mass of blood that might once have been a rat. Lois wondered what could have gotten into that cage and mangled the little creature.

"I see you're admiring my pets." She jumped slightly at being discovered. Brad was walking toward her with a delightful smelling mug of tea. "Here we are. Ginseng and cinnamon."

"What was this?" she asked, casually pointing toward the cage. "Something sure got to it."

Brad sat the cups down and frowned past the wires. He moved to the operating room, pulled on a pair of surgical gloves, and carried a small stainless steel tray over to the cage. He opened it and gently removed the remains of the animal. "You'll have to excuse me," he mumbled, already lost in the work at hand. "I have to study this immediately."

She watched him move into programmed action, completely oblivious to her presence. He turned on the surgical lamps and moved a large magnifying lens into position. He hunched over the animal and deftly began to dissect it.

Lois occupied herself by cleaning the lab while Brad worked. He spent nearly an hour in total commitment to the destroyed animal. She glanced at him occasionally and realized that he had no idea that she was still there. She had cleaned the cages and was refilling the last water dish when he finished his work.

He stretched his neck and grimaced in pain as the discarded surgical gloves fell into a plastic lined trash can. "Oh, I'm so sorry. You didn't have to wait for me. My research tends to occupy my mind to the point of rudeness."

She shrugged. "No problem. I kept busy while I waited."

"I can see that you did." There was genuine appreciation in the tone of his voice. "This is the part of the work I can do without, the cleanup."

Lois felt her heart pounding. This was the opportunity she had been hoping for. His answer to her next question would make or break her chances of someday winning Dr. Brad Richardson. "Why don't you quit doing the chores and concentrate more time on your research?"

He turned toward her with a slight frown, rubbing the back of his neck. "I'm not sure what you mean, Lois."

"Why not make me your assistant. I'll do the cleaning and feeding, type your notes, answer the phone and anything else that needs done." When he hesitated she added, "I don't have a hunchback like the legendary Igor but I can fake a limp if that would help."

Brad smiled wearily. "I do have an assistant in my budget but I never took the time to look and no one has ever asked."

"Someone's asking now."

"Yes, so you are. I'll tell you what," he exclaimed, "if you can rub the pain out of my neck I get every time I'm done bending over that operating table you've got the job."

Her fingers ached with fatigue but the effort was worth it as twenty minutes later Lois had the job.

She recognized Brad as a very special and different person. He was a medical doctor so his intelligence could hardly be questioned, but he was a man possessed with the desire to stay young. Restaurants were not permitted in his life as he claimed there was no way of knowing what was put into the food. Additives or preservatives of any kind were poison. Temperatures in rooms had to be precise, even the speed he walked was calculated to decrease the ravages of age.

Her first month was taken up by studying hard to stay in school and learning his every move. Lois knew that her plan would be totally in vain if part of Brad's regimen included abstaining from sex, but she considered the risk worth the value of the prize.

Near the end of their second month of working together she discovered something she would not have believed possible. Brad had not only never attempted to get her into bed but he didn't even flirt with her. Lois discovered a second unbelievable fact; she had fallen in love with him. The girl that swore no man would tie her into a house full of children had fallen for a middle aged man who feared death and didn't even seem attracted to her.

She became so frustrated with her feelings that she decided to play her trump card and either win or lose the game. The opportunity came during one quiet afternoon. All of the work seemed to be caught up, a very rare occurrence, and they were sitting in the small kitchen eating yogurt.

"Have you ever loved anyone?" she asked, her heart pounding in nervousness.

He raised one eyebrow with a puzzled look. "Forgive me for being so dense but I presume you mean love like other than my parents."

Lois blushed and studied the contents of her dish. "Yes, I mean a woman, a lover or a wife."

"Years ago I was married." He appeared to be ready to speak again but stopped and began eating.

"Where is she now?"

"She died."

This was not going well at all. She had made him uncomfortable at a time when his mood should be relaxed, but Lois plunged ahead. "Does your research permit making love?"

He relaxed a little bit and almost smiled. "Why live to be four hundred if you don't enjoy it. What the devil are you driving at Lois?"

She glanced up shyly, wondering why she felt like this. Usually she could just be blunt and tell a guy she wanted to go to bed with him. "Why haven't you ever made a pass at me?" she blurted.

His other eyebrow went up, registering considerable shock in his face. "Because you're less than half my age and, well, ... oh boy," he said, rubbing his face with both hands.

"I'm sorry. I shouldn't have said anything."

"Don't be sorry." He leaned forward and grasped one of her hands. "I'm very flattered Lois. You're an incredibly beautiful woman."

"All right then." She lifted her head and caught his eyes, the old confidence returning. "I want you to know that I want to make love to you Brad. Please don't make me wait forever."

That was enough for now. She squeezed his hand and with a smile got up and took their dishes to the sink.

She mentioned their conversation several times during the next few months but he kept avoiding the issue. Lois had reached the point of total frustration and considered leaving school and going home in an attempt to forget him, and with this thought in mind she decided to try one last time.

"Brad, I'll be twenty one years old tomorrow. Either I pack a bag and move in with you tonight or I pack the bag and leave Ohio. Which will it be?" She hoped he wouldn't notice that her lips were trembling.

He did not hesitate for an instant. "I have an extra key to my house in the cabinet in the next room. I'll get it for you."

TWO

Soft music drifted from the clock radio into the bedroom. Room darkening shades kept the early morning sunlight outside, with just a small amount of gold brushing past the edges of the window where the shade wasn't fitted quite right.

Most of the items in the large room were very old, and a trained eye would have recognized the bedroom suite and roll top desk to be priceless antiques. The thick carpeting seemed to defy its ancient roommates by being the only new decoration.

Brad cautiously lifted his left eyelid in his usual morning ritual. He surveyed his surroundings without moving his head and then opened the right eye to permit a full view. He felt pleased that the music level had been set perfectly to awaken without causing an ear piercing scream. He also noted that the blinds were permitting precisely one half inch of light on each side to enter the room, exactly as he had installed them. Room temperature was exactly seventy-eight degrees, the temperature that caused, if his research was correct, the least amount of deterioration.

His fifty two year old body was solid as a result of rigorous exercise which included light weight training and stationary running on a treadmill. Before moving from the bed, Brad flexed each body part slowly and carefully, concentrating on the blood flowing to each fiber of his body. The entire procedure took exactly fourteen minutes. He then rolled quickly to the floor and blasted through sixty pushups in about as many seconds. Without pause he rolled onto his back and did sixty sit ups.

Jumping lightly to his feet, he paused to stare at the woman lying in the bed. Her long blonde hair was spread out on the pillow so perfectly it appeared to be staged for a picture. The soft gray eyes were hidden behind closed lids, giving Brad the opportunity to concentrate on her full lips and the overall beauty of her face. Brad idly wondered when time would claim her beauty and demand a breakdown of the muscle. By forty five she would need a face lift, but for now she was absolutely magnificent.

Brad had put her off for quite some time, fearing that a physical relationship could taint their professional interaction, but she finally wore down his resistance. After last night he found little trouble in convincing himself that sex with a younger woman could be used as part of his research. Perhaps the aging process could be further retarded by this close physical contact.

Brad reluctantly pulled his eyes from Lois' face and moved toward the shower. Even in the bathroom his research was put to practical use. Perfumed deodorant soaps could dry and age skin, thus only Ivory was found in the bath. Creams and lotions created from natural ingredients kept his skin oiled and supple. His only concessions were deodorant to prevent being offensive and shaving because he personally detested facial hair.

Every aspect of Brad Richardson's life was geared toward extending not only his existence on this earth but making it healthful and enjoyable. A major federal grant, private contributions, and a generous budget from Ohio State University where he served as a researcher concerning the aging process. He felt sure a breakthrough was close, if only the federal people would permit him to use human subjects without all of the red tape. Why should some wasted wretch in a nursing home care if some test killed him. Death was reaching out anyhow, most of them were in such pain that death would be a welcome release. Brad was convinced he could not only halt but reverse the ravages of age. Federal regulations would slow his progress but the time would come.

These thoughts were flashing through his mind as he emerged from the dressing room knotting his necktie. Lois still slept peacefully in the same position, completely oblivious to the noise Brad made while preparing for work. She told him the night before to reset the alarm when he left because she slept like the dead. Music would not work; the abrasive screech of the alarm would be needed. He marveled at the ability to shut out the world and idly wondered if that capacity would increase the length of youth. Brad kissed her on the cheek and quietly moved through the house toward the front door.

He walked to work each morning, the three story campus area house he purchased four years ago being exactly one mile from his office door. Rush hour traffic jammed High Street as he turned the corner and moved faster than the automobiles. His only class of the day was over before ten, leaving the bulk of his time for research, his only reason for existence. Students saw his class as an easy three credits, which was entirely Brad's fault. He taught the course only to qualify for the government grant and felt that to give less than an average grade to a student would be unfair because if he didn't care why should the student. Word spread quickly that anyone who showed up for the lectures got no less than a "C", consequently the course was filled every quarter. Occasionally someone would show genuine interest, which was how he met Lois.

His usual preoccupation caused him to walk past the sciences building, the delay nearly making him late for his class. Sixty totally bored young people sat through his lecture to receive their passing grade, not realizing that he had no idea who was there. He took no role and made no attempt to memorize faces.

He simply graded tests, giving the higher grades to the students that wrote the most sensible answers. The fraternities and sororities had a field day as Brad never wasted his time changing test questions or lectures, so every Greek house on campus had all of his exams on file. Brad knew it, but he just didn't care.

The hour crawled by with nearly physical agony. Brad considered the class fairly successful as only five people fell asleep.

THREE

Lois was feeding the mice as he entered the lab, the muscles in her shapely calves straining slightly as she bent over the cage. Brad felt his heart sink slightly at the sight of her, and he dreaded this moment in a bittersweet way. He was happy to have discovered Lois as a lover but still feared their new relationship would spoil their ability to work together in the lab.

"Good morning Brad," she said with a slight smile. "All the mice are well but we lost a dog during the night."

"Which one," he asked as relief flooded through him. Of course nothing would change in the lab. She could forget the night and be a professional during the day, or at least he desperately wanted that to be true.

"Molly," she answered, moving toward the dog cages. "Looks like the same problem."

"Oh no," Brad whispered as they reached the cage. Inside laid a decidedly dead toy collie. The paper in the bottom of the cage was covered with blood that still dripped from the dog's ears, mouth, anus and genitals. The eyes had virtually exploded from their sockets and hung to the head gruesomely by thin cords of muscle. The cage was dented in several places where the frenzied animal had attempted to escape when the pain struck. The dog looked even more grotesque from the unnatural bulging of muscle that seemed universal in Brad's studies. The physical development increased at an unbelievable pace until the animal increased its strength tenfold. Early in his research a dog broke from the cage and nearly destroyed the lab before its insides ruptured and sprayed blood for thirty feet. Stronger cages were promptly installed.

"I'll clean it up," Brad said.

"No, never mind. You start the dissection." She winked at him and unlocked the cage. "This doesn't bother me."

He really believed it didn't. She was really a very good assistant, never a complaint when nasty jobs had to be done. Brad thought that the animals' death might be harder on her, but Lois seemed to have no trouble dealing with it. She deftly pulled the animal through the small door of its prison and promptly deposited it on the examination table. She seemed not to notice the blood on her laboratory coat, and soon calmly began to remove the gore from the cage bottom. Brad turned his attention to his own duties, quickly dissecting the dog for immediate and future study.

What seemed like ten minutes became actually an hour. Lois brought his attention back to his overall surroundings with a gentle touch on the shoulder. "Is it the same as the others?" she asked.

Brad's shoulders straightened painfully as he moved away from the dissected animal and removed his surgical gloves. "Yes, I'm afraid so. Incredible muscle development, at least fifty percent reduction in age, then suddenly the entire endocrine system goes wild. This dog reproduced blood so fast his body literally exploded from the pressure."

"Just like the monkeys and mice."

"Yes. Just like." He felt the first twinge of a headache and knew he was letting the pressure get to him again. Stress was a killer and Brad Richardson was not at all ready for death.

FOUR

Darkness had covered the city with a blanket that was comforting for some and fearful to others. Dishonesty can be enhanced by the lack of light as Thomas Maywood of Maywood Nursing Home could testify. He was helping to unload an unmarked truck in the alley behind the kitchen. His ledger books showed the shipment to be prime beef costing the government one dollar fifty cents per pound and Thomas Maywood Two dollars ninety cents a pound, a neat little subsidy that helped promote better food for our aging and ailing senior citizens who are confined to a nursing home. The half rancid horse meat being delivered actually cost one dollar per pound, saving Thomas not only his share of the expense but netting him money on each order.

"Don't these old geezers ever say nothing about the taste of this slop?" questioned the driver of the truck. "Stuff's so rotten already the dog food plant won't take it."

Thomas smiled despite the unaccustomed sweat that was dampening his lightly starched white shirt. "Most of them are already as dead as this meat," he scoffed. "This whole place smells like twenty years worth of puke." His smile quickly disappeared as he realized the old blue collar mannerisms had emerged. Thomas Maywood liked to think he had risen above his old days of bilking elderly people with his traveling home improvement service. Sure he changed angles when the police in six states were looking for him, but he felt that the nursing home business made him respectable. In reality Thomas Maywood was a punk.

"Well, all I know is this pays better than the fertilizer plant," the driver was saying. "Besides, I can rake a nickel a pound off the top from the boss. I guess we all end up happy, huh?" He chuckled. "Ain't it great? The govn'ment feels good cause they's helpin' folks. My boss feels good 'cause he gets better money from you for rotten meat than at the fertilizer plant. I'm happy 'cause I get my pay and a nickel a pound on the sly. You're happy cause you're gettin' cheap meat. The old geezers don't care 'cause they're half dead anyhow. Ain't life great?" The truck driver flashed a yellow grin and spat a brown a stream of tobacco juice into the darkness.

Thomas had regained his white collar composure and only smiled slightly. The truck was soon unloaded, the driver paid, and darkness had again triumphed over honesty. Thomas washed his hands and face and returned to his ledgers. Hours were spent not only hiding the discrepancies but also looking for new ways to increase unreported income while reducing expenses. The ledgers had no way of telling him that a new source of income would soon be within his grasp.

FIVE

Libraries were always a favorite place for Lois. The quiet helped her to enjoy the mix of odors from new ink and molding pages. The wealth of knowledge was almost overwhelming. She had once considered reading every book on the shelves at the small library back home but even that tiny building held too much to conquer.

She wasted thirty minutes enjoying her senses, as was her custom, before she began the task at hand. She held a list of nursing homes copied earlier from the yellow pages of the phone directory. Brad had instructed her to call each one and ask for the name of the director. Only one asked why she wanted to know, and Lois followed instructions to the letter and responded that she was interested in placing her mother.

Her visit to the library was to check the city directory and criss cross to get home addresses and telephone numbers of the nursing home directors. Brad was very secretive concerning her purpose of obtaining the information so she did not push for an explanation. Armed with the necessary data she reluctantly left the library and returned to the lab. She had just finished typing the information in her usual ultra efficient way when Brad came in with three new monkeys.

He quickly placed them in cages that were recently occupied by animals that had exploded from within after hours of maddened frenzy. Every alteration in his formula ended in this gruesome result. "Did you get the information?" he asked without as much as a greeting.

"And good afternoon to you, Dr. Richardson," she snapped. She was angry at being left out of this portion of his research and knew she was being too touchy, but didn't at this point exactly care.

"I'm sorry Lois," he soothed. "You know how I get sometimes." He patted her hand affectionately. "If I'm not careful I get consumed with my work."

She melted slightly and replied, "I know how important it is to you and I don't really object to your dedication. What upsets me is you're shutting me out." She paused to force back the tears. "My problem is I love you more than you love me." The tears began to tumble down her cheeks despite her fighting them back.

Brad looked at her with astonishment. "I guess I hadn't realized it but I don't show how much I love you too." He stepped forward and took her into his arms.

"I don't know what I would have done if you hadn't said that," she said, her voice muffled into the fabric of his shirt. "I've never felt like life was a thing to fear before but suddenly I don't know what to do, all I can think about is not having you."

He rocked her gently back and fourth, his right hand gently patting her back. "How could you think an old fossil like me would be foolish enough to give you up. For goodness sakes I'm the one that should be frightened."

"Don't be," she said, lifting her head up and looking into his eyes.

"That's a deal," he said and kissed her gently. "From now on we're a team."

"A team," she echoed. "Through thick or thin."

SIX

Robin Slane was the perfect example of a preppie. He nearly always wore a suit to class with an occasional compromise during August. The suit coat could be left behind but the necktie remained knotted securely in place.

Robin lived at home with his parents in a fashionable suburb of Columbus. He was never a football or basketball star as his father had hoped; the only teams he captained were debate and chess. Physical exertion was not a desirable activity and his pipe stem arms and sunken chest stood out like beacons to this philosophy.

Mrs. Slane thought her boy was absolutely marvelous. She protected him from the world at every opportunity, which created many arguments in the elder Slane's bedroom. Even at seven years of age Robin understood his father's late night screaming at his mother. He had learned to read by five and used a dictionary to look up words like 'fag' and 'queer', which helped him to understand what his father thought of him. After hearing the constant fighting for most of his life, at the tender age of fifteen Robin Slane decided to find out if his father's worst fears were correct. They were.

He didn't get caught until the night of his junior prom. His parents went to the country club and were not due home until after midnight. Mrs. Slane got a migraine at eight thirty so they were home by nine, but she quickly forgot the headache when she walked into the family room and discovered Robin and Ernie Jacobs making passionate love in front of the fireplace.

Mr. Slane threatened to kill them both as his wife screamed hysterically between throwing up on their genuine bearskin rug. Ernie grabbed his pants and ran in terror when Mr. Slane produced a pistol from the desk in his study.

No one was killed and the rug was cleaned, but plans to send Robin to Harvard were scrapped. He would go to Ohio State and live at home where he could be watched. Psychiatric care was instituted at once and the problem was never mentioned at home again.

These events eventually brought Robin to the door of Dr. Richardson's lab. Because he was such a perfectionist with his studies Robin worked each course he enrolled in like his life depended on it. He wanted to maintain his perfect 4.0 grade average and wasn't about to mess that up on this course. Robin spoke to his teachers during the term to determine what they were looking for and asked to be notified if his average dropped below an A.

Experience taught him that the best approach was to drop in with no appointment. The conversation was kept shorter and the professor had less time to prepare a sermon. He turned the doorknob and felt the latch release. The door stuck so he pushed with almost all the might his spindly arms could produce and virtually fell into the room. Lois often forgot to lock the door as farm families never found the need to do, and of course old habits die hard.

Robin pushed the door firmly closed and walked toward the cages. He glanced into the kitchen as he passed and stepped into the faint light of the cage room. The sun was casting eerie shadows through the thick wire of the cages. No dust floated in the air as the electronic air cleaner filtered to near purity. He quickly scanned the room in a vain attempt to find the doctor.

Robin suddenly felt the tiny hairs on his back raise with an unexpected jolt of fear. Something was seriously wrong in this room. He knew that was foolish but his legs wanted to run. He slowly turned on the balls of his feet to face the doorway to freedom and . . . . safety?

The animal that faced him might at one time have been a chimpanzee or a large monkey of some kind, although now it was distorted with muscle bulk unlike anything Robin had ever seen. Flecks of blood mixed with the saliva dripping from the corners of its mouth and the eyes were almost human as they glared at Robin with obvious hatred. Each of the huge arms ended with hands that clutched a large dog whose spine had been broken.

Robin gasped with terror and began backing toward the far end of the room toward Brad's open office door. The creature reacted with instant rage and deftly tore the dogs into pieces, shaking its arms and showering the large room with blood and flesh. It bounded toward Robin before the boy's thin legs could move him closer to the door.

The dogs were flung aside as the creature grasped Robin's arms near the shoulders. They instantly separated and the collarbones broke. Pain had barely caught up with this movement when the creature pulled both arms from Robin's body. He fell to his knees with a voiceless scream and died the next moment when the creature kicked its foot through his upper body like stomping a paper cup. It then crushed Robin's skull before rupturing internally itself, exploding across the room.

Brad returned minutes after the carnage to a sight that even a doctor's stomach wasn't meant to take. Blood and flesh virtually covered the cage room. His eyes swept the cages quickly to determine which animals had escaped. Three cages were destroyed, a dog with no name, a dog named Lucky, and Patsy the chimpanzee. He'd had great hopes that Patsy would be able to withstand the treatments, being the closest animal to human.

The blood left the floor more sticky than slippery as Brad moved toward the chimp, fighting the churning in his stomach each time his crepe soled shoes sucked free. He idly wondered how the chimp's arms became detached when he froze with a small scream escaping through clenched teeth. The corpse with no arms was human.

He would later feel shame that his immediate horror was not for the life that was lost but for the future of his research. Funding instantly vanished when human life was lost. With no hesitation Brad rushed to his operating table and drew on a pair of surgical gloves. He took a roll of heavy plastic from a storage cabinet and cut a large piece which was laid across the table. He dragged the body that was smashed beyond recognition, placing it and the arms on the plastic. Having rolled it up Brad turned his attention to the room. He pulled the fire hose from its glass case and removed a drain plug from the floor. Nearly an hour later the worst was cleaned up and the lab looked wet but normal.

He dialed his home and Lois answered after one ring. "Dr. Richardson's residence, may I help you?"

How lovely her voice sounded. How absolutely absurd to think of such a thing at a time like this. "Hi hon."

"Oh, Brad. You're late and my meatloaf is beginning to look like a brick."

"Sorry, but I dropped into the lab and found Patsy."

Her tone of voice expressed her sorrow. "How awful. Is she dead?"

"Yes, quite a mess I'm afraid. I'm going to clean the place up and do the dissection before I come home. It'll be late."

"Why don't I come down with a sandwich? You know the mess bothers you and you can get on with it while I clean up."

"No, I'll do it." He hoped he hadn't seemed too anxious. "You get some rest and I'll take care of everything. I kind of need some time to sort through all of this. You know I had high hopes for Patsy."

"Yes I do and I'm sorry. Okay Brad, I've got a history exam to study for anyway. Remember I'm still a student."

"I know," he laughed, trying to act normal and knowing he was making a mess of it. With luck she would think he was just upset about the chimp.

"Well, I'll see you tonight."

"Yes. Maybe around twelve."

"Okay. Call if you need me." She hesitated. "Brad, are you sure I can't help?"

"Positive. Go study history and I'll see you later." He replaced the phone before she could protest further. Darkness was about an hour away, and then part two of his plan could begin.

He busied himself by cleaning the cages and replacing the food soaked by the fire hose, but the plastic encased body kept pulling his attention like a magnet. He thought he saw the form move several times and fought down the hysteria attempting to overcome him.

Finally the sky darkened, providing the security Brad needed. He left the laboratory and walked to a large staff parking lot. His car was seldom moved as he walked nearly everywhere, and besides the well lighted lot provided better security than the alley behind his home.

The late model Ford came quickly to life despite the weeks of inactivity. His plastic parking pass slid neatly into the slot, a magnetic strip activating the wooded gate. He reached the lab in moments, parking near the sidewalk but outside the direct glare of the street light. Brad jumped from the car and quietly pushed the door closed to snuff out the courtesy lights. He walked quickly past the lighted display window of the bookstore and was soon in the shadows of the laboratory entrance.

The body was still in the position he had left it so he set aside his earlier fears that it kept moving. He pulled it from the table and quaked inwardly when the plastic crackled like gunshots. The burden was incredibly light as he placed it on his right shoulder and moved again into the darkness. The bookstore display case was his greatest concern as he was forced to expose himself to its light but fortunately no one seemed to be in the area.

Moments later his trunk lid banged shut and he entered the car with relief, his hands shaking so badly he had trouble finding the ignition with the key. He pulled away from the curb and drove toward High Street. A horn honked behind him and Brad looked into his rear view mirror. His heart nearly stopped as he saw a police car with flashers on following closely behind. He forced down the panic and pulled to the curb. A uniformed city policeman soon appeared at his window.

"May I see your driver's license please, sir." More a command than a request.

Brad fought to control the tremor in his voice. "What did I do wrong officer. I'm sure I wasn't speeding."

The officer took Brad's license and briskly pushed it under the clamp in the clipboard. "Would you get out of the car sir. I'd like to show you something." Brad reluctantly climbed out and followed him to the rear of the car. "You have a tail light out. Probably just a bulb but I'll have to write you a warning."

Brad nearly laughed with relief as he waited for the paperwork to be finished. He was soon on his way and considering himself quite lucky.

A large apartment complex was Brad's destination. He eased the Ford next to a large dumpster and after looking about to insure that no one was outside, fitted the proper key into the trunk. He lifted the body from the car and unrolled the plastic into the dumpster, body parts softly landing in the trash. Brad folded the bloody plastic into a small package, which he placed in a garbage bag and secured with a metal twist tie. The garbage bag he tossed into the passengers seat and then drove back to the school parking lot. His plastic card admitted him into the reserved area and soon he was walking toward home.

The bloody plastic hid inside the garbage bag which was tucked under his arm. A large can sporting the message Keep Your City Clean became the new home for the garbage bag. Brad reached his door at exactly twelve o'clock. He realized his clothes were drenched with sweat despite the chill air. Lois was reading in bed as he entered the bedroom, her classic beauty touching his heart as it often did.

"Did you get everything taken care of?"

"Yes. Same old problem." He was in the bathroom striping for a shower. "Did you get any studying done?"

"I'll ace that test for sure." She raised her voice to be heard over the noise of the shower. "I've got something for you."

"Oh, what is it?"

"Just come out and I'll show you," she teased.

Moments later Brad came into the room toweling his hair dry. "What is it you have . . . ." His voice trailed off as he walked toward the bed.

She was holding a large bowl of dried fruit pieces. "I know these are your favorite and with no dinner I thought we'd have a snack."

Brad's stomach clenched in objection to the thought of food after the evening's gruesome work; unfortunately he had to act as normal as possible. "How thoughtful," he said with a smile and walked wearily to the bed.

SEVEN

The police radio scratched on with noise that could only be deciphered by a veteran officer. Lieutenant Charles 'Sandy' Gibbs picked up each word effortlessly as he moved his unmarked police car onto Livingston Avenue. Sandy was one year away from thirty years with the force, twenty two of them in homicide. His wife had wanted him to retire after twenty five years but he had resisted. Everyone went at twenty, most quit by twenty five, but thirty years as a policeman was a real accomplishment. Martha wanted to live in Florida each winter to escape the ice and snow covered roads but Sandy had to have it his way. This February ninth would make it exactly one year since her accident. 'Watch for ice on bridge' the sign said. She had watched but still lost control of the car and fell one hundred feet to her death. If he had retired they would have been in Florida during that ice storm.

"Lieutenant Gibbs, call control," the radio rasped.

He thumbed the mike control. "Gibbs, roger." A twist of the dial brought a new frequency on the radio. "Gibbs to control." Static answered his call. "Gibbs to control. Are you there?"

"Keep your shirt on Sandy." There was very little noise on this frequency.

"What can I do for you Cap?" Sandy was speaking to Captain Dale Salinski, perhaps the toughest cop in the Midwest. No one told Polish jokes around Captain 'Ski' as he liked to be called. Rumor had it that a rookie cop was once overheard by Cap telling a Polish joke. Ski took the kid into his office and he disappeared. Some claim Ski killed him, but Sandy knew the story wasn't true because he started the tale twelve years ago. In return for making him a legend Sandy was permitted to call him Cap.

"How close are you to East Main?"

"I'm on Livingston now around the two thousand block."

"Good." Sandy could hear him spiting tobacco slivers from the ever present cigar. "There's an apartment building at 3140 East Main with a body in the dumpster. I've got them on hold over there until you see what's happening."

"I'll check it out." Sandy turned the dial back to normal frequency. Cap hated it when he did that. The conversation was always finished but Cap wanted to officially end it and Sandy always beat him to the punch.

Traffic was light until he was two blocks away from the murder scene. Cars suddenly jammed all four lanes, many of them abandoned by their drivers who wanted to get a cheap look at violent death. Sandy silently cursed the traffic control officers that had permitted this to happen. He pulled into a nearby parking lot and walked toward the apartment building. Barricades had been set up near the dumpster but the crowd was practically smashing through for a closer look. After fifteen minutes of pushing through the throng, Sandy was past the sawhorses and glaring at a very nervous sergeant.

"Call in twenty more officers," Sandy grated. "Get someone on a bull horn and move this crowd back. Tell them we'll hit them with tear gas if they don't move."

The sergeant eagerly went about his task and soon a certain semblance of order was restored. Sandy surveyed the entire area with dismay. There was trash everywhere. The curious had virtually emptied the dumpster, destroying any possible clues. He spied the nervous sergeant barking orders and waved him over. "How the devil did this happen? The civilians have torn this place apart."

"Yessir. This is the way we found it. It seems that some kid found the body and his parents called the press, waited an hour and then called us. The jerk said he wanted on the news. By the time we got here the place was crawling with people. We can only find one arm for Pete's sake."

"How do you know both arms were there?"

"Someone told us they saw a bunch of kids carry one off." The sergeant swallowed sourly. "Pretty sick huh?"

"Yea, sick. Check it out and see if you can find it. How did you let the traffic get so screwed up?"

The sergeant stared at the blacktop. So many people had just left their cars we couldn't get any cars through. We almost caused a riot when we moved them this far back."

"Incredible," Sandy murmured. "Look, don't worry about it. You did your best with what you had to work with."

"Thank you, sir." The sergeant was visibly relieved that someone was understanding of his problem.

The lab people were finishing their work and dozens of photographs were taken. Sandy took mental photographs, using his trained eye to look for tiny clues. He finally gave up in frustration because of the destruction of the murder scene. The body itself was amazing. Animals killed on the road sometimes look this bad after cars had run over them, but this was the worst human he had ever personally seen. A hole had been blasted through the center of the torso. The arms were torn off, with one still missing, and the head was crushed like an eggshell.

"Pretty messy huh?" Sandy looked up to see Dr. Joe Lucas, the county coroner. "I wouldn't be surprised if we find out some kind of machine did this. I'll check extra carefully for machine oil and sharp cuts."

Sandy shook his head. "I don't know Joe. Something tells me this one is going to be bad. Maybe some irate husband or something. Maybe it's just the condition of the scene, I don't know."

Dr. Lucas shrugged. "The only way we'll know for sure is for me to get to work. You finished with the body?"

"Yea, I guess so. Maybe I can get something out of his family. This thing sure wasn't for money; his wallet was intact with credit cards, ID, and fifty-three dollars cash. He's just a kid, turned nineteen last month."

"They get knocked off a lot younger than that, Sandy." He placed a gentle hand on his old friend's arm. "Why does this one have you so spooked?"

"I don't know, Joe. It's just this bad feeling I can't shake. Probably nothing."

"Well, I'll call in the lab report as soon as I get it. That will give you the general idea before you read all the fine print."

"Thanks Joe, I really appreciate that." Sandy watched as the crew gathered up the broken body and placed it in the ambulance. He waited until most of the crowd left before heading towards his car. Reporting deaths was distasteful business so he put it off as long as possible.

Sandy shook his head as he pulled into the Slane's drive. These people had the home he only dreamed about, but how much would it mean with their son dead? He had done this many times and never knew quite what to expect. Some people cried, some fainted, others just said thank you. The moment he met Carolyn Slane he knew he had an emotional woman.

She invited him into her home before he even had the opportunity to introduce himself. "Please come in. How may I help you?"

"Are you Mrs. Slane?"

"Yes I am."

He was so nervous that it transmitted to her, and Sandy saw her regret at having been so hasty to invite him in. "I'm a police officer." He quickly pulled his identification from his pocket and watched her face go from relief to worry again in one fluid motion. "Is your husband at home?"

"Yes but what is it? What did we do?"

"You did nothing wrong Mrs. Slane. Could you get your husband for me please? This would be much easier if I could talk to you together."

"It's Robin isn't it. He's been arrested." Her voice was trembling.

Sandy said gently, "Please. Your husband."

She moved nervously to the stairway and shouted up, "Charles, would you please come down to the library?"

"Just a moment," the muffled voice replied.

"Please follow me." She led the way to a large room that was a perfect stereotype for a man's study. Bookshelves covered three walls and were filled with perfectly lined books. Behind the desk were college diplomas and various civic awards hung with obvious pride. "Please, sit down."

"No, thank you. I'll stand."

Charles Slane came into the room and raised his eyebrows at the sight of his nervous wife. A powerful looking man, he turned his attention to Sandy as the only obvious cause of his wife's distress. "I'm Charles Slane." He did not walk over to Sandy and offer a welcoming hand. "How may I help you?"

"My name is Charles also, sir. Detective Lieutenant Charles Gibbs. I have come today to give you some news that is never easy and always hard."

"Oh, Robin." Carolyn Slane was starting to swoon already. Her hands moved to her mouth.

Charles Slane moved instantly to her side and circled her waist with his arm. "Easy dear, easy," he whispered.

Sandy felt some relief as he suspected she would be a fainter. "This is not easy for you to hear so I'll be as direct as possible. Your son has been killed."

Slane did not even seem to notice that he was holding the limp form of his wife. He had not moved an inch and stared blankly ahead with his wife draped over the back of his arm like a wet towel. "How was he killed?"

"Sir, your wife."

"Oh." Slane deposited his white faced wife on the leather sofa. "How did it happen?"

Cool and calm. Just as Sandy suspected he would be. "We don't know yet, however, there was definitely foul play."

"Foul play. You mean my son was murdered."

"Yes sir."

Carolyn Slane moaned and suddenly sat upright on the sofa. Moments later she began to cry. "May we continue this later Lieutenant?" her husband asked.

"Yes, I suppose we can. I'll have to ask some questions later on you know. You and your wife can be extremely helpful in giving us information that should help us to catch your son's murderer."

Mrs. Slane finally spoke. "What makes the difference? Robin's dead."

"The difference, Mrs. Slane, is that if we can catch who did this, hopefully I won't have to repeat this conversation to another family. I'll call tomorrow." He left the two grieving people and gratefully moved into the cool air outside. This one would be messy. He was sure of it.

—

EIGHT

Brad was fifteen minutes early for his meeting with P. Osgood Nash. Everyone came early out of plain fear of being late when the President of the Board of Trustees asked to see you. His signature determined where the money for research went and Brad had always been given a generous portion of the monies available. Brad was convinced that Nash feared death even more than himself. Despite his early arrival Brad was not invited into the office until precisely nine o'clock, the time his appointment was scheduled.

"Brad, Brad come in." Nash was a tremendously fat person who would probably die before he was sixty if his lifestyle didn't change. "I read your latest report and as usual I want you to explain it in Layman language. Sit down and relax."

Brad slid his lithe frame into the uncomfortable chair provided for guests. Nash let his bulk drop into a large desk chair that almost screamed in protest when the pressure smashed into its frame. Brad idly wondered how many times each day that chair was forced to accept such abuse, and how long it would survive.

"Thank you sir. Actually, very little has changed since we last talked. I truly feel that we're stuck until we can move on to human subjects. I'm convinced that the genetic makeup of animals makes it possible to achieve only temporary results. My serum works, but after a certain point the body becomes destructive. Human makeup is different enough that I would like to find out if the process would react differently."

"The problem is, who wants to be the first human subject," Nash said. How about trying it on yourself Brad?" The chair groaned as the huge body shifted forward for emphasis.

"If I died, a lot of research would go down the tubes." Brad smiled faintly. "Only a desperate person would try something like that."

"What if I told you we had a large gift that is meant to specifically be given to anyone who would submit to your tests."

"That of course would be nice, but the government isn't likely to agree. Besides, if someone dies his family would sue and ultimately the research would be banned." Brad's heart was pounding with fear. This was not what he wanted to hear. "Do you have any suggestions Mr. Nash?"

30

Nash leaned back again and the chair groaned in protest. "I think that's your problem Brad. I have available two hundred and fifty thousand dollars to anyone who would be willing to help us move forward by offering their body. The authorities should not be involved and lawsuits are not acceptable. Can you handle it?"

"I have already researched this area and can buy a lot for our money."

"I'll have the money transferred to your account."

"I think this will have to be a cash deal," Brad said. "We won't want receipts or any written record of the transaction."

Nash raised a hand. "I don't want to hear any more. How you handle this is your affair. Pick up the cash here at noon tomorrow." Nash heaved himself out of the chair, and Brad suppressed a smile at the thought of the relief the chair must have felt.

When Brad reached his office he went immediately to his files and pulled out the nursing home list Lois had prepared. The next portion of his investigation had to be done himself. No one could be trusted with what he would do, not even Lois.

He retrieved his car from its customary spot in the facility lot and drove downtown to the courthouse. Nearly six hours were spent in researching public record information. Despite the eye fatigue that he felt, he was excited by what he found. He returned his car and walked home, barely ten minutes later than usual.

"Is that you?" Lois called from the kitchen. She was taking the meatloaf from the oven, Brad's favorite meal.

"It sure is. Do I smell what I think I do?"

"Absolutely. The baked potatoes are ready too." She smiled brightly as he entered the room. "The best meal for the best man."

He smiled in return and kissed her deeply. "Speaking of best man, we ought to be thinking of using one."

"Why, Doctor." She forced her voice to not tremble. "Is this a proposal?"

'I guess it is."

"You know, when I first met you, my purpose was to use you for a year or two and then move on, and I'm just telling you the truth. That seems to be the way my life has been up to now."

"How do you still feel after six months?" he asked. Things have moved pretty fast."

"I told you before that I've fallen in love with you. That's why I had to tell you my original motive. I don't want any skeletons popping up. I should tell you too what my past was like."

31

"Hold it." Brad held both hands up to emphasize his point. "I'm not telling about my past so I don't want to hear yours. Look, why don't we see how both of us feel after another six months. If you still feel like making this thing permanent, we'll get a judge and do it. Is that a deal?"

"That's a deal. Say, I've got a swell idea."

"Good, let's hear it."

"Let's eat later. Right now I just want to hold you."

Brad took her hand and they walked toward the bedroom. "Nothing tastes better than a cold meat loaf sandwich," he said with a smile.

NINE

Maywood nursing facility was obviously one of the poorest maintained in the city. The lighting system was very inadequate and many of the safety features did not actually function. The hallways were cleaned weekly instead of daily and about half of the proper number of nurses were on duty. The staff doctor came in once per week and was an alcoholic. State inspectors were bought off for fifty dollars a month, much less than the cost to make improvements.

Brad was waiting in a dingy reception area. He stood as the chairs looked too dirty to sit on. Thomas Maywood almost slithered into the room, hunched forward and looking up at the taller man. Brad noted he looked like a nervous mole.

"Dr. Richardson?"

"Yes." He accepted the small, dry hand and almost grimaced at the dead fish response.

"How might we serve you?" A loved one perhaps that needs our services?"

"Actually Mr. Maywood, I feel that I can help you. May we talk in your office?"

"Of course. How rude of me." Maywood opened his office door with a flourish.

Brad waited until both men were seated before speaking again. "I have a proposal for you, Dr. Maywood." He pulled an envelope from his pocket and removed twenty fifty dollar bills. "I would like to give you the opportunity to earn this money tax free very easily. Are you interested?"

"Well Doctor, I'm not sure." Maywood licked his lips at the sight of the money. "This whole thing sounds kind of funny to me. I have to be concerned with my reputation you know."

"Look Mr. Maywood, don't make me get out your rap sheet." Brad's voice was cold. "You've been chased around this county enough, I can imagine how many cities would like to get hold of you."

"Then let's cut the crap" Maywood suddenly snapped. "What do you want?"

"I want to study certain of your residents. They can have no family and must be very old. That's all you need to know."

"Can any of this be detected by any other Doctor?"

"Yes. I would have to become their only physician."

"Too complicated. The money you're offering isn't worth it, plus Doc Clem comes in every week and might pick something up. He's a drunk but I can't take any chances."

"What are you paying him?"

"Too much. He probably kills half the people here."

"I'll be the staff doctor for half of what you're now paying. That not only eliminates the problem of anyone detecting anything, but your profits increase."

"Maywood narrowed his eyes and smiled with half of his mouth. "I'll pay you the same as Doc Clem but you'll give half back in cash. Then make that thousand dollars a one time payment of ten thousand and we've got a deal."

"I'll give you seven thousand."

"Ten. This is not an auction sale."

"Agreed." Brad stood to leave. "When do we begin?"

"Tomorrow. Bring the money in cash."

Maywood made no effort to get up so Brad left the office and made his own way to the exit. He shook so badly with excitement and nervousness that he was forced to wait for several minutes before he could drive.

He arrived at the lab to find Lois cleaning the blood from a cage. A mass of torn flesh was in a pan on the surgical table.

"Hi," she said in her typical bland reaction to the gore she was facing. Brad patted her rounded buttocks as he passed her. "Be careful Doctor. We'll lose our office professionalism," she gently chided.

"I was worried about that you know."

"I could sense it. What changed your mind?"

"I guess it isn't very important since I've fallen in love with you. In fact we seem to work together even better."

She stopped her work and stared at him as he prepared to work on the dead animal. "Thank you darling. That means a lot to me."

"You're a very special person you know." He released the moment by returning to his work.

"Brad, these animals are getting stronger. Did you see that cage? That was a spider monkey and it almost tore these bars apart. What would happen if one of these animals escaped?"

His forehead instantly beaded with sweat. "Why do you ask?" he said carefully.

"Oh, I was just wondering. If they have all that strength and as crazy as they go wouldn't they hurt someone if they got loose?"

"They won't. We'll get better cages, would that be okay?"

"Yea, that would make me feel better. Who would be blamed if someone got hurt?"

"No one." His shirt was now soaked and he felt real fear. "It would just be an accident."

Sandy was a very typical cop. He wouldn't leave anything sit too long. His car was parked outside the Slane home and he was patiently waiting for them to return from the funeral home. Police officers worked on several cases at once and time was critical, but he did not want to let this one go. Years of living the life of a policeman had given him certain instincts that could not be denied. This murder was not isolated. There would be more.

A late model Cadillac pulled into the drive. The garage door whispered open and the car disappeared inside. Sandy left his car and trudged up the long sidewalk as the garage door floated shut as if to keep away his intrusion. Charles Slane answered the door after several persistent rings of the bell and glared at Sandy with almost open hatred. Sandy was used to the reaction, after all he reminded them of the violent way their son died.

"Come in lieutenant."

"Thank you." He continued as he followed his reluctant host toward the library, "I have to get some information about your son. This can help to give us the answers that we need."

"I know. It's just that our son is in a closed casket because his body . . . ." He broke off his sentence as his wife opened the library door and walked into the room. She looked absolutely horrible with red swollen eyes and contrasting white complexion. Her legs wobbled as she walked.

"Good morning Mrs. Slane. I'm sorry to have bothered you but I truly need your help."

"Yes, of course." She waved a limp hand. "Charles and I talked about this last night. Whoever did this must be caught so this thing never happens again."

"Tell me about your son. Did he have a lot of friends?"

"Not that many," she replied. "Robin was very quiet. Most of his life was spent studying."

"He had good grades in school?"

"Excellent. He had perfect grades all through school. College was no exception."

"How about sports?"

"He wasn't very active," Mr. Slane volunteered. Our son wasn't exactly sickly, but he preferred chess to football."

"He also led the debate team and was president of the Latin Club," his mother proudly added. Her moment of joy quickly faded. "Now he's gone."

The telephone interrupted any further comment and Charles Slane picked up the study extension. "It's for you Lieutenant."

"Thank you. This is Gibbs."

"Sandy, this is Joe Lucas."

"Joe, could I call you when I get back to the office? I'm into something pretty important here."

"I don't think this can wait. We found dog and monkey blood all over this kid."

"What did you say? I couldn't have heard that right."

"You sure did. Hair too. Not only that but his skull was crushed by hands."

"Isn't that impossible?"

"It was until now. The marks on the head were definitely made by ten fingers. Even a gorilla wouldn't have had that kind of strength. Besides, a gorilla would have had bigger hands. Sandy, that kid's head was crushed like an egg."

"Boy, oh boy," Sandy murmured. "Look, I'm going to have to think about this one. Could the hands thing have been faked?"

"I suppose so but I don't think that's the answer. People have been known to do some amazing things when they're crazy or just in a rage, but this is incredible. I mean a skull."

"Okay Joe, thanks. Send me the report." Sandy replaced the phone and paused with his hand resting on his chin. He turned to look at Charles Slane. He was a powerful looking man that was definitely an athlete. "Are you an active man Mr. Slane?"

"Active?" he said. "In what way?"

"Do you play sports?"

"Handball and weight lifting. I try to stay in shape."

"How much can you bench press?"

"Two forty. Why do you ask Lieutenant?"

"Just curious. Do you have any pets?"

"No," Mrs. Slane answered.

"No dogs, cats, birds, fish or anything?"

"Robin was allergic to fur. He used to want to be a veterinarian but gave that up when he discovered his problem. Twenty minutes around an animal with hair and his eyes would swell shut. He had some very violent reactions."

"Do you folks practice any particular religion?"

"We're Methodist."

"Was Robin into any fraternities or offbeat religions or studying many kinds of animals?"

"Why are you asking us these things?" Carolyn Slane interrupted.

"It's all part of our investigation," Sandy answered gently. "I'll try not to ask anything that I don't really need to know."

"We're not aware of any weird religions and Robin avoided animals. Fraternities didn't interest him because he didn't get along with people.

"The next question I have to ask. Did you get along well with your son?"

Carolyn Slane jumped and her eyes opened wider. Her husband quickly spoke. "He was our boy and of course we loved him."

"There was nothing that you weren't happy about concerning your son? No girl trouble or anything?"

"No," Mr. Slane shot back. "No girl trouble. Just the typical parent child disagreements."

"Okay. No more questions. I would, however, appreciate one more thing. Make me a list of anyone who might know Robin or groups he may have associated with. I'd like to send in a team to check his room for clues too. I promise we won't make a mess. Oh, and I would like a grade transcript and a list of this terms classes."

"Anything that would help. Is that all, Lieutenant?" Mr. Slane walked toward the library door in an effort to end the meeting.

"Yes, I'll let you go now. Thank you for your help." He walked slowly toward the door that Charles Slane held open, not wanting to leave yet as something felt undone. He turned at the door and looked at the slain boy's mother. She looked practically comatose. "Mrs. Slane, did you suspect your son was involved with drugs?"

"Look, Lieutenant," her husband fairly shouted. "Our son was the victim, not the criminal. Please stop trying to tarnish his image. He's gone now, let it be."

"I understand your anguish but I can't ignore any possibility. Your son was murdered. Whoever did it must be captured or he may kill again. If someone had a grudge against your son we may be lucky and it won't happen again, but if he was killed by a maniac it will happen again. I don't like to embarrass your family but I'll do whatever is necessary to catch a murderer." Sandy turned and left the couple in silence. He hated himself instantly for losing his temper. These people had been through a rough time and had the right to be upset.

He heard his radio crackling halfway down the drive and hurried to answer the call. "This is Lieutenant Gibbs."

"Sir, please call control."

"Roger." He turned the dial to Captain Salinski's frequency and announced himself. The speaker answered almost instantly.

"Sandy, what the devil did you say to those people?"

How had he heard so quickly? "What's the problem Cap?"

"The problem is I just called their home to talk to you and Mr. Slane slandered your parentage and hung up on me."

"They objected to me asking personal questions. Maybe I leaned too hard."

"Well, never mind. Haul your butt in here quick. We've got a break in this case."

"Yea, what's that?"

"We've got a kid here that claims he knows who killed Robin Slane."

The boy was young, probably near the Slane boy's age. He was very nervous, which wasn't a surprise as officer John Tainor was watching over him. He was a man mountain and did not hesitate to speak his mind.

"Hi young man." Sandy offered his hand and received a firm handshake. "I'm Lieutenant Gibbs. I'm told you have some information for us."

"Are you in charge of this case?"

"Yes, I am. Anything you have to tell us can be taken care of through me."

"Come on kid," Tainor bellowed. "Spit it out and quit wasting our time."

"John, I'll handle this please." His look was hard. "Go on son. What's your name?"

"Ernie Jacobs."

"You know who killed Robin Slane?"

"I sure do. It was his old man."

"How do you know, Ernie. Did you see him do it?"

He hesitated. "Well, no, but I think it had to be him 'cause he tried to kill Robin and me once before."

Sandy spoke very softly. "How about telling us about it Ernie."

"Do I have to tell it in front of him?" Ernie gestured toward Tainor. "I'd rather just tell you."

"There should be two of us to hear this Ernie," Sandy soothed. "Why don't you just go ahead and tell us about it."

"Well, Robin's dad caught us in their house one night. He got a gun and chased me out, then went around screaming that he'd kill us both."

"Wait a minute kid." Tainor couldn't keep quiet any longer. "Why couldn't you be in the house. Were you smokin' dope or something?"

"No. We were, you know, we cared for each other."

"John, I'll take it from here." Sandy stood up and moved closer to the nervous boy. Tainor was trouble, a mean man who was not inclined to be anything less than a problem with what Sandy knew was coming. He waited until a glowering Tainer left the room and then said, "Is that the way it was Ernie? Did Charles Slane catch you and Robin together and kill him?"

"Well, not right then he didn't. Like I say, he went wild and swore he'd kill us both, but Mrs. Slane was crying and stuff so I figure he decided he'd wait.

I thought I'd better get in here before he comes after me next. Can I have a drink of water?"

"Sure." Sandy moved to an old refrigerator in the corner and pulled out a bottle of water. The boy took a long drink before he continued.

"Tell me something Ernie, and believe me I'm not trying to be smart or anything, but did you and Robin ever get involved with animals?"

"No, we weren't sick or anything we just loved each other. Some people are into pain and apparatus and the like, but that can be straight or gay people. Robin and I weren't into anything weird; we really just cared for each other. Robin and I had dated for quite some time, so I think I'd know if he was into anything else, especially if it was strange. He was just a regular, nice guy."

"How about drugs?"

"Not us. Robin didn't want his mind screwed up. He wouldn't even drink a beer."

"Okay Ernie. We'll put a police guard with you if you want while we investigate Mr. Slane."

"No, thanks. The people I socialize with would get awful nervous with a cop around. I got a friend who said I could hide out with him for a while."

"Fine," Sandy agreed. "I'm not sure you have anything to worry about anyway. Leave the address and phone number with Officer Tainor where we can reach you." The young man left his office and Sandy dialed an extension. "Vic, this is Lieutenant Gibbs. There's a kid out there with John Tainor. I want him tailed. Right, twenty four hours." Never leave a stone unturned.

There was a sharp knock on his door and a very young, uniformed officer stuck his head in. "Excuse me sir, but Captain Salinski wants to see you right away."

Sandy rubbed his temples in a vain attempt to chase away the headache that was starting. "Thank you. I'm on my way."

Cap was spitting strings of tobacco from his mangled cigar into the waste basket. "Well, fill me in on what you've come up with."

Sandy sat down wearily and carefully outlined the facts and speculations as he knew them. Cap listened intently and scratched a note or two, but made no attempt to interrupt his Lieutenant's report. Nearly an hour later he completed his report and waited for a reaction.

"I can't tell exactly from what you've told me but I'd have to say Slane is a prime suspect."

"I think so too Cap, but a couple of things bother me. If he didn't kill them on the spot when he caught the boys, why would he do it later after his rage died down. And why didn't he kill the other boy too? Or at least first."

"Maybe he held off at first because his wife was there," Cap suggested.

"Perhaps," Sandy agreed. "But, then there's the animal blood. That sounds like ritual murder to me. And the violence too. Why not a bullet in his head?"

"Is he strong enough to crush a skull?"

"No one is according to the coroner, but he's a powerful man so I suppose he could be as likely as anyone."

"Do you want to pick him up?"

"No, I don't see any reason to. I'd like to dig around some more into the kid's life. The college kids sometimes get into weird things so I'll try that angle. I think some crazy did this."

"If that's true it will happen again." Cap's tone was somber because he respected Sandy's hunches.

"Yea, I believe it will."

"Put some extra time in on this one Sandy."

Sandy moved toward the door. "Count on it Cap."

TEN

"I'm heading for the nursing home," Brad stated as he pulled on his coat. "I shouldn't be more than a couple of hours."

"I still don't know why you agreed to take this job," Lois argued. "You're too busy now and you haven't worked with patients for years."

"That's exactly why I want to do this. I'm a doctor. I miss helping people, and besides I've gotten rusty. What if my research money should dry up, we've got to eat you know."

"Well then why don't you let me go with you. I'm not a nurse of course, but I could help."

"Look Lois, we've been over all of this before. I need you to keep things caught up here so we don't get even further behind. Besides, you need some extra time to study. Now stop pouting."

"I'm not pouting," she pouted. "Go on, I'll see you later this afternoon."

Brad kissed her and left. She stuck her tongue out at the closed door and angrily stomped over to the cages. She cleaned and fed the animals more quickly than usual to work off her anger. She walked toward Brad's office where her books were waiting for several hours of much needed study. She heard a slight click and turned to see what unusual sound had occurred. Climbing from an unlocked cage was a mongrel dog that Brad had picked up at the animal shelter several weeks ago. The animal had virtually doubled in size as a result of Brad's experimental injections, all of it muscle.

Lois turned back toward the dog without hesitation. She had never feared any animal. "Hey, it looks like I forgot to lock your cage old fellow," she said gently. "Let's get you back inside now."

The dog turned to face her and Lois instantly froze. Its eyes were wild and bloodshot. Blood and froth dripped from its throat and the huge muscles tensed to strike.

"Easy fellow." She felt raw terror as she backed toward the office door. The dog matched her step by step as she moved. Lois backed to the last cage in the room and slowly reached for the latch. She gently lifted the latch and moved back two more steps, opening the cage door as she moved. The dog uttered a horrifying howl and bounded towards her. Lois hit the open cage hard and then ran for the office door. She glanced over her shoulder as she ran to see what was coming. The dog reached the last cage in two bounds and was instantly attacked by a huge cat that leaped from the cage Lois had opened. Although much smaller than the dog, the cat was just as heavily muscled. Lois reached the office door easily and turned, totally fascinated, to watch the struggle that began.

The two animals were tearing huge chunks of flesh and fur from each other and the noise was deafening. The cat was scoring heavily as it was much quicker than the dog, but size and power soon prevailed. The smaller animal was caught under the dog who unleashed a primal scream, before severing the cat's jugular vein with one bite. A second bite removed its head completely.

Lois was caught in a trance induced by horror from watching the battle and was slow to react when the dog instantly lunged toward the open office door. She jumped at the movement and slammed the door closed just as the dog reached her. The doorjamb cracked with the pressure of the onslaught and the enraged animal began tearing large pieces of wood from the door.

The bathroom door was the last refuge if the office door was destroyed and no weapons were in sight. A large piece of wood flew into the room followed closely by the howling animal. Lois reacted to her only possible chance of survival and ran into the bathroom. She realized the hollow door would serve as only a temporary refuge and looked about frantically for some means of protection.

Part of the door cracked away as the dog lost no time in coming after her. In desperation she opened the medicine cabinet and began throwing items across the room in her terror stricken search for help. A straight razor lay on the top shelf and was almost thrown aside in her haste. She almost dropped it as a large portion of the door exploded and the upper body of the dog blasted into the room. The powerful back legs churned in an attempt to complete the entry while the front legs clawed at the tile floor in an attempt to gain a better foothold.

Lois opened the razor and reached for the animal's throat. The dog lashed out and caught the blade in the corner of its mouth. She pulled hard on the handle and deftly split the right side of the dog's mouth. The wound missed the muscles and the enraged animal continued to struggle and bite at its intended victim. Loss of blood from the cat fight and razor seemed to have no effect on its incredible strength.

The door gave completely away and the dog fairly tumbled into the small bathroom. This movement probably saved Lois' life as the dog fell into the room on its back. Using one quick motion she slid the razor across the dog's exposed throat. She jumped on top of the toilet seat to avoid the thrashing feet as the animal died.

Very carefully she stepped around the dead animal and through the splintered door. She quietly walked through the lab and went into the small kitchen near the entrance. She very slowly closed the door and propped a chair against the doorknob. Having assured herself that the door was secure Lois promptly collapsed.

Thomas Maywood escorted Brad through the nursing home, introducing him to the staff and residents. The place was incredibly filthy and the elderly people were not treated with respect or decency. Most of them had minor problems such as bed sores that could be corrected with proper care. Over half either had no families or no visits from loved ones. Brad had twenty people to choose from in starting his work.

Marsha Perrin was his choice. She had terminal cancer and would not live long anyway. Her pain was intense and she often asked to die. Brad realized that her medication and disease could affect his study but he felt better in choosing a person that was effectively dead anyway to begin his experiment.

Her room smelled so badly he nearly vomited. Body waste and rotting flesh mixed into the air so heavily that his chest hurt with the effort to breathe. She was heavily sedated and had absolutely no knowledge of Brad's presence. He failed to find an adequate vein in her shriveled arms to inject his serum, and finally located a usable area on the back of her leg. He injected either death or the possibility of centuries of life.

He started a new notebook that would be kept separately from his other research. He would keep it with him always and hide it in a secret place in his office at night. Lois would never see this portion of his work. The risks were tremendous but the possible rewards were incredible. The Germans committed many cruel acts by experimenting with the Jews, but medical science advanced more during those years than any other period in history.

Where does the blame truly begin or end. Although thousands of persons were tortured, millions have lived longer and more productive lives as a result of the research. These thoughts helped Brad to justify what he was doing, although in his heart he knew horrible wrongs never make an acceptable right.

Weekly visits would not be enough, daily would be necessary at first, maybe weekly later. One positive result he would get from this place would be the assurance that care would be improved for these people. He discovered that people were laying in three day old bedclothes and had no control over bowel movements. Medication was often missed or possibly even was sold on the streets. The agony and suffering at Maywood Nursing Home was medieval.

Brad gratefully gulped fresh cool air as he left the dingy building. He had stayed longer than he had anticipated as he personally supervised the changing of sheets and bathing all of the residents of the home. Maywood had complained that his laundry bill would go up, but Brad insisted that the work be done. The attendants were angry with the work load but figured things would soon return to normal.

He felt good as he drove toward campus. Many people felt better and his experiment had its first human subject. Absolutely nothing could ruin this day. He was carefully measuring his walking speed as he left his car and felt every fiber in his body hum with life. He pushed at the stubborn lab door and whistled a small tune as he closed it behind him.

"Lois, are you here?" he called and walked into the cage room. Blood and flesh was smeared across the floor and tracked to the broken office door. "Lois," he repeated. Moments later he discovered the dog in a large pool of blood on the bathroom floor.

He ran from his office, slipping and falling down into a pool of blood. "Lois where are you?" he shouted and the animals started getting nervous. The dogs began barking and monkeys chattered and leaped about in their cages.

Maybe she had left. She could be at home right now Brad thought. He ran toward the front door and noticed the closed kitchen door. "Lois are you there?" he called out. The door had no lock but still refused to open. Several minutes of pushing finally dislodged a chair and Brad rushed into the room. Lois was sitting on the small countertop by the sink with her knees pulled under her chin.

"Honey, are you all right? Why didn't you let me in."

"I forgot to lock a cage." Her eyes peered over her knees. "That animal almost tore me to shreds. I let a dog loose and than finally had to cut its throat. Then I came in here and fainted. I woke up, climbed in here, and haven't moved since. Come touch me so I can move."

Brad walked over to her and gently pulled her down. She hugged him so tightly that he could barely catch his breath. He squeezed her in return to help her feel comforted. "You're okay now. I'll take you home and then come back and clean up."

"No, I think I can do it."

"Absolutely not. You're going home and I'm giving you a sedative. First though we have to clean up a little and make sure we wear coats when we walk home. We're both covered with blood."

He helped her to prepare herself to go home, recognizing she was still in shock. Her silence bothered him because he didn't want her to think too much about what had happened. She could become too frightened to return to the lab or even worse, she might connect the Slane boy's death with the animals. Brad hadn't even known who the victim was until he read the story in the papers.

"Spring is here isn't it," she said dreamily on their walk home.

"Yes, it's very beautiful," Brad agreed. Anxious to keep her talking he continued, "Hopefully we'll be turning off the furnace soon. We'll open the windows and let the fresh air in."

"Don't do that please," she gasped. "They can get in if the window is open."

"Who can get in darling?"

"The animals." Lois picked up their pace, ruining Brad's heart rate for walking.

"Can we slow down a little?"

"Hang your walking speed," she shrilled. "Your bloody whole research nearly got me killed. I can't live a million years if I'm dead can I?"

Several people were openly staring at them and Brad lowered his head in embarrassment. Fortunately they reached home a few minutes later and no further incident occurred. Shortly thereafter Lois was enjoying a dreamless drug educed sleep.

Brad left her to rest and walked back to the laboratory to clean up the mess. He shook his head sadly and bitterly wondered what he was doing wrong. He had changed his formula dozens of different ways and the problems still existed. Maybe his theory was wrong. Maybe the human race was meant to die after eighty years. The fear gripped the pit of his stomach whenever this thought struck home. He could not be wrong. Death had to be conquered.

He was not finished until nearly midnight. The telephone in his office sounded hollow as it rang. Brad answered on the third ring and grimaced at the voice on the other end of the phone.

"Hi Doc. Charles Maywood here. Ready to earn your pay?"

"What's the problem?" Brad was too tired to give a sharp retort.

"We got a dead one. That means you got to come over and sign a death certificate."

His heart pounding, Brad asked, "Who is it?"

"Marsha Perrin."

"I'll be right there."

She looked very peaceful in death. The pain was gone and Brad could sense a true physical relief. Maywood had opened a window and the smell of cancer was softened slightly by the brisk spring air.

"I went ahead and called Wilsons."

"They do most of the county burials don't they?" Brad inquired.

"Yea, nobody asks them no questions cause they've got the best price in town. Frank Wilson hasn't embalmed a welfare case in ten years. He plants them in a pressed board box, makes the price low, and saves the taxpayers money. He's a bigger crook than you and me Doc." Maywood chuckled, pleased that he was making Brad angry. "They tell me he still cremates for the Mafia. Burns them up and flushes them down the toilet."

Brad refused to strike up a conversation as he knew Maywood was just trying to bait him. He did, however, pick up a vital piece of information that would help him with his research. He made a mental note to visit Wilsons the following day.

The paperwork was completed and the body was removed by two o'clock. Brad was physically and mentally exhausted. He parked his car outside his house instead of leaving it at the faculty lot, something he had not done in years. Lois slept soundly and appeared to not have even rolled over in her sleep.

Although fatigued Brad could not sleep. He was a doctor, dedicated to preserving life. One person was definitely dead because of his research and a second might have died sooner because of him. The morning music from his alarm clock filled the bedroom and still Brad had not slept.

ELEVEN

Brad gently shook Lois awake around ten that morning. She appeared well rested and the color had returned to her cheeks. "How are you feeling?" he asked.

"I feel a lot better than you look," she replied. "Didn't you sleep well?"

"Not like I should have. I guess there's been a lot happening that isn't very nice. The whole thing upsets me. If you would have been hurt . . . ."

"But I wasn't" she interrupted. "I made a mistake. It was my fault and it won't happen again. After all that I can promise those cages will stay locked."

"Good. I was afraid the whole thing might ruin your desire to stay with the research. I've really come to rely on you at the lab Lois."

"Let me shower and brush the morning out of my mouth and you can prove it to me by buying me brunch."

Brad smiled. "Not so fast. I'm late already. My class will think they can take the day off."

"So let them. What could be so terrible about one day?"

"If I let you do this to me I'd end up spending my life not working." He kissed a soft shoulder. "Now I've got to go."

"Oh all right," she panted. "I can see you're not captivated by me any more and here we aren't even married yet."

"Don't worry about that." He smacked her rounded bottom and moved toward the door. "That couldn't happen."

He went through the motions that morning, fatigue making him feel his age. Brad cursed himself as he thought about the time it would take to regulate his bodily functions back to age regression.

Twenty minutes before his lecture was scheduled to end Brad dismissed the class. His mind felt so full of fatigue and concern that he could no longer continue.

Forcing himself to fall into his proper walking speed, Brad left the building and walked toward his lab. Perhaps an hour or two nap would be helpful.

"Excuse me Dr. Richardson?"

Brad glanced over his shoulder, hardly noticing the man scurrying along in an attempt to keep up with him. "Yes I am. What can I do for you?"

"How about slowing down a little for starters. I'm too fat and old to keep this up."

Brad stopped and took a good look at a middle aged man that looked like he had been mugged. His threadbare suit was at least one size too large and wrinkled beyond belief. A stained necktie helped to hide a shirt that was probably once white but had long since turned a dingy gray. Brad wondered if the tattered hat or the worn shoes were supposed to help the suit look better.

"Thanks Doc. Let me catch my breath a second." He held one hand up in a pleading gesture and with the other pulled a small leather case from his pocket and opened it, showing Brad a police badge. "I'm Lieutenant Gibbs from the police department. Just a second." Sandy took several deep gulps of air before continuing. "Wow. I knew these lousy cigarettes were bad but I guess I never realized how bad until I tried to catch you."

"What can I do for you Lieutenant? I'm in rather a hurry." Brad's heart was pounding with fear, wondering why the police suddenly were interested in him.

"I appreciate you're a busy man but this is very important. I believe you had a student named Robin Slane?"

"Why yes, I believe so." Brad was suddenly wide awake, the adrenalin beginning to pour through his body. "The news said something about him being killed didn't it?"

"Yes, unfortunately that's true. I've been assigned to investigate his actions leading up to his death. Strictly routine."

"Why do you want to talk to me?"

"I understand Robin came to see you the day of his death."

"No, I don't believe so. He was in class that day but I didn't talk to him."

"That's interesting. Several of his classmates told me he was going to talk to you about his progress in the course."

Brad was sweating. "Perhaps he went to my office but I wasn't in."

"He was going to your laboratory as I understand it Doctor. You spend more time there than at your university office don't you?"

His head reeling, Brad fought to collect his thoughts. "I'm required to officially have an office in the Bristol building but I never use it. All of my students come to my lab office."

"Say, could we go over to your lab? I've got some more questions and I'd like to see where you do your work."

"Surely. It's not far." Brad was fighting to control himself. How did the police connect him with the death? He had been so careful. He fought down the urge to ask a lot of questions about the boy's death, deciding it would be better to not show that much interest. "Lieutenant, has anyone ever told you how much you look like Columbo?"

"You mean that Peter Faulk character?"

"Yes. I can't resist asking you that." Hopefully small talk would help.

"You know Doc, I think every cop in the country dreams about being that good. Do you really think I look like him?" Sandy was genuinely pleased.

"I don't mean that in a derogatory way," Brad hastened to say.

"Oh no offense taken," Sandy beamed. "I consider that connection an honor."

"Here's my laboratory." Brad was relaxed somewhat, feeling slightly comforted in the fact that he had pleased the lieutenant. "Would you like a cup of herb tea?"

"No thank you." Sandy was quickly taking in the surroundings of the laboratory. He noticed the cages and walked to them almost eagerly, noting the variety of animals which included both dogs and monkeys. "Do these animals ever get violent?"

"Brad's mouth went dry and his heart began pounding again. "No, of course not. They're quite harmless." Fortunately none of the animals were currently in advanced stages of treatments so they all looked quite normal.

"Do these animals ever leave the lab?"

"Never. Their every move must be monitored or the research could be altered. My assistant or I check them daily. Since all our research is done here there's no reason to ever take them elsewhere."

"You're doing age research aren't you?"

"Yes I am."

"Could you tell me more about it? I'm really interested."

"Surely. Come into my office and I'll give you the basic idea."

"I'm not taking too much of your time am I?" Sandy stopped at the entrance of the small office. "You're so busy I could come back some other time."

"You're doing Peter Faulk again Lieutenant."

Sandy Grinned sheepishly. "That obvious huh?"

Brad smiled in return. "I can almost remember the episode. Sit down please."

"Thank you. Do you really think you can help people live forever?"

"We're sure working in that direction. There are probably fifty different people in the world doing serious research concerning age. We're not going to turn mortal man into a god but there is no reason people shouldn't live three or four hundred years."

"Kind of like the people in the Bible," Sandy interjected.

"Exactly. I don't know what their secret was but some of them lived a healthy and productive life for centuries."

"Maybe they got special help from God."

"Or maybe God was a super intelligent being from another planet that gave them the proper drugs to keep them alive."

"If that's the case Doc why doesn't He still give people the treatment?"

"Maybe he's dead."

"You mean you're one of those God is dead people Doc?" Sandy frowned. "That's not a pleasant thought."

"I don't personally believe that theory, although there are some gerontologists that think maybe that could be true."

"Geron what?" Sandy scratched his head.

"I'm sorry. A gerontologist is the fancy name for someone who does age research. One fellow in Russia believes the spaceman God theory. He thinks the man had perfected it to the point that he lived for several thousand years and then died. That's why you don't see much in the way of miracles anymore. Most people in my field are legitimate though. This guy's a crackpot."

"Leave it to some blasted Red to come up with that one" Sandy glowered. "Those people are afraid to believe."

"Personally I agree Lieutenant. There are several theories that are being worked on. I happen to believe mine is correct or of course I'd be working on another one."

Sandy stretched his legs in front of himself and tried to relax in the stiff backed chair provided for guests. Brad had purposely chosen an uncomfortable chair as he had discovered that students spent less time when they came to discuss his course. "Tell me about some of the other researchers. Why are there so many theories?"

"Well, I suppose it's because they all make sense, that is they all have a reasonable argument. I just believe my research makes more sense. But let me answer your questions. There are six theories that I know about. The most pessimistic one says we're all doomed because nature automatically weeds out a species with age to make room for the young."

"If that's the answer everyone else is wasting their time," Sandy replied with a frown.

"That is if it is correct. I don't happen to think so. Another concept is that we self destruct. Our white blood cells battle disease but forget with age what is bad and what is good. Eventually we destroy ourselves."

"That sounds logical. So that's what you're studying?"

"Patience Lieutenant. I'll save mine until the last."

"Sorry." Sandy shuffled uneasily in his chair, not realizing he had been disciplined by an expert, a school teacher.

Brad continued without comment. "Another theory is that chemical changes take place in the body that confuse proteins and forces them to read incorrectly. A similar idea is that impurities build up in the system and create disturbances.

Eventually cells mutate and we age. Some researchers believe body cells make mistakes when they divide. As years go by the mistakes create gray hair, wrinkled skin, and ultimately death."

"All that makes common sense," Sandy interrupted again.

"Indeed. That's why they have researchers and get grant money to study the possibility of them being the truth. My theory is based on the pituitary gland. I believe the endocrine system begins to malfunction at about twenty five years of age. The pituitary gland controls the endocrine system and just starts to produce age related substances. This is the point when our body starts the death clock. Eventually we'll develop a drug that reverses the effect."

"What makes you think you're right Doc?"

"Some of the things I've been working on have been successful" Brad said with pride. "I've doubled the life span of several microscopic life forms and my animal tests are encouraging."

"Do your students ever help out here at the lab?" Sandy's eyes narrowed ever so slightly, his only giveaway when he went for information in a case.

"I only permit my fiancé' to work with me."

"Is she here today?"

"No, she has classes today."

"Then she is a student."

"Yes. She expressed an interest in the work when she was taking my course. I gave her the opportunity to work with me and I'm happy to say she is not only an able assistant but we fell in love."

"Kind of a storybook romance eh?" Sandy smiled. "What is her name?"

"Lois Henderson."

"Could you tell me where I might reach her other than here at the lab?"

"Try calling her at home." Brad reached for a piece of paper and wrote down his home telephone number. "She is usually there until nine or ten in the morning."

"Excuse me Doc, I .... uh ..." Sandy hesitated.

"Yes Lieutenant?"

"Well, isn't this the same number the facility directory lists as your home?"

Brad leaned back in his chair and chuckled. "Come on Lieutenant, this is the twentieth century. Lois lives with me."

Sandy shook his head and grinned. "Sorry Doc, I guess I'm a little old fashioned." He stood up much to the relief of his back and said, "I've kept you much too long. I really don't even need to talk to Miss Henderson but you might warn her that I may need to ask some questions later on. If you tell her in advance I won't be as likely to scare her."

"No problem." Brad stood and walked toward the front of the lab as a sign of dismissal. He turned to find out why the lieutenant was not with him. The detective was near the animal cages, stroking his chin thoughtfully. "Is there something else Lieutenant?"

"Hum? Oh, excuse me Doc." Sandy held out a hand and shook his head in confusion. "I was just wondering, why should any of these ideas on old age be correct. Whatever made anyone consider all this?"

Brad sighed and walked back toward his office. "Come here and let me show you something. He pulled a textbook from the top of his filing cabinet and turned to a color photograph near the middle of the book. "Take a look at this."

Sandy had returned to his seat and now reached out for the heavy text. He frowned at the pitiful sight before him. There were several color pictures of very small people. Each were in advanced stages of age with wrinkled skin and balding heads. "Very old dwarfs. So what's the point Doc?"

"The oldest person on that page is twelve years old." Brad paused until Sandy closed his astonished mouth. "It's a rare condition called progeria. The body ages ten times faster than normal for no apparent reason."

"Okay." Sandy closed the book to avoid the pleading eyes. "So what does this prove?"

"If people can age too fast there must be an imbalance that causes it. Whatever causes that to happen should be, must be, able to stop completely or reverse itself. My job is to find out how. Personally, I'm convinced my theory is the correct one. Some day Lieutenant, man will live for hundreds of years."

Sandy narrowed his eyes slightly. "Except when someone kills."

Brad fought the fear that again crept into his throat. "That's your job to stop Lieutenant."

Sandy stood and moved toward the door. "We each have our jobs Doc. Let's hope we both get lucky."

TWELVE

The Capitol was a cheap excuse for a newspaper making a vain attempt to break into the Columbus market. They never hesitated printing half truths in exchange for flashy headlines. Someone had put the daily issue on Sandy's desk with the front page headline circled in red: PROMINENT LOCAL ATTORNEY PRIME SUSPECT IN MURDER.

"What the . . . ." Sandy sputtered.

'An informed source has informed this reporter that Charles Slane, father of the young man murdered on Columbus' east side is the prime suspect in the investigation. The younger Slane was a reputed homosexual and was discovered by his father. Our source states that the elder Slane threatened to kill his son. Attempts to reach Lieutenant Charles Gibbs, chief investigator in the case, for comment have been unsuccessful.'

"That stinking little scumbag," Sandy hissed. "He couldn't wait to run to this rag."

"Lieutenant, Captain Salinski wants to see you."

"What? Oh, okay." Sandy looked up at the young policeman standing near his desk. "Thank you."

He walked to Cap's office and walked in without knocking. His superior officer had shredded the end of his cigar in anger and frustration. "How in thunder did this get out Sandy?"

"Hi Cap. I'm having a nice day too thank you," he said dryly.

"Cut the crap. How did this get to the press?"

"It had to be Ernie Jacobs. After that idiot Tainor was done insulting him he probably did it for spite. I can run him in and harass him a bit but it wouldn't do much good."

"No, don't waste your time," Cap growled.

"If we start leaning on him the little jerk will probably cause more problems. Say, you don't suppose he did it do you?" Cap looked hopeful.

"No such luck. I think I know who's responsible but I have no concrete proof so I'll keep my theories to myself. In the meantime I'd better get over to the Slane's and play my hand. Maybe they haven't heard about this yet."

"Bob Zelno from The Capitol has been trying to get in touch with you."

"He can stuff it," Sandy growled. "Let that clown sit."

—

53

"Okay but call him back sometime today or he'll print whatever the public wants to hear."

"He will anyway Cap, but I'll call him later today."

"Let me know what happens with Slane."

Charles Slane had spent an hour staring at the front page of the paper. His secretary had called and suggested he go out and buy a copy. He shook so badly he had thought he would have to call his wife to drive him home from the drug store but somehow he had gained enough control to drive the five blocks home.

The world now knew that his son was gay. Any moment that scruffy little detective would show up and take him to jail for a murder he did not commit. Even if he was cleared his life and business would be ruined. Only one answer came to his tortured mind.

He went to the garage and took a new rope from a nail on the wall. He tied one end of the rope over a beam on the exposed ceiling. A small folding chair enabled him to reach the rope comfortably and form a hangman's knot. Slane was forced to stand on tiptoe to fit the noose around his neck. The fibers burned his skin and stuck him like the quills of a porcupine but it felt somehow comfortable and he was comforted by its snugness. He slowly pulled himself up with his hands on the rope and with a violent kick the chair flew into a corner. He took a deep breath and relaxed his arms.

The rope immediately tightened just above his Adams apple, cutting like a razor into the soft flesh. His feet were nine inches from the floor and would not touch despite his frantic efforts. The pain was blinding and he wanted it to stop. This was a mistake and he wanted down. He reached frantically above his head and pulled with all his might in an attempt to relieve the pressure on his neck. He pulled one hand on the noose and released his tortured lungs with a gasp.

"Help. Somebody help me," he screamed. "Don't let me die please." His arms were strong but not powerful enough to permit him to hold his weight with one arm while the other clawed the rope from his throat. Each time he loosened the rope enough to fit the noose over his head, Charles' arm would fail him and the knot would tighten.

For fifteen minutes the struggle for life continued. Charles grew weaker after each frantic effort to remove the noose. Finally he could only relieve the pressure by exerting all of his strength with both arms on the rope above his head. The skin on his hands peeled off from the friction and blood slicked his grip. He could pull himself up with his arms, bunch up the muscles in his throat to loosen the noose slightly, inhale and exhale several times, and than his arms would give away to pain and fatigue, instantly closing his throat to any passage of air. After a total of twenty minutes his entire body was screaming in pain.

Saliva dripped from his open mouth and soaked the front of his shirt. His hair was wet with blood from his torn hands sliding down the rope. No strength remained to call for help during each moment of breathing.

Nearly thirty minutes of the death struggle went past. Charles attempted to raise his arms for another pull on the rope and discovered they would not move. He kicked his feet frantically in one last fear crazed effort to break the rope or to touch something solid. His lungs burned like they were on fire and pain flew as fluttering butterflies throughout his body. Two minutes ticked by before he stopped seeing flashes of light and razor sharp stars no longer flashed past his eyes and he blacked out. This brief time was spent in a voiceless, airless scream for mercy that was not heard. His tongue had swelled and lolled from his mouth in a blackened impression of a rock star from the band Kiss. His stomach muscles contracted and forced half digested food toward his mouth, only to have the escape route blocked by the squeezing rope.

In his darkness Charles could feel his heart pounding in a desperate effort to send oxygen to his brain. The vessels and capillaries in his eyes ruptured and filled their sockets with blood. Three minutes after he lost consciousness his bladder and bowels voided themselves and Charles Slane was dead. Forty seconds later the rope broke and released its burden.

A County rescue squad responded to a hysterical call from Mrs. Slane. She had come home from a ladies club meeting and found her husband in the garage. Recognizing the scene involved murder or suicide the squad called the police. Sandy received the message by radio moments before he came within sight of the Slane home.

"Blast it all anyway," he murmured as he plodded toward the open garage door. The two paramedics were packing their equipment as Sandy approached, pulling his identification from his pocket. "Lieutenant Gibbs from homicide. What have you fellows got here?"

"Boy that was quick. We just called in a minute ago." The young EMT looked amazed.

"I was on my way when you called." He walked into the garage and stared at the purple face of Charles Slane. His eyes were so bulged that Sandy doubted that a mortician could close them for a funeral. "Looks like a chicken suicide," he commented, more to himself than anyone

"What's that?" One of the paramedics had followed him into the garage and stood across from the body, starring with open curiosity.

"Happens a lot. Some guy ties a rope around his neck and kicks a chair out from under himself. He suddenly decides he made a mistake and tries to back out. The problem is he's got a rope around his neck and his feet won't touch the ground."

"How did his hands get so torn up?" the paramedic interrupted.

"That's why they call it chicken," Sandy continued patiently. "The guy's hanging there and changes his mind, you know chickens out. The only chance he's got is to reach above the knot in the rope and hold his weight with his arms. That will loosen the rope a bit and let him breathe."

"Can't he use one hand to take the rope off his neck?"

"Not even if you've got an incredible amount of strength. Most people can barely pull themselves up enough to get any slack. After a few minutes of holding the rope the hands get torn up from the friction. They'll get to the point where only a few seconds can be tolerated at a time. Eventually he can't do it any more and chokes to death."

The paramedic uttered a low whistle. "What a lousy way to die."

"It can take a long time, but remember something son. Any way is a lousy way."

"Really." The paramedic left the garage to help his partner prepare the report before they left the scene. Two patrol cars arrived and Sandy walked out to give orders to the men.

"Call in the teams and check this all out."

"Yessir," the young officer replied. "Do you need anything else before they take the body?"

"No. I'm done here. Just let them take him after the Coroner gives the okay." He walked to the front door and rang the bell. A neighbor answered the ring. "I'm Lieutenant Gibbs from the police department. May I speak to Mrs. Slane?"

"Just a moment. I'll see if she's up to it."

Moments later Carolyn Slane came to the door. She was ashen white but had regained her composure. "Please come in Lieutenant," she said in a very small voice.

"Thank you," he said softly and moved into the quiet wealth of the home. "I'm very sorry Mrs. Slane. Not only about your husband but the fact that this story got to the papers. I want you to know we had nothing to do with that."

"I know you didn't Lieutenant." She smiled sadly. "It was the Jacobs boy wasn't it."

"Probably, although we can't be sure. Did your husband talk about this with you?"

"No, but I knew if the story about Robin ever got out he couldn't take it. Then when it added that he was a suspect . . ." She didn't need to finish the thought.

"I know Mrs. Slane. If it's any small comfort to you I'm sure your husband was in no way connected with your son's death."

"Then you know who murdered my boy?" Her voice sounded hopeful.

"Personally, I think I know, but proof I don't have."

"If you know why don't you gather up the evidence and arrest him." Her voice rose in frustration. "Everyone will believe Charles killed his own son unless you catch the scum that did this."

"Take it easy Mrs. Slane. I'm not telling you these things to upset you. I'd hoped you would be somewhat comforted. If my theory is correct, and I emphasize it is only a theory, it may be almost impossible to prove guilt."

"Then the case will never be solved?"

Sandy shrugged. "Possibly not. I'll have to take a lot more than theories to the D.A. to get him to act on this. The fact is I possibly will never get the proof I need."

"Please try Lieutenant." Her voice was pleading. "I want my husband's name cleared."

Sandy stood up and walked toward the front door. "I promise I'll do my best. Good-by."

He found himself clenching his teeth as he reached his car. Sandy was convinced that Dr. Richardson had something to do with the Slane boy's death. One or more of those animals killed that boy. Nothing else fit because every move the victim made had been studied and documented. Obviously every single event could not be traced but as far as could be determined the animals at the lab were the only nonhuman contact the boy had.

A man that was as busy as a doctor would never have been so cooperative and willing to take the time to explain his work so thoroughly. The good doctor was hiding something and Sandy, being the good cop that he was would wait for him to make a mistake. Maybe a tail would be in order. He made a mental note to ask Cap for more manpower.

He considered stopping at The Capitol and pushing that little pimple Zelno into printing a retraction but realized that could make things worse. "Aw, what the heck" he growled and swung his car toward the south side offices of The Capitol.

The visitors parking area was empty so he parked in front of the main entrance and ran up the front steps to prevent any of his anger from cooling. A young girl with large breasts and a low neckline sat behind the receptionist desk. She beamed a flawless smile and said in a voice that could be in a commercial for sex, "May I help you sir?"

Sandy bit back the typical 'can you ever' comment and instead dug out his badge. "Lieutenant Gibbs. Is Bob Zelno in today?"

The girl leaned forward to peer at the badge. He permitted the girl to take her time studying the badge. She finally leaned back and said breathlessly, "Yes sir. Wow, the police huh? A lieutenant too."

"Is Mr. Zelno in?" he repeated. A great body but her brains were in Cleveland.

"Oh yea. Sorry." She picked up a telephone and dialed an extension. "Mr. Zelno this is Ruby out front." She paused a moment and then giggled. "You never get tired of that one do you Mr. Zelno. There's a Lieutenant Gibbs from the police department here to see you. Okay thanks." She replaced the receiver and leaned forward again. "He'll be right with you."

"Thanks," he replied. With great effort he turned his head and gazed out of the window. He half smiled as he noticed the hurt look on her face out of the corner of his eye. She slowly sat back and adjusted herself in a prim and proper manner.

"You can sit over there if you like," she said coldly.

A tall, good looking young man burst into the lobby. He smiled and stuck out a hand that looked like it could wrap around a basketball. Sandy noted in dismay that this man was impossible to dislike. "You're Bob Zelno."

"I sure am Lieutenant. Am I getting that well known already?"

"Not really. I just figured since I asked for Bob Zelno and you came running that you must be Bob Zelno."

"My, my he said with a broad smile. "The police department has trained you well."

"I'm trying to stay steamed at you Mr. Zelno," Sandy replied. "Unfortunately you've had some courses in charm yourself. You're a hard man to hate."

"Come on Lieutenant." Zelno looked genuinely hurt. "What did I do to get you angry?"

"You killed a man."

"I don't know where you get your information Lieutenant but someone is lying to you. I've never killed anyone in my life."

Sandy felt his anger growing again and was grateful. "You wrote a slanderous story about a man and his son. The man couldn't take the scandal and hung himself in the garage."

"Oh my . . . . Slane!"

"That's right. You should have called me before you wrote that story and gotten the facts."

"Wait a minute. Are you saying his son was not gay?"

"No I'm not. What I'm telling you is Charles Slane was not a suspect and as far as I'm concerned is dead because of your story."

Zelno was visibly upset. He ran a shaking hand over his face and had suddenly lost his boyish charm. "He hung himself? Well, maybe he did kill his son."

"No way Zelno. The case isn't solved but we're sure Slane didn't do it. Are you going to write a follow-up story and explain why that man is dead?"

"Okay Lieutenant. Did you just come here to make me feel bad or is there some official reason for your visit?" His dancing eyes had turned cold.

"I guess that's the main reason I came. I'd also like to know who fed you the sordid details."

"I can't tell you that. Sources are confidential you know."

"Sure, I know. Well, tell your old pal Ernie Jacobs I said hello."

Zelno raised his eyebrows and smiled slightly, some of his composure having returned. "If you knew already why did you ask?"

"Because I wasn't positive until now. Thanks Zelno." Sandy walked away and glanced over at the receptionist. She had taken in every word and was staring wide eyed with her mouth hanging open. Sandy walked over to her desk and leaned across so he could speak quietly. "By the way Ruby, you've got the greatest body I've ever laid eyes on."

She flushed and smiled shyly. "Gee, thanks Lieutenant."

Sandy shook his head and smiled. "Have a nice day sweetheart." He walked out of the building without another glance at a miserable Bob Zelno.

THIRTEEN

Frank Wilson looked like anything but a crook. He dressed well and presented himself as a distinguished looking middle aged man. Brad looked around the spacious surroundings and wondered if he was making a mistake.

"Dr. Richardson."

Brad turned to see a man that looked nothing like he would have expected. Respectability almost oozed from him. Maywood could be wrong unless looks were very deceiving. "Hello. Are you Mr. Wilson?"

"Indeed I am. How may I help you?"

Brad decided not to make him the offer to cover up any unusual looking deaths. The risk didn't seem worth it. "I just wanted to come by and see your facility since so many of our nursing home patients come here. I must say I'm impressed."

"Thank you sir." Wilson touched his fingers together and bowed slightly. "I would be more than happy to show you our embalming and makeup room if you wish."

"No, that's not necessary thank you. I really just wanted to drop in for a bit and look around. Thank you for your courtesy."

He offered his hand and Wilson shook it with a warm, firm grasp. "Dr. Richardson, don't go yet. Would you please step into my office for a moment?" He guided Brad toward a large but sparsely furnished office. He gestured to a chair and moved behind his desk as Brad sat down. "Maywood called me and said we might be able to do some business. He must know you pretty well because he said you might be nervous and back out without talking to me. Dr. Richardson, if there's money to be made I want in. Can I make myself any clearer than that?"

Brad took a moment to let the shock wear off and then smiled. Good old Maywood had led him in the right direction after all. "Very well Mr. Wilson, there is some money to be made, and I might add very easily."

"Good. I should have said that I don't want anything that could cause problems for my business. I have certain business associates that would frown about that."

The mob Brad thought. "Don't worry about that. In fact this must be strictly between us."

"That's fine with me. What is your proposal Doctor?"

"You get all the County burials from the nursing home if I'm not mistaken."

"That's correct."

"Death certificates are signed by me. All you have to do is not ask any questions if the cause of death I list does not appear to be accurate."

"In other words if someone comes in with a bullet between the eyes I don't question heart failure as the cause."

"That's right. There won't be any bullet wounds but some of the bodies could be rather, shall we say, gruesome."

Wilson nodded and held one finger up in mock discovery. "Why don't we cremate them? That eliminates any further evidence and so long as they don't have family it wouldn't be questioned anyway."

Brad smiled in appreciation of the solution to his problem. "That would be absolutely perfect. Perhaps we should make that a policy for all welfare deaths unless a family member objects."

"Fine by me doctor except you'll have to pay a lump sum to get the job done so we won't have to argue about which body needed to be burned and which didn't."

"We can arrange that any away you wish Mr. Wilson but believe me if the service is necessary you will be able to tell immediately. If any deception were possible I wouldn't be offering to pay you for your discretion. I'd just cover it up."

"That's a good point. How will I be able to tell so easily?"

"The body may have exploded."

"You mean like being hit with a bomb?"

"Yes, or the entire inner body could rupture, which would cause the body to bloat and turn purple."

Wilson whistled softly. "I guess that couldn't be hidden too well. Say, is this some disease I could catch or something? All the money in the world isn't worth cancer."

"There is no disease of any kind involved here. No harm could possibly come to you."

"Okay Doctor. I'll take your word for that. How much are you able to pay?"

With great effort to remain calm and appear relaxed Brad said, "I thought five thousand would be a fair sum."

A well manicured hand waved through the air in firm rejection. "You sure didn't think hard enough Doctor Richardson. Try thirty thousand."

"That's not at all reasonable," Brad countered. "There will be very few and hopefully none that die this way. Ten thousand would be more like it."

—

"If you thought there was much chance that my help wouldn't be needed you wouldn't be here Doctor. Fifteen thousand."

He realized that Frank Wilson was vital to the continued success of his work. There was a good chance that no one would die, but how could he take the chance. He could risk no more dumping of bodies.

"Come on Doctor Richardson, stop daydreaming. Do we have an understanding?"

"I'll bring the money tomorrow morning. Would eight be too early?"

"That would be just fine. Cash of course."

"Of course."

Sandy scratched his head thoughtfully as he watched Brad leave the funeral home. Something was not right about this whole thing and he had determined to find the solution. The animal connection had to have come from the lab and he felt with a gut instinct that the doctor knew exactly why that boy had been killed.

Officers from the detective bureau would take over the surveillance in a few days but Sandy always started the watch himself. He learned a lot by observing the habits of a suspect. He wanted to feel a part of Doctor Richardson's life.

He had already determined that the doctor drove his car very little as a quick check of the odometer showed just over seven thousand miles on a four year old car. The life of a campus professor seemed to engulf the man. Very little outside activities were tolerated until, that is, the death of Robin Slane. Suddenly the good doctor was involved in a nursing home and a funeral parlor. Pretty low quality places too.

Sandy followed his prey to the campus faculty parking lot and then to the lab. He considered his options carefully and decided to continue with the Peter Faulk act. He walked through the door of the small building without knocking and tried to look as rumpled as possible.

"Hey Doc, anybody home?" Sandy suddenly lost his poise completely and realized he must look like the village idiot. Standing before him was perhaps the most beautiful woman he had ever seen.

"My goodness are you alright?"

She even sounded beautiful. Sandy shook himself back to reality and readjusted his Columbo look. "Gee, I'm terribly sorry. You're just so blasted beautiful that I lost myself for a minute," he said honestly. He was pleased that she seemed embarrassed and lowered her eyes shyly.

"Oh gosh." Sandy held his hand up in a gesture of self admonishment. "I'm so stupid. See, you've still got me shook up." He produced his badge and held it out for her to see. "I'm Lieutenant Gibbs from homicide."

"Pleased to meet you Lieutenant. I'm Lois Henderson. Brad told me about your investigating that poor boys death. Have you any suspects?"

"So you're Miss Henderson. For goodness sakes no wonder the Doc is so proud of you and there I go again shooting off my mouth a mile a minute. No, unfortunately this thing is beginning to look like one of those cases that never get solved." He smiled and hoped he wasn't being too corny. "Is the Doc around?"

"Yes, he's in his office. Just go on back."

"Thanks." Sandy paused and looked at Lois with slightly narrowed eyes. "Did you know the Slane boy Miss Henderson?"

"Call me Lois and no, I didn't."

"Do you spend a lot of time here at the lab?"

"Sometimes I feel like most of it," she said with a smile.

"Did he ever come here to the lab?"

"Never when I was here. Brad uses his office here for interviews but he seldom has any."

"So if Robin had wanted to talk to the Doc he would have come here."

"Probably, but like I say he was never here when I was."

"Thanks Lois. And call me Sandy."

Her smile was warm and pleasant. "That's a deal Sandy. Good luck in finding that killer."

"Have you found him?" They both started slightly at the sound of Brad's voice.

"I didn't hear you walk up Brad. Sandy came by to ask you some questions about Robin Slane." Why did she feel guilty about talking so intimately to this police officer.

Brad gave her a puzzled look when she mentioned the lieutenant's first name. He turned his gaze from her and said, "What more can I do for you Lieutenant? I've told you everything I know about the boy which is frankly precious little."

"If you'll excuse me I've got some work to do," Lois interrupted. "Sandy, it was really nice meeting you. Good luck with your investigation."

"Thanks Lois. You take care."

Brad felt a sharp pang of jealously and immediately shook it off. Lois couldn't be attracted to this scruffy old man, but despite his self-assurance he found that he disliked the man. "What do you want from me Lieutenant? I'm pretty busy today."

"Sure Doc, I'll only take a minute. The reason I stopped by is I'm kind of over a barrel here. I've got a dead boy and absolutely nothing to go on. We've pretty much reached the point where we'll have to give up and let this one lay unsolved. I don't like that Doc. I don't like that at all."

"I can understand how you feel Lieutenant. Still, how can I help any more?"

"Those animals of yours. Does this stuff you give them make them any smarter?"

"No, I don't think so." Brad began to put up his mental guard. This man was a powerful adversary and could not be underestimated.

"Then there's no way any of these animals could escape and then come back."

"Well, that doesn't take any great brain Lieutenant. Any house pet can leave for a period of time and then return home with no problem. The reason that it's unlikely any of my animals could do such a thing is their cages are kept locked and the door to the lab is locked when someone isn't here."

Sandy's eyes narrowed more than usual before he spoke again. "I'm going to level with you Doc. I don't think that boy could have been mutilated like that by a human. For goodness sakes his head was smashed like an egg." Sandy paused a moment for effect and then quietly said, "The only connection to animals in that boys life was here Doc. He came here to see you."

Brad was fighting an impulse to run. As absurd as that would be his brain was absolutely screaming at his feet to move. "Maybe he had a pet, or maybe he was into some kinky sex thing with animals." His voice was too high, not at all natural like an innocent man would react.

"No way Doc. You see he was allergic to animals. The kid couldn't take twenty minutes within three feet of one. I figure your lab animals must be the answer."

"But if my animals did anything here I'd know it wouldn't I?" Brad's armpits itched so badly he wanted to scream but he forced his arms to remain at his sides.

"Yea, I guess you would." Sandy raised his eyebrows and smiled. "Well, I'll be seeing you Doc. I got to run." He paused in the doorway. "By the way, do you keep any kind of record on the animals that die?"

"Yes, it's all in my research notes."

"Would you let me see them?"

"No. The information in there is worth a Nobel Prize. No one gets those notes."

"Okay Doc. No problem. No one would believe I was the Nobel type anyway" Sandy said with another grin. He left the lab without another word.

Brad watched him until the door closed and then rushed for a glass of water. He dropped the paper cup three times before he could control his trembling hands. Could he know? Of course not, but how had he figured it out? The questions flew through Brad's head with fear and confusion.

"Darling are you alright?"

He jumped and blinked his eyes as he noticed that Lois had come back to the kitchen. "I'm fine."

"But you're shaking, and you're covered with sweat. What in the world is the problem?"

"I guess I don't feel too well. Maybe it's the flu," he lied.

"Why don't you cancel the afternoon and go home." She gently rubbed his temples. "Maybe you'll feel good enough later to take me dancing."

"You know I love it when you talk about fun," he mumbled, turning to face her and openly admiring her beauty. "I feel better already. Why wait for tonight to dance?" He buried his face into her hair and sniffed the clean fragrance.

"Slow down Doctor," Lois said as she pushed him away gently but firmly. "You're the one who didn't want the office work and recreation to get mixed up. You go home and rest and I'll see you later. Now go on."

Brad glowed with the emotion he felt for this young girl. Moments ago he had been nearly hysterical with fear and now he suddenly felt calm and in control again. "You're right as usual. Can you do the temperature checks and rotate the cultures?"

"Yes darling. Go home." She walked him toward the door.

"Oh wait. That cat in cage nine needs an injection today. Why don't I . . . ."

"I'll do it as soon as you're out the door," she interrupted. "I can handle everything. Now go."

She fairly pushed him out the door and stared for a long time at the floor after he left, lost in thought and wondering what she should do. Something about the Slane boy's death completely rattled him. That detective scared Brad to death. She had never seen him so upset. Lois knew he was a good, honest person, but his research was more important than anything. Would he cover up murder to protect his project? If one of the animals had escaped there was no way the police could call it murder, but that would not have made the university officials any happier. They would shut the money off immediately. Lois knew that the animals would kill when they reached their advanced stages of madness. She shivered at the memory of her narrow escape that day in the lab. Those animals would have truly torn her apart.

Brad's notes were kept in a safe in his office. He had never told her the combination but she had watched him open it several times and had memorized each number. After only a moment's hesitation she went to his office and minutes later was pulling a thick notebook from inside the safe. She leafed through it quickly and soon found the date near the Slane boy's death. His notes were printed in the typical perfect way he did all things. The bottom of a page contained the exact date of the boy's death. Lois turned the page and saw the following days date with a brief explanation of tests and results of experiments done that day. There was no page in his book covering the day of Robin Slane's murder.

Her heart fluttered slightly and her stomach churned with fear as she replaced the book and began to busy herself in the lab. She realized that Brad knew what had happened to that boy. Her only question was what to do, confront him with her suspicions or try to forget. She truly loved him and wanted to support him in every way, but she also needed his trust. Lois finished her work but instead of leaving for home immediately went back into Brad's office and began to cry.

Sandy waited patiently across the street until he saw Brad leave. He followed at a safe distance and watched every move Brad made with an eye trained to see something, no matter how small, that would provide a lead or an answer. He knew Doctor Richardson had something to do with Robin Slane's death. The man practically wet his pants when the animal issue was pushed. Sandy had seen the cover-up for guilt and fear too many times to miss such obvious reactions. The man knew and wasn't telling.

The boys death and the Doctor's fear of ruining the research he had done by admitting to the cause did not irritate Sandy as much as the death of Charles Slane. If an animal escaped and killed the kid that was a tragic accident that probably could not have been helped. Doctor Richardson's desire to keep it quiet was even understandable as he could lose his research money, but because of his silence another man was dead. And what about Mrs. Slane. She could be next if she can't come up with a reason to live. No. the truth had to come out. Cap would probably pull him off the case and onto something hotter sooner or later, but until that happened Sandy Gibbs would be right on this guy's butt.

Brad reached his home and disappeared inside. Sandy positioned himself in a nearby alley, settled back against a building, and waited.

FOURTEEN

Leonard White had been somewhat of a lowlife for much of his seventy eight years. His father left the day he was born and his mother spent the next fifteen years kicking Leonard around to get even. She probably would have kept it up for a few more years but Leonard finally buried a steak knife in her throat. Five years in prison presented the world with a frightened, ruined young man. After being sexually assaulted in prison over three dozen times Leonard was more of a shell than a man, and unfortunately his mind was permanently twisted. He managed to get by with only two more trips to prison where he decided that he might as well make money with his body and sold himself repeatedly as a prison prostitute.

Leonard 'retired' when he was released from prison at fifty seven years of age and went on welfare. Maywood nursing home was given the responsibility of providing care at public expense two years before Brad started giving him injections. If any family members existed they could not have cared less about a sick old man that soiled his sheets four or five times each day.

Life had become a fog of pain and dreams for Leonard. The experience was almost pleasant as he was used to pain and the dreams were about things he had wanted to do and be when he was younger. People had always treated him like trash and Leonard's fondest wish for most of his life was to be able to hurt someone else like he had been hurt. His drug induced dreams showed him towering over his enemies and thousands of people bowed down before his cruel hand.

His veins were full of holes where countless numbers of needles had injected pain killers and liquid nutrition. He had been in a light coma for weeks when the first treatment began and had no way of knowing that a drug traveled through his blood and slammed into his pituitary gland with enough force to kill many people. What he did realize was the incredible strength that seemed to electrify every muscle in his body for just an instant, a change so extreme that his eyes flew open and his withered hands clenched the metal bed frame with the power of twenty young men. The effect was gone as soon as it came and the coma returned with its lovely dreams of death and suffering.

Brad turned his head to reach for the bag containing his equipment and missed the reaction of the old man. His fingers relaxed the instant he turned back toward him or Brad may have noticed the imprints of Leonard White's fingers bent into the bed frame.

He connected the life monitoring equipment and noted that his subject was operating slow but normal. He drew blood for several tests in the lab and then rechecked all of the equipment before leaving the room.

Thomas Maywood was standing outside the door as Brad emerged, flashing his constant nervous smile. Brad felt his stomach turn at the sight of the slightly yellowed teeth and the smell of cheap hair tonic. Maywood had been taking a keen interest in Brad's activities and generally had been getting in the way. Several people were getting injections and Maywood was trying to keep track of his charges. He felt a little uneasy with the situation, not knowing how many people were being affected by Brad's experiments.

"Maywood, will you please stop lurking around every room I'm in," Brad snapped. "You've got to get off my back and let me work. I'm paying you enough to demand some privacy."

"Now wait a minute," Maywood whined. "I didn't realize you were going to be so secretive. You could be playing Dr. Frankenstein with every patient in this facility."

"Let's go to your office," Brad suggested. "I don't think we want everyone in this facility hearing what we're saying."

The two men walked to Maywood's cluttered office without further comment but began their argument in earnest the moment the door closed. Maywood pointed toward the closed door and shouted, "Look Buster, anytime I want you out of here you're gone. You may be paying me but I've decided the risk is too great without knowing what the devil's going on."

"You wouldn't understand what I'm doing even if I tried to explain it to you," Brad shot back.

"Now wait a minute." Maywood's face had turned a deep red. "Don't talk down to me."

Brad suddenly realized that he was fighting a battle that could not be won. He had an ideal setup here and did not want to damage his research because of a petty squabble. Quickly he said, "I'm sorry. I really was not trying to talk down to you. My research is a study of the ageing process. I know that's putting it simply but all of the details really are difficult to grasp if you're not a medical doctor. I think my work is safe but I don't want to wait for all of the government red tape to clear."

"What about the Perrin woman?" Maywood interrupted. "She croaked the minute you started working on her."

"She was an old woman for crying out loud. I don't think there's any way my first treatment could have hurt her in any way, there just wasn't time. Look Maywood, I don't want to get into trouble any more than you. I'm not going to treat anybody that has relatives or someone who cares for them, just like we agreed. Anyone that dies while I'm working on them for no matter what the reason will be taken care of by Wilson. Can't we just drop this subject and trust each other that much?

"I would be very foolish to cross you in any way," Brad reasoned. "You're not only giving me a way to continue my research but if anything happens you can claim you didn't know what I was doing."

"Hey, that's right." Maywood beamed. "I never thought of that. How can I know what a doctor is doing since I don't have a medical degree?" He seemed to be extremely pleased with this new realization. "Okay Doc. Everything's fine now. Just keep my money coming okay?" he chuckled.

"Sure, no problem," Brad answered with a smile. "If we're going to be into this let's get along okay?" He extended his hand and Maywood grasped it warmly. "Now I'd better get back to work."

"Oh sure Doc you go ahead," Maywood beamed, pleased with his new found sense of security. "Go slice the old buzzards to ribbons," he laughed.

Brad just smiled and walked out of the office. He went into the room of a female welfare patient named Janet Laird. Before preparing an injection of his serum he reached into his pocket and removed a tiny recording device. He reversed the tape and played back a small portion of his conversation with Thomas Maywood. The recorder had worked perfectly. He sighed with satisfaction as he placed the tape in his medical bag and began to prepare Janet Laird for renewal of her youth.

Janet had always been a gentle person who believed people should take care of each other and not permit all of the suffering that goes on in the world. Her husband had been a self employed cabinet maker who had not believed in pension plans or in women working. His plan had been to work all of his life because he loved what he did and made a comfortable wage doing it.

The plan worked well except that he died at sixty years of age, leaving a wife with no job skills or even children to help support her. Welfare was the only possible way Janet could exist. Life had been difficult. Hunger and cold became a common problem which caused health problems that were not treated properly due to the lack of money. Although she was only seventy years old she was sent to Maywood as a ward of the State.

Some of her hours were clear to her. Memories consisted of pleasant summer evenings waiting for her husband to come home for a large dinner, and of cold winter nights cradled in each others arms. She sometimes awakened and reached for him, momentarily wondering why he was not by her side. Fortunately the bulk of her long hours were lost in a dreamless sleep.

Her senses were somewhat more alert than many of the bedridden people at the nursing home so she opened her eyes at the slight pain of the needle entering her arm. Brad's face would not focus properly due to her failing eyesight but it really did not matter as she had learned to accept the small indignities the old must suffer at the hands of their keepers. She felt a speck of heat swirling through her veins until it ended in an explosion in the front of her head. Janet's eyes cleared and she saw the face of Satan leaning over her body. Her right arm shot forward with inhuman speed and grasped the Devil by the throat. "Die you scum," she rasped as the withered arm tensed and delivered the power of a twenty year old athlete. Satan's face contorted with pain and began to flail away with its arms into the air.

As quickly as it began the strength left her arm. Her eyes again blurred and the face became a blob as her arm fell uselessly to the bed. The entire action left her exhausted and she fell into a deep sleep.

Brad fell to his knees, gasping in pain and clutching his bruised throat. An instant more would have crushed his esophagus. Her strength had been so incredible that his entire force could not remove her thin hand from his throat. She lay quietly sleeping, looking so frail that death could overtake her at any moment. He was rather badly frightened but forced himself to continue the task of hooking up the monitoring equipment. Her vital signs were completely normal.

Still shaken, he left the room and headed toward home. He needed the protection of its quiet familiarity so badly that he parked on the street outside instead of returning his car to the faculty lot. Much of his tension and fear left when he turned the lock from the inside and turned wearily toward the bedroom.

Lois was stretched over the width of the king size bed reading a book. She moved a bookmark into place and carefully placed the novel beside her before speaking to him. "Brad, I'd like to ask you something."

"First tell me hello," he said with a smile. "I'm going to have to slow down a little bit. I feel like I never see you any more."

"That's right," she replied. "Maybe we don't know each other well enough."

He didn't catch her meaning and reached out for her hand. "We sure haven't lately. Let's get to know each other better right now."

She pulled from his embrace and shook her head almost violently. "No not now. I mean we really have to talk Brad. I'm serious."

—

He walked slowly to the window and looked into the limbs of an oak tree that was close enough to touch if you leaned out just a bit. A mother robin was feeding three naked babies. Brad knew what was coming and wished for the next five minutes to disappear as much as that mother robin must have wanted her babies to never again be hungry. Somehow he knew that Lois had suspected his connection with Robin Slane from the moment the police came snooping around.

"Brad will you look at me." Her tone was a request, not a demand. "I want you to tell me about that boy that was killed."

Moving away from the window was an actual physical effort. His heart pounded into his ears with an almost alarming ferocity. Ironically he found that the fear of destroying Lois' love was greater than the threat of discovery by the police. "First I want you to know that I love you." He desperately needed a drink of water to help wet his lips. "You are more important to me than my life or my research."

Tears slid slowly down her cheeks. "I love you too my darling. Nothing that could have happened can change that. Please tell me about it."

"Apparently he came to see me about his school work. How he got in with no one there I'll never know but . . . ." He paused to swallow the lump that had risen in his throat. "There was an escape, like what you went through. He was torn apart." Brad's legs began trembling so severely that he was forced to fall into a nearby chair. "I cleaned everything up and took his body to that dumpster."

Lois' face was so pale that she looked bloodless. "Why in the name of all that's sensible didn't you just call the police. This wasn't murder."

"Of course it wasn't, but a death would have ruined my research. The university would jerk that money so fast I wouldn't be authorized to buy paper clips."

"But darling, an innocent man hung himself to escape the shame of his life."

His head hung in shame. The tears sliding down the bridge of his nose fell onto the front of his shirt. "I know, but how could I have known how all of this would come out. I thought the police would just end up considering this another unsolved murder." He paused to wipe his nose. "I just had no way of knowing Lois."

She rolled from the bed and kneeled in front of him. His hand tasted of salt as she pressed her lips to Brad's clenched fists. "Nothing can be done about what's happened. Our only concern is that detective whose been hanging around. I think he suspects something."

He lifted his head and looked into her eyes. "Then you'll support me?"

"Of course I will," She insisted. "I not only love you but I also believe in your work." She smiled and squeezed his hands. "Get hold of yourself before aging starts again. I don't want that teenage expression 'my old man' to turn out to be true. Now come on and smile for me."

He managed a feeble upturn of his lips that looked more like a grimace than a smile. He wondered if he should tell her about the nursing home work and quickly decided to tell her. Lois could be of great help in gathering and testing data. "Can you really trust in me?" he asked hesitantly.

"Brad, I meant every word I said. Your research will someday enable scientists to work for hundreds of years on an idea. Think of how many breakthroughs were halted because the researcher died of old age. I don't care how many notes he kept, a certain amount of insight dies with him. I firmly believe that someday life may be almost eternal because of your work."

He looked into her eyes that were moist with the emotion of her little speech. "Listen to me carefully. Could you justify the death of more human beings to advance the work I'm doing?"

Her eyes widened with surprise or horror, Brad was not sure which. After only an instant of hesitation she reached out and took his face gently between her hands. He could barely hear her whisper, "I will follow you to the depths of Hell if you ask me to."

Brad reached up and pressed her hands even more firmly to his face. He sighed deeply and said, "My work at the nursing home involves working with the residents. I've injected seven people so far, one of which died." He paused for her reaction and got none so he pressed on. "I don't know if my treatment caused her death. She might have been as good as dead anyhow. That's actually what I'm aiming for, people who are going to die anyway."

She pulled away and looked at him intently. "Won't the director of the nursing home get suspicious if one or more of these people start getting younger?"

"No, I've paid him off."

"Oh Brad," she exclaimed, "is that safe?"

"I think so. After all, he's taken the money so he's implicated himself in everything I do." His heart pounded with relief that she was saying things to support and not condemn him. "I've even made arrangements at a funeral home for no questions asked death certificates and cremations."

"Is this all really necessary darling? I mean the risk of human life."

"You answered that question yourself," he said with a smile, "when you talked about the scientists dying and people in general living hundreds of years. The very people that I'm going to use have no families and are as good as dead anyhow. I think they would want to not only have a chance to live but help all of mankind at this point in their lives."

"Of course you're right," she said. "What can I do to help?"

———

72

"The first thing you could do is promise to go to the court house with me tomorrow."

She gave him a puzzled look and then shrugged her shoulders. "Of course I will, but what are we going to do there?"

"Pick up a marriage license."

He said it so simply she wasn't at first sure she had heard him right. "Did you just say marriage?"

"Only if you really want to," he answered.

"Can't we make them open for us tonight?" she cried and fell into his arms.

A weary police officer stood across the street in the shadows and watched the bedroom light flash off. Sandy was using his day off to continue his information gathering. Cap had ordered him to mark his files as an unsolved murder and begin his work on a case that could be cracked. He knew without doubt that the answer to the Slane boy's death was safe within that darkened bedroom. He also felt in his guts that more people would die if he didn't find the proof he needed, and one thing that Sandy hated was the death of innocent people.

"Go ahead Doc," he whispered. "Enjoy your freedom while you can because old Columbo the second is gonna' lock your butt up." He moved toward his car with a renewed spring in his step at the thought of solving another crime.

FIFTEEN

Five more residents were placed in the treatment program because of the success with Leonard White and Janet Higgins. Neither had shown any signs of improvement but Brad considered their stability an important breakthrough.

Janet knew something was happening because she discovered her mind was much more alert than normal. The constant pain was nearly gone and she actually sat up in bed once. Why all of this was happening she could not understand, but she thought it would be wise to keep all of this to herself.

The doctor came often and took tapes from the equipment attached to her skull and sunken chest. She knew her increased activity would show but decided there was nothing that could be done to prevent that. Maybe this was the normal way to die, a last burst of energy just before the end. After all she had never gone through this before.

She kept having wild dreams, so wild that normally they should seem like nightmares. She kept seeing young men and hated them so badly her brain ached. Feeling like a wild animal she hunted these men and found no rest until she attacked and destroyed them, tearing great chunks of flesh from their bodies and drinking the hot sticky blood.

Janet felt that during her wakeful hours the dream should terrify her but for some reason looked forward to the nightly excursion in the bizarre. This must be the prelude to death.

Brad noticed the change on the tapes after three weeks. White had not responded either way but the Higgins woman showed rapid brain and respiration activity. She must have been awake often but she had either been in a light coma or was playing possum each time he visited her room.

He decided to have the first two subjects transferred into the same room to better monitor their progress. When White was being prepared to transfer from the gurney to a clean bed Brad produced a tube of ointment used to treat bed sores. His experience had been that nothing really helped them much but the ointment at least prevented infection. His eyes widened at the discovery that the skin was clear and smooth. Not even the trace of a scar was there to indicate prior damage.

An attendant noticed the change and shook his head. "Boy Doctor, whatever that stuff is you been 'usin sure works. Maybe we should try it on all the folks with sores."

"Yes of course," Brad muttered. "We'll have to try that." Cleaning people and attendant's who changed sheets and bathed the patients were a constant worry to Brad. He could not pay off everybody to remain quiet about any odd changes, besides the risk grew each time he admitted any wrongdoing to someone. Fortunately Maywood paid so poorly that he was able to hire only the least qualified people who knew little about health care. His main concern was that someone beside himself would find the remains of a subject.

Room nine held just such a gruesome sight. A female ninety four year old lay in her bed bloated beyond recognition. She had nearly every vein and artery burst from within. The body did not explode like the animals but the intense pressure had forced a massive amount of blood to flow from her nose and mouth. Brad was making his rounds and walked into the room. He paled at the sight of the swollen corpse and the almost black blood that seemed to cover the entire bed. Another resident living in the room, also one of the subjects of his experiments, awoke and turned her head toward her roommate before Brad could draw the curtain that separated the two. She bolted upright in her bed and opened her mouth in a voiceless scream, forgetting in her horror that cancer had claimed her vocal cords six months before. The shock was so intense that her heart instantly stopped beating and she fell back on her pillow, joining her roommate in death.

His instincts as a doctor pushed Brad to her side. After checking for a heartbeat he prepared to begin life saving action. Suddenly he paused. Saving this miserable old wretch would create a witness to a death that he did not want to explain. She would probably die soon even if she were revived, that is presuming he could even bring her back. Surely there was justification in permitting her to pass on for the good of his work.

He left the room quickly, locking the door to prevent anyone from discovering the bodies. The storeroom contained several body bags. He took two and returned to the room, locking the door this time from the inside. He wrapped up blankets and sheets soaked with blood and placed them in the vinyl bag with the body. The two women were so emaciated by age and sickness that the task was a fairly easy one. They were almost birdlike in weight.

Most of the blood had been contained within the bedding, so the cleanup was a simple task. Only about twenty minutes passed before the entire incident appeared to have never happened. He left the room, locking the door again to prevent anyone from seeing the bags.

He dialed the funeral home as he wound the necessary document into a typewriter. Sweat suddenly beaded onto his forehead as the tension began to sink in. The telephone rang only once before being picked up.

"Wilsons. May I be of service?" the smooth voice almost purred.

"This is Doctor Richardson." He reached for his handkerchief to rub at the sweat stinging his eyes. "Is this Mr. Wilson?"

"Yea it sure is." The speech and tone instantly lost the smoothness it had a moment ago. "You got some business for me?"

"Yes I do." Brad swallowed hard, his stomach churning in protest.

"Regular or special."

"One regular, one special." He pulled a waste basket closer to him as his stomach soured further.

"I'll be there in twenty minutes. Have the death certificates ready."

"I'm typing them now," Brad said duly but the line was already dead. He leaned over the basket and almost vomited but was able to hold himself back. He quickly finished the forms and went outside to wait for the hearse. The cool air helped his head to clear and soon he felt better.

A long, obviously well used hearse soon pulled into the drive. Frank Wilson looked as perfect as ever, each hair groomed into place. He left the engine running and walked gracefully toward Brad. His voice was almost a whisper as he was so used to speaking softly but clearly to mourning visitors. "Let's get with it. I've got three to get ready for tomorrow morning.

"This way." Brad's shoulders slumped from the burden of so many innocent deaths. Despite his constant rationalization the guilt he felt was often staggering.

They entered the room and Wilson unceremoniously tossed a bag over his shoulder. Brad winced and then lifted his small burden with tenderness and respect. "I'm carrying the one that needs special treatment," he said as they reached the courtyard.

"It doesn't make any difference. I'm going to burn all of the nursing home bodies to eliminate possible suspicion. If there's ever a problem the officials won't question standard procedure, but they would wonder why we're burning certain ones. I'll just throw them in the oven together and flush the ashes."

Brad handed him the necessary paper work and turned back to the Nursing home with a heavy heart. His whole existence was dedicated to helping people and prolonging life. He suddenly wondered how he had gone too far to turn back. The lives that had been sacrificed would have been truly wasted if he quit now.

The walls in the hallway of the nursing home looked dirtier than usual as Brad continued his rounds. The suffering seemed worse than usual and the injustice of life more intense. He longed for the comfort of home and the soft, soothing voice of Lois but forced himself to complete his rounds.

White and Higgins were the last two he needed to check for the day. By the time he reached their room his depression was almost physical. He opened the door and suddenly stood erect, stunned into immobility. Janet Higgins was standing in front of an open window; her arms stretched high above her head. She shook herself like a dog coming out of the water and bent over to deftly touch her toes.

Brad noticed her arms and legs were not covered by the flimsy hospital gown. Many of the wrinkles were gone, the skeleton thin skin and bones were filled with flesh. She turned toward him and gasped in surprise at the sight of him. Her face was not young, but she could have easily passed as someone in her early sixties.

They stared at each other for a moment until the shock wore off. Janet broke the silence with a voice that was filled with both terror and excitement. "Are you the doctor?"

"Yes I am," Brad answered quietly. He moved slowly into the room and closed the door.

"What is happening to me? Should I be grateful or will I just be disappointed when I wake up tomorrow morning and discover this was all a dream?"

"I assure you you're not dreaming. The thing I can't tell you is if your condition is temporary or permanent," he said truthfully. "You are the first human being that has responded like this to the treatment."

She flexed her arms and wiggled the very fingers that a few short weeks ago were twisted with arthritis. "I want to know what you are doing to me but I also sure don't want you to stop." She frowned and narrowed her eyes. "You're not going to stop are you?"

"Absolutely not. I hope that before we're done we'll have your physical age at around twenty five or thirty."

"Will I get my figure back? I was quite a dish in my day you know."

Brad smiled, relieved that he didn't have to be concerned with a confrontation with the woman. She obviously liked what was happening to her. "The only problem at this point is that you're supposed to be close to death and here you are ready to go dancing."

"I don't know if I'd go that far," she laughed, "but I sure feel terrific."

"Well, I don't think we're ready to unveil you to the world just yet and I don't think we want some orderly getting a look at the new you. I think tonight you'd better come with me and we'll get you a new place to stay."

"Great," she exclaimed. "The best thing that could happen to me is getting out of this place." She held up one hand and added, "On my feet that is."

"I couldn't agree with you more," he said. "Now let me check you over and give you an injection that will keep your age going in the right direction."

"Inject away. Anything that works."

A quick call to the funeral home took care of the problem of her disappearance. "Two thousand buys you a case of mixed up records Doc. You just fill out the death certificate and I'll forget that I didn't get a body."

Brad hung up the phone with mixed emotions toward Wilson. He was grateful that the man was willing to take his money in exchange for silence but he would rather his motives were for science. For a moment he thought about the trouble he was in. Would the world forget a few deaths in return for the fountain of youth? It really didn't matter. No price was too great to pay for the answer to death.

He returned to his subject with the serum and prepared to inject her. "How long will I have to take these shots?" she asked. "I've always hated shots."

"I hate to keep saying I don't know but I truly can't answer most of your questions. I plan on injecting you daily until we lower your physical age to the late twenties. After that we'll stop until you start again. That should pretty much tell us how often you need a booster."

"Then this whole thing is pretty much hit and miss," she complained.

"Pretty much, yes."

"Then this thing could kill me as quick as it makes me young."

"That's correct."

"What other choice is there?"

Brad shrugged. "We could stop now, you'll probably soon revert to your actual age and, at the rate you were going, you'll be dead in six months."

"I'm not seventy two yet you know. A lot of people live to their nineties and I've been almost two years on my back in this hole."

"Part of the reason I picked you was I knew you wouldn't live much longer anyway, so actually you should be glad your health failed. Being younger probably is the reason you're progressing so well and, besides, would you rather be a healthy thirty year old or a healthy eighty year old."

"You doctors have an answer for everything," she said with a smile. "When do I get out of here?"

"Tonight. I'll walk you out like you're a visitor. We're not even going to tell Maywood about this."

"How can I just disappear? Won't someone wonder what happened to me?"

Brad hesitated for a moment, trying to decide how much he should tell her. He decided that her trust was important and only the complete truth could guarantee a solid relationship. "On paper you died this morning," he said simply.

Her face registered the shock. "Wow, you must have some really heavy connections. Is this the government or something?"

"Yes and no. It's a university funded project with backing from some government agencies, but even they don't know I'm doing this. I've acted totally on my own."

"Well whatever or however I'm glad you did it."

"I think I'll have you stay at my university lab until I decide when to introduce you to the world. Do you think you can restrain yourself and stay hidden for a few weeks or months?"

"That's going to be tough. After all, it's like being reborn and I'd love to have some fun."

"And soon you shall," he consoled. "Maybe you could go out at night a few times to keep down cabin fever."

"Whatever you say. After all I do owe all of this to you." She twirled around in glee at the ability to feel good again. "I'll just save up my energy for a while and then just tear this town apart."

SIXTEEN

Three weeks seemed like years when you felt and looked like a person in their early forties. The injections helped remove literally several years each day. Her only side effect was headaches and some nervousness which Brad attributed to boredom.

Janet had all of the comforts she could ask for. Anything she wanted, Brad was quick to supply and brought it to her with promises of a quick release from seclusion. Television had become boring and the caged animals were the only company she had most of the day.

Lois had become a fast friend and visited often. Janet knew that she had been sent to help fill the empty hours and help her to be content with staying out of sight, but the two had developed a genuine liking for each other.

The animals liked being set free to roam the laboratory and Janet spent hours playing with them. When she knew Lois was coming to visit she locked them away because her friend was frightened by their freedom. Janet asked her often why she feared the creatures but her only answer had been a vague story about once being frightened by some of the animals.

On one unusually balmy evening she was especially bored as television failed to hold her interest, and even the small creatures playing on the floor were not adequate diversions. She went to the bathroom and took a shower in the stall that Brad had installed especially for her use. A full length mirror hung on the back of the door and she wiped the steam from it to view her naked body. The wrinkled skin was now smooth and taut. Her legs were almost too muscular, with a shapely buttock area accenting her lower body shape. Even as a youngster her stomach had never been this hard and she was especially pleased with her overall solidness.

The bottom line was she looked better than at any time in her life. She was still admiring her assets when a flash of white hot pain struck her forehead with such force that she abruptly sat down on the bathroom floor. Moments later she arose, and almost in a daze slipped into a revealing slit skirt that Lois had given her. She added a silk blouse that she left three buttons undone, showing off her ample breasts. She smiled at the thought of how she would affect men again, and laughed aloud at the fun it would be seeing a good looking man's face when he discovered that she wore no underwear.

Janet's vision blurred momentarily as she shook her head to clear it. The door to freedom appeared to stand at the end of a long, narrow tunnel and suddenly she realized that she must have air. Small animals scattered as she ran toward the door that not only constantly stuck very tightly closed but was locked from the outside. The entire casing and even the door itself was constructed of heavy metal. She turned the knob and pushed, listening to the sound of rivets giving away and the screech of metal tearing and bending.

The lock fell into several pieces and the door itself buckled away from the frame. Janet barely glanced at the wreckage as she burst into the cool night air, breathing huge gulps of it gratefully. She regained her composure fairly quickly but was somewhat bewildered to find herself several blocks from the laboratory.

High Street in the Columbus, Ohio campus area is famous for its night spots. She looked in both directions and realized that all of the blazing neon indicated that she was there. She walked into the nearest bar and sat on a high stool, permitting the slit in her skirt to reveal her leg almost to the waist.

"What will it be," the bartender asked, staring openly at the straining front of her dress.

"I don't know," she purred. "It depends on what the gentleman is willing to buy me." She turned to a young, strikingly handsome young man two seats from her.

"Oh boy," he muttered under his breath at the sight of that long leg falling out of the dress. Moving down beside her and visually attempting to take in everything he spoke to the bartender without moving his eyes. "Give the lady anything she wants."

"Sloe gin fizz," she replied and leaned over to touch his hand. She smiled as the young man's right eye began to twitch. "Let's not stay here long."

"Yea right". He swallowed hard. "We can even skip the drink if you want to."

"Now let's not overdo it. I haven't had a drink in a long time and I plan to at least finish this one." She drank it in two huge swallows and reached across to squeeze the inside of his arm. "Let's go."

They left the soft lighting in the bar to the sign lit brilliance of the street. Janet noted with satisfaction that her young man was sweating. It was nice to once again have that effect on a man. He lived nearby in a small apartment over a clothing store. Although the decorating was definitely done by a man the rooms were surprisingly neat and clean. No dishes lay stacked in the sink and the double bed was made with military style hospital corners.

"Well, this is my place," he began awkwardly but stopped abruptly as he watched Janet in one fluid motion strip the skirt and blouse from her body like a peeled banana. "Oh my . . . ." he began but again was stopped as she pressed her mouth to his.

She lay back on the bed in total comfort, enjoying the effects of complete satisfaction. The desire had never left with old age, only the attraction and the strength had failed her. The young man had been an excellent lover, but then so had she. Strange desires began to suddenly rush through her, ruining the comfort she had just felt. Her head began to throb again and control of her actions began to fade. She rolled on top of the young man and sat up, straddling his stomach with her naked body.

"Sweetheart," he murmured, "you're fantastic but I'm only human. I'm afraid I'm done for the evening."

"No you're not," she said quietly and deftly drove her fingers through the middle of his chest. She felt his heart beat into the palm of her hand and squeezed firmly, smashing it to a pulp. Her eyes widened and his mouth fell open just as a stream of blood poured over his face.

Janet emitted a low growl from deep in her throat and began tearing him apart. She split his head in half like a ripe melon and threw the pieces across the room. She tore the arms and legs from their sockets and completely pulverized the trunk of the corpse. Only then did she relax, the burning in the center of her forehead somewhat relieved. Covered with blood, she walked to the bathroom and turned on the shower. She didn't seem to notice that only the cold faucet was on and the water contained absolutely no heat as she stood watching the blood washing from her body and rushing down the drain.

Minutes later she slid into her dress that had miraculously escaped the bloodbath and quietly left the apartment.

She awoke on her small bed in the laboratory to the sound of Brad's voice. She was naked, the crumpled dress flung on a chair.

"Good morning," he called. "Are you decent?"

"No," she answered. "Let me get to the bathroom first will you?"

"Sure. I'll make some coffee while you get freshened up."

Brad busied himself in the kitchen with the coffee pot. Every time he saw this woman his heart began to pound. His theory was correct, his treatment was effective. Age had been conquered.

Suddenly Brad heard a scream that could have broken thin glass. He bolted from the kitchen and reached the bathroom in seconds. Janet was curled up on the floor completely naked. Her skin was wrinkled and the flesh hung with flab. She lifted her wrinkled face in agony and tore at her hair. It was snow white.

Brad had feared he would have to send her to a hospital as massive doses of sedatives had initially failed to quiet her screams. Finally the sheer volume of the drugs quieted Janet sufficiently to permit him to examine her. "You've recently had sexual intercourse," he said matter of factly, "and by the smell of your breath you've been drinking."

"Yes," she said with no emotion. "I couldn't stand the solitude any longer and I just went out on the town."

"I noticed the door was broken. What happened to you out there?"

"Nothing really. I went to a bar, had a drink, let some guy pick me up and take me home. That's all. It was great by the way."

"Janet, we have no idea how things like that affect your treatments. The alcohol or the sex could have caused the reversal of your progress."

The medication was causing her to drift into sleep, but suddenly her eyes cleared and she grasped Brad's wrist so hard he winced in pain. "Can you make me young again?" Her voice held real fear.

"No problem," he lied. "I can have you back to normal in a few days. Right now you get some rest."

"Thanks," she murmured and fell instantly into a deep sleep.

He gave her a triple dosage of serum and hoped for the best. The guesswork behind all of this was maddening but research traditionally advanced more rapidly quite by accident. He made careful notes concerning her condition and noted that within minutes after her injection many of her wrinkles were gone and her hair had only streaks of gray. The hair change was the most curious of all. Exposed hair is dead and should not be affected by the treatments but strangely enough it reacted to the age changes. Within hours she had returned to a beautiful woman in her early forties. The alcohol had to be the reason. Brad finished his testing and notes and checked the damage to the door. "At least the door doesn't stick any more," he mumbled to himself and made some mental notes of what he would need to fix the latch. The last thing he wanted was maintenance coming around and wanting to know what had happened.

He checked Janet's vital signs before leaving and felt assured she was fine. The sedatives would keep her asleep for hours. He covered her gently and thought how much she looked like Sleeping Beauty. Once again the rush of excitement pulsed through him as he considered his accomplishments. Life would continue for centuries, just like in the days of the Old Testament.

The barking, scratching and general howling of the caged animals in the laboratory pulled him back to reality. Lois had entered the door and the animals thought it was time to be fed. "Brad," she said breathlessly, "is she alright?"

"Yes, I've given her a sedative." He paused to kiss Lois warmly. "How did you know anything was wrong?"

"You haven't heard the news?"

"No, I've been working and didn't even think of the radio. What in the world is wrong?" Fear began to grip at his throat.

"A young man was murdered last night, torn to pieces. Did she do it Brad?"

"I don't know," he said. Suddenly he was very tired.

"She's strong Brad. I mean really incredibly strong. I've seen her bend inch thick metal with absolutely no effort."

"I know, the same as the animals. But that doesn't prove anything."

"Brad, the animals get violent too" she said quietly.

"I know darling," he murmured. "I just don't want to think that she's capable of murder."

"Maybe the guy attacked her or something," Brad suggested. "She can't understand her own strength."

"She claimed she just picked up a guy in a bar, had some fun in his apartment and came home. No comment about killing anyone for crying out loud."

"Could she not remember what happened?"

"I suppose that's possible." He rubbed his eyes. "I sure hope we're not running into trouble. Blast it Lois all I want to do is help the world. How many people have to die in the process?"

She sighed and put her arms around his neck. "The bottom line, doctor, is that some may have to die so lots of others may live."

SEVENTEEN

Except for a severe headache right between the eyes Leonard White felt better than he had in years. He walked around his room and tried to understand why he felt so strong.

A trip to the bathroom answered his question. He was either dreaming or dead as the face in the mirror over the sink belonged to a young man. A quick inspection of his body revealed the fine tuned muscles of a weight lifter. He thought he must be in heaven to have such a build as he never looked this good in his younger days.

He waited impatiently for someone to come in his room and tell him exactly what was going on. He had searched every drawer and found no clothing to replace the open backed hospital gown that was in need of a washing machine. Leonard occupied himself by taking a long hot shower and washed out the soiled gown in the sink. He sat on the edge of his bed in the nude and calmly waited for the garment to dry.

Night was descending upon the room when he dressed again and prepared to leave on his own. A key slid into the lock just as he approached the door. He backed away in sudden terror as he realized the unknown was about to enter into his world. Leonard stood in the middle of the room and tensed his bulging muscles in preparation to do battle.

Brad's eyes widened as he pushed the door open and faced the frightened young man. He glanced at the empty bed and quickly assessed the situation. "You must be Leonard White," he said softly and held his hands palms up to be less threatening.

"Right. Who the devil are you? Pun intended too mister."

"Well you can relax," Brad insisted. "I'm not the devil and you're not dead."

"Then how did I get this body? The last thing I can remember I was a sick old man."

"And so you were. Why don't we both relax and I'll tell you about it."

"I suppose I might as well," Leonard agreed. "If you are the Devil I guess I couldn't whip you anyway."

"Don't worry," Brad chuckled. "Are you hungry?"

"Famished. Problem is I don't think I'll get into too many restaurants in this outfit."

"You're right. Why don't I go out and pick up something for you to wear. By the way, I'm Brad Richardson, your doctor."

"Glad to meet you. Hurry with those clothes will you? The only thing that's keeping my curiosity in check is my need for a steak."

Brad contacted Wilson before returning with a suit of his own clothes and arranged for another death without a body. His excitement was almost impossible to contain as he thought about a second success in his research. The time would soon come to unveil his work to the world.

Leonard was waiting patiently as Brad unlocked the door and handed him the suit and shoes. "I hope you can at least get these on until we get to a clothing store," he commented.

"The suit is pretty close to the size I used to wear but then I didn't have muscles like this back then. The shoes will be too big."

"I'll explain the reason for the muscles on the way to the shoe store," Brad explained. "I hope you won't mind staying with a very beautiful woman for a few days. Of course both of you will have adequate privacy."

"Wait a minute Doctor. You're hitting me with too much too soon. One minute I'm an old man on my deathbed and the next I'm covered with muscle and moving in with a beautiful woman."

"You're absolutely right, I'll slow down." Brad walked toward the door and motioned for his confused patient to follow. "Let's get you those new clothes and some food and I'll explain on the way."

"Good." He led the way into the corridor. "First tell me why I'm young again."

"Have you ever heard of a gerontologist?"

"I couldn't even pronounce that."

The two men walked into the early evening coolness and Brad directed the way toward his car. "In very simple terms that's the study of the ageing process. Several different theories exist, but the one I prescribe to is commonly called The Death Clock. For some reason after our early twenties the pituitary gland produces age related substances and eventually we get old and die."

He paused to let this idea penetrate and unlocked his passenger door. He looked carefully for a reaction on Leonard's face and, after seeing no change of expression walked around the car and slid behind the steering wheel. The car backed into the travel lane of the parking lot and moved onto the highway before Brad continued. "You were near death, basically from old age, and I figured you wouldn't care either way if you died from an experimental drug or heart failure."

"So what you're telling me is you've found a way to reverse my age and now I'm going to be young and live forever?"

"Not necessarily. This whole thing is brand new and strictly experimental. All I really know is that for you and one woman it worked. Her change was gradual and yours was almost overnight. I'm finding out more as we go along."

"Is all this legal?" Leonard asked. "I mean can you just work on people any way you want just because they're old?"

Brad pulled into a shopping center and parked near a clothing store. "Using you was completely illegal and I'm sure I could have gone to jail if I had been caught."

"Wait a minute," Leonard interrupted. "You said could have. What if someone complained now?"

"You're living proof that it worked." Brad turned toward him with a smile. "I don't think the man with the answer to eternal life is going to be sent to prison do you?"

"I guess not," Leonard answered thoughtfully.

"Come on, let's get you some new clothes."

Little was said by either man as they entered the shopping center and picked out a modest variety of clothing and shoes. Brad noted to himself that some tailoring would be necessary for most of the items to fit properly over the massive muscles.

Their next stop was a rental center that fortunately was open later in the evening for a foldaway bed. Leonard lifted it into the trunk of the car with one hand as effortlessly as moving his arm.

"Imagine an old guy like me throwing a forty pound bed around like it's nothing. This is one part of this whole thing that's really great. I feel like I could crush this car like an aluminum can."

Brad didn't comment as he was somewhat concerned that he possibly could crush an automobile. Leonard would discover such things soon enough. Control over his subjects was important and brute strength could help create an even greater feeling of independence. His major club to hold over their heads was he had the youth serum and they needed injections on a regular basis to survive.

"Who's this girl I'll be staying with?" Leonard inquired as they drove toward the laboratory. "Do I by any chance know her?"

"I suppose it's possible. She was at the nursing home with you. Her name is Janet Higgins."

"No, but of course I was pretty much out of it when they took me there. I really don't remember much of anyone. You say she's a real looker?"

"She certainly is. We discovered that with her, alcohol reverses my process really quick, but the serum brings her youth back just as quickly."

"Will we have to take the treatment forever?"

"I don't know," Brad answered truthfully. "So far we have had to maintain regular injections to prevent remission with Janet. Right now, I'd presume so, but time will tell."

Brad's car pulled up to the lab and the two men entered the building. Several of the animals were playing with Janet near the cages and she did not hear them come in. She had recovered from the drug induced sleep and her youth had returned. They stood quietly in the hallway for several moments enjoying her candid movements with the animals.

She had become beautiful again, the muscle tone in her solid body adding to her sexual attraction. Her eyes were what especially haunted Brad as they were the lightest blue he had ever seen. He often looked as deeply as possible into them and almost imagined that they were transparent. Occasionally she would become displeased with something and the soft beauty became stone. The change could not have actually been a physical transformation and yet his arms exploded into gooseflesh whenever he witnessed the change.

He pulled himself from the trance she held him under and walked into the cage room. Leonard shook his head and quickly followed. "Janet, how are you feeling?" he asked.

She looked up with no sign of being startled and smiled. "Wonderfu,l thank you. I seem to be back to normal."

"Good," he exclaimed. "I want you to meet someone." He motioned Leonard to his side as he was still standing in awe of her beauty and was acting a bit like a young lovesick schoolboy. "This is Leonard White. Leonard, meet Janet Higgins."

"My pleasure," she said with and extended her hand. Leonard awkwardly thrust out his arm and grasped her hand. Brad noticed a shocked, almost pained expression on both of their faces. A tremendous flash had driven like a band of fire around both of their heads that was impossible to detect with the naked eye. It left a strange yearning in both of them that could only be satisfied by privacy. Janet was trembling from the intensity of the feeling.

Brad waited for a moment while the electric moment seemed to fade somewhat, not wanting to impose upon their private wordless exchange. "Janet," he said and when she did not immediately respond repeated "Janet".

She started and blinked her eyes. She looked at him dumbly and said, "What do you want?"

Brad, a bit taken aback, plunged ahead. "Leonard has gone through the same process as yourself. I need a place for him to stay and I was wondering if he could stay here with you."

"Of course," she said without hesitation.

"We can place some partitions on this side of the room so you both can have your privacy. You can work the bathroom arrangements between yourselves so there won't be any modesty problems."

Her eyes had moved back to meet Leonard's. "That will not be a problem. We also don't need the partitions."

Brad raised one eyebrow and smiled. "Uh, where shall I set up the bed?"

"Over next to mine," she answered without shifting her gaze.

He unfolded the portable bed and slid it alongside Janet's as instructed. He turned to tell them where the additional bedding was stored but remained silent as he saw them standing toe to toe, gently touching each other's face. Brad became caught up in the trance himself and quietly stood by watching as they very slowly began to kiss each other, their eyes remaining locked together as if welded in place.

Brad finally wrenched his mind free and began a quiet exit as he realized both people were oblivious to his presence.

EIGHTEEN

Sandy jumped aside as a young police officer ran by him, head down and hands over his mouth. Vomit was streaming through his fingers. Sandy looked quickly at his suit to insure no damage was done and walked into the apartment. An older uniformed officer met him just inside the door. "Good evening Lieutenant. You're putting in some long hours today aren't you?"

"Tell me about it Sam. What we got here?"

"Brace yourself for this one sir. There's a guy in there torn to bits. I mean this guy looks like someone was making dog food with him."

"That explains that kid coming out of here wearing his lunch."

The older officer waved his hand in disgust. "Rookies. Why can't they recruit people man enough to swallow it back down when they see this stuff?"

Sandy clapped him on the back. "They just don't make 'em like you and me anymore Sam, that's all. You can't recruit what isn't made."

"Guess you're right Lieutenant," he agreed, "but none the less this is a bad one."

"Thanks Sam. I'll swallow hard."

He really wasn't prepared for the sight he beheld in the bedroom. Gore was a part of a policeman's life but this was incredible. A blood covered head lay detached from the remains of the body. Sandy knelt and looked closely at it, trying to determine sex or age from what was left, but the mutilation was too extreme to be sure.

With pounding heart he surveyed the scene, convinced that this was another result of Dr. Richardson. Maybe the doctor himself was a madman and went around destroying people, but where did the massive strength come from? "Have the lab boys finished?" he asked to no one in particular.

"Yessir," answered a young man taking pictures for the file. "Left about ten minutes ago."

"Hey Sam," Sandy shouted through the closed door. It immediately popped open and the officer stuck his head into the room. "Call the lab and ask them if they found or looked for any evidence of an animal in here."

"An animal?"

"Yea and if they didn't look get them back here. And find out where Joe Lucas is while you're at it."

"Save your dime." Dr. Lucas was standing behind the officer, patiently waiting to get through the door. "Oh brother," he exclaimed at the gruesome sight in the room. "Have we got another Robin Slane here?"

"I'd bet my badge we do," Sandy answered. He motioned the doctor toward the bed. "Look at this torso. Torn to pieces just like before."

"Well, anything that got this violent and is covered with hair would definitely leave some behind. If we've got our killer monkey working here I should be able to tell." He pulled a stainless steel probe from his bag and carefully moved pieces to various angles. "The damage this thing does is incredible. Animals don't normally mutilate without eating, besides which monkeys aren't, for the most part, meat eaters. It's almost like this one kills for fun."

"There's got to be an answer here somewhere Joe. If we don't find it soon we're going to be seeing a lot more of this."

"You're really convinced of that aren't you? You said the same thing after the Slane boy."

Sandy rubbed his eyes wearily. "Every cop that's been around very long starts to get hunches. Lots of them never amount to anything, but occasionally you get a flash that lets you know for sure you're right. If we don't solve this one lots of people are going to die."

"Haven't you any ideas as to who could be behind this?"

"That's the heck of it Joe. I'm absolutely convinced. Problem is I can't prove it."

"Ah yes," the doctor said sympathetically, "the old catch twenty two."

"Yea no kidding." Sandy shuddered and moved away from the remains. "Look, I've got to get out of here before I join that kid throwing up in the bushes. Let me know if you connect this with an animal."

The doctor was already almost lost in his work and waved over his shoulder. "I'll call you Sandy."

The veteran officer still guarded the door as Sandy walked toward the welcome outdoors. He touched Sandy's arm and nodded toward the young policeman standing near the curb at the street. "Say Lieutenant, maybe you can talk to that kid for a minute. He feels pretty low about blowing his lunch and all that and he really is a pretty good kid."

"Why Sam," Sandy chided, "are you getting soft in your old age? A few minutes ago you were talking about these sissy rookies we've been recruiting."

"I guess I'm just an old softie. Hey, he really is a good kid."

Sandy smiled and winked as he walked toward the street. "You're one heck of a good cop Sam. Not many can be that tough but still care."

The older man blushed but was obviously pleased with the compliment. "Thanks Lieutenant. From you that means a lot."

He couldn't be more than twenty two or so Sandy thought as he walked toward the still shaky and white faced young man. He flashed back a moment to the first time he had seen death. A drunk driver had run a red light with a pickup truck and literally ran over a small sports car. The amazing thing was the lack of blood on the young girl that was killed in that car. She had a look of absolute horror frozen on her face. Sandy had taken one brief look and passed out. He woke up to the stench of an ammonia capsule and a bemused look from a paramedic. It took him months to live that one down.

"How you feelin' kid." He placed a reassuring hand on the slumped shoulder. The smell of vomit made his own stomach roll dangerously.

"I guess I really blew it in there. I never realized anything could be so sickening."

"Was this your first messy one?"

"Yea." The young officer passed his hand over his mouth. Traces of his lunch still clung to the back of his hand. "Maybe I'm not cut out for this work."

"Look, uh, Speakman is it?"

"Yessir."

"I'm Lieutenant Gibbs. Look here Speakman. You just saw the worst mess I've ever seen in my whole career. Chances are you'll never see one this bad again."

Speakman looked up hopefully. "Really?"

"Really. You could go through your whole career and never see another dead body let alone a mess like this. Look here kid, don't let this get to you. You don't have a legitimate gripe until you blow someone away. Then you can puke your guts up and talk about quitting."

"Have you ever killed anyone Lieutenant?"

He had him on a different subject, definitely a move in the right direction. "I had ten years in and never even had to pull my weapon, then one night I was on special assignment to patrol the near north side. Someone was breaking into local pharmacies and carrying off drugs. He knew what he was up to because he only took stuff that messed up his mind."

"You had your junkies to deal with too," the rookie inserted. He was beginning to regain his color.

"Sure we did, they just didn't get the press like you see now. I was on foot patrol and was walking in the alley around inside like some blamed bull elephant."

The rookie was genuinely interested now, and leaned against his cruiser for increased comfort as he listened. "The guy wasn't even trying to hide it?" he asked.

"Nope. Now that I think back on it I suppose the guy was half crazy for a fix. I went around to the front of the store and there the door was wide open. I put three hot loads in my gun, left three regular, and just kind of tip toed inside."

"Wait a minute. You used hot loads?"

Sandy joined him in leaning against the car. "The bleeding hearts today will have your badge right now if they know you're using hollow point bullets with an extra load of gun powder in them. I've heard of those things going through steel doors thanks to the extra punch."

"They can cause some pretty wicked damage," the kid added. "They flatten out and spread when they hit."

"Listen son, I had no idea how much damage they'd do until that night. I went into that store and we saw each other at the same time. I leveled my gun at him and this guy actually wet himself. I mean these light tan slacks turned dark right on the spot. I told this punk to freeze and he just dropped his armload of drugs and pulled a forty five out of his belt."

"Geez," the rookie inserted. His color had completely returned. "What did you do?"

"Well here I was," Sandy emphasized, really warming to his story, "probably just as scared as the junkie. I yelled at him to put the gun down but he just hit the safety. I figured at that point this Bozo was going to kill me so I jerked off two rounds as fast as I could pull the trigger. You would have sworn a cannon went off. The first shell hit his chest and blew a five inch hole out his back. The second hit him flat on the nose and just completely eliminated his face. I want to tell you I took one look at that mess and threw up for ten minutes. I couldn't eat for a week."

After a moment's pause the rookie took his queue and said, "But you got over it right?"

"Darn right kid. I got over it because if I didn't I'd have had to get out of the business and I happen to love being a cop."

"I guess I do too."

"Then you'll be alright." Sandy pushed away from the cruiser. "All you have to do is love being a police officer more than you hate seeing death. Hang tough okay?"

"Yessir. And thank you sir."

"Don't thank me," Sandy said over his shoulder as he headed for his car. "Thank a fellow officer that cares." He jerked a thumb at Sam who was coming down the steps of the apartment.

Sandy felt good about himself as he reached his car and saw the two police officers, the old and the new, talking about the horrors of the job. That very thing kept men on the force and not needing counseling for job stress. His task at hand jumped back into focus as he pulled away and remembered his next stop. The laboratory was only minutes away and it held the answers to these murders. He pulled up to the curb and sat for a moment while trying to gather his thoughts. Letting animals loose to kill people just didn't make sense. An accidental escape was one thing, but that surely wouldn't happen more than once. You would think security would be tightened down hard after the Slane boy's death. The other possibility was the laboratory animals had nothing to do with either death and he was leading himself down the wrong path. Many a good cop had been so sure of their 'hunch' that an obvious fact completely escaped detection.

He shook his head and climbed out of the car. "Maybe I'm just too old for this" he muttered to himself and wearily trudged toward the metal door. The knob refused to turn as the new lock was in use. Sandy walked slowly around the building, trying to hear sounds from within. A muffled noise could be heard near the rear but he couldn't determine if it was animal or human. He reached the front door again, pulled a credit card from his wallet, and deftly slid it between the door and its frame. He glanced around and was reasonably sure no one was looking. The lock leased easily under his practiced hand and he pushed gently. The buckling of the door when Janet had pushed her way out eliminated the sticking so the door swung easily open.

Growling, animal like noises were coming from the office area. Sandy pulled his service revolver and moved slowly toward the sounds. He silently prayed that his ammunition wasn't too old. Regulations dictated new bullets every four months but most detectives never bothered to change them. After all, it was the street cops that had to worry about using a weapon.

His mouth went dry and sweat broke out on his forehead as he moved toward the sounds. He figured that this is the way Robin Slane died, a laboratory animal escaping and waiting for something to attack. Well, Robin didn't have a .38 police special with him. Sandy wiped his hand across his brow to remove some of the perspiration and inched slowly toward the open office door.

A cage rattled and Sandy almost shot a dog that was trying to push his nose through the links for a pat on the head. Sandy breathed deeply and moved forward, his hands trembling slightly. A soft light was coming from the office and the animal noises increased with intensity. Two steps to the left placed him directly in line with the open door. He crouched slightly with his pistol leveled at arms length. He gasped involuntarily at the scene in the room, not sure if he was seeing violence or love.

Two naked people were intertwined on the floor, tearing and biting each other with such violence that blood was flowing from their many wounds. His initial instinct was to rush in and save the woman from the attack, but he quickly realized that the groaning and snarling was not based upon fear and pain, but actually was the product of passion and lust.

He watched for several minutes, completely entranced by the incredible power of their lovemaking. Finally the spell was broken and he quietly slid toward the exit, embarrassed that he had invaded their privacy. The couple raged on, oblivious to any outside influences. Sandy closed the door and walked to his car, trembling so violently from the adrenalin pouring through his veins that he feared he would collapse.

The car seat was a welcome relief as Sandy fell behind the wheel and composed himself for a moment. Having decided that he had seen enough for one day he finally started the car and headed for the nearest bar, hoping to drink away the days events.

Leonard and Janet lay on the bare floor of Brad's office, the small bed completely forgotten and turned on its side in one corner of the room. Both were completely exhausted and covered with bruises, scratches, and blood. Neither had the strength to even speak for several minutes, then finally Leonard struggled to his feet. He righted the small bed and helped Janet over to one edge and then he fell across the other.

"I hurt you pretty bad didn't I?" he asked. His eyes slowly took in her bruised and swollen body.

"You should take a peak at yourself," she replied with a half smile. "A normal man wouldn't have lived through what I just did to you."

He looked at his own naked body for the first time. Long scratches etched his torso with large red welts forming around them. His face felt tight and swollen. Despite the pain, however, he felt strangely satisfied and calm. Leonard had never been a great lover but the past few minutes had been the most incredible experience he had ever felt.

"I guess you did remove a considerable amount of my skin," he said. "I'm afraid we've splashed some blood around Brad's office."

"We can clean that up," she replied.

He nodded in agreement. "What about the scrapes and bruises? They're going to be pretty hard to explain to him."

Janet stood up, stretched her arms above her head, and walked toward the bath room. "You'll be healed over in about an hour."

"Do you mean we regenerate that quickly?" He was astonished.

The shower burst into life. She shouted over the noise of the water, "That's right. Brad said part of our getting younger is a regeneration of cells. Anything old or damaged gets replaced."

Many of the welts were already gone and the scratches were itching furiously as the skin began to smooth over. Leonard watched the process with fascination until Janet emerged from the bathroom still naked and looking magnificent despite her own healing wounds.

A long hot shower returned most of his strength and he emerged from the bathroom to find her dressed and relaxing in a chair. "You're almost back to normal," he said.

"You too." She smiled and motioned to another nearby easy chair. "Sit down and let's talk a bit. I'm kind of anxious to find out what someone else thinks about all of this, and what we're going to do."

He settled into the chair before replying. "I guess I really don't know what to think. This is kind of like a new lease on life; I mean I ought to be dead by now. I'm an old man for crying out loud."

"Do you feel like a freak?" she asked.

"No, just fortunate. I like the prospect of eternal youth."

"What about side effects? We could really become creepy you know."

He shrugged casually. "I don't care. I just want to live."

"You can't make love like we did with an outsider you know."

"An outsider?" he injected.

"For some reason that seemed to be the thing to call them." She hesitated for several moments before plunging ahead. "I spent some time with one. I remember going to bed with him and the next thing I knew I was back here."

"So you had a blackout. That's a small price to pay for life."

She jumped up and began pacing around the room. "You don't understand. I had the strangest feeling when I got back, a sense of satisfaction that goes even beyond sex."

"I guess I don't follow you."

"I know, this is hard to explain. I guess the only way to explain it is I think I know how a cat feels when she gets a mouse. A taste of death was in my mouth and I liked it."

Leonard stared at her, openly drinking in her beauty. "You gave some guy the time of his life and feel good about it. There's nothing wrong with that. You just had a blackout and now you're scared. Just forget about it."

"That's not all there is to it. I don't know what happened but . . . . I just don't know how to explain."

"I tell you what," he suggested, "why don't I go out one of these nights and see if I have the same problem."

She brightened somewhat. "Not a bad idea." Her face fell as quickly as it had brightened. "I'm not really sure if I want you to be with another woman. Isn't that awful? I'm jealous already."

"Now don't become a possessive female," he said.

"Oh I won't," she said with a smile. "Besides I think you're going to find that once you have a taste of this you'll want more. I know I do."

"I'll check it out," he said softly. "I'll check it out soon."

NINETEEN

Lois felt a combination of emotions that ranged from worried to proud. Brad had decided to unveil his success to P. Osgood Nash at a ten o'clock meeting this morning. He was so excited that he hadn't slept all night, completely disrupting his personal anti-aging program. She noted as he dressed that he truly looked his age today. Large dark circles half mooned his eyes and his face seemed to sag and wrinkle.

"Can you get into trouble for faking death records and using human subjects?" Lois pulled her legs up and rested her chin on her knees. "Couldn't you go to jail for that?"

Brad smiled and winked. "Do you really think Ponce de Leon would have been punished for discovering the fountain of youth? Public opinion will be so much in my favor that the authorities won't dare touch me. Oh, I suppose a few will try but they won't get away with it."

"What about the nursing home administrator and the owner of the funeral home?"

He sniffed indignantly and shrugged. "The irony of it all is that those two slimes will not get touched either. How can the authorities come down on them and not me? I don't know. Any way whatever happens to them they deserve."

She leaned back against the bed's headboard and felt a small measure of reassurance. "Should I be there with you this morning?"

"I don't think it's necessary darling. Besides you've stayed in bed too long for me to wait. I still have to pick up Leonard and Janet."

"Has she fallen for him?" Lois asked. "She seems to have that far away look in her eyes when I talk about him."

"I think you're exactly right. He looks after her like a palace guard. Has Janet ever told you anything that she might have been embarrassed to say to me? Like female problems or emotions or something?"

Lois shook her head. "Never. Why do you ask?"

Brad picked up his coat and came to the bed. He kissed her on the cheek before answering. "Every small detail could make the difference in the success of this project. They may be doing well but I still have to consider the results very unstable. I'm late so I'll see you later."

"Good-by my darling. Give old Osgood heck." She watched him stride out the door and didn't lose her smile until she heard the front door latch.

Brad paced himself perfectly despite his fatigue and arrived at the lab on schedule. Janet had never looked more radiant, showing ample cleavage thanks to the low cut dress purchased for the occasion. The dress was slit to mid thigh to accent her shapely legs.

Leonard had attained boyish good looks with his transformation and looked like a fashion model. He wore a custom suit that accented the wide back and narrow hips of a body builder. Brad had given him a short sleeve shirt to show off his massive arms when the coat was removed.

Brad sensed that they were as nervous as himself and attempted to relax them. "Be natural and charming. Just your very existence will knock him off his butt so just relax."

"It's kind of hard to do that when one man holds your future in his hands." Leonard's voice was hard. "This guy could bring the whole thing down and put us back to our old selves. Pun intended."

"Nash has spent a lot of trust money on this project. He's a politician" Brad reassured. "He will know exactly how to sell you to the world. Besides public opinion will keep you young."

"Well, let's get it over with."

Brad ushered them across campus to the Trustee's office. Janet still had not spoken when they sat in the plush chairs of the waiting room. The secretary entered with a smile and motioned them to enter Nash's office.

"I can't do it." Janet's voice was shrill with tension.

"Don't lose your grip now," Brad began.

Leonard grabbed her arm and pulled her aside. He whispered something in her ear, she nodded, and all of the tension drained out of her face.

The trio walked into the office like they owned the world. Brad discovered that he was suddenly more nervous than he had realized and hoped that his voice would not break when he tried to speak. Nash pulled his bulk from his desk chair and it seemed, as usual, to sigh with relief.

"Come in Brad." His tone was light but cautious. "I understand you have some important information for me. I presume this gentleman and lovely lady have something to do with this news?" His eyes openly undressed Janet.

"Mr. Nash." Fortunately his voice came out even. "I would like for you to meet Leonard White and Janet Higgins. Mr. White is seventy eight years of age and Ms. Higgins is seventy."

The smile slowly slid from the fat man's face and his eyes narrowed. "I want you to know Doctor I am not a man easily amused by humor directed at a serious subject. In other words I won't put up with a bunch of phony crap." He dropped into his chair and a caster splintered like broken glass. Nash ignored the resulting tilt of his seat and glared at his embarrassed guests.

Brad cleared his throat before continuing. "I can document everything that I've done. In fact I've broken the law to accomplish my goals. All of the details are in this report I've prepared."

The silence in the room became suffocating as they waited for a response. Nash finally waved Janet toward the front of his desk. She came forward and leaned toward him, exposing a large amount of cleavage. "Are you really seventy years old?" he rasped, never moving his eyes above her neck.

"Absolutely," she purred. "I not only have my beauty returned but there are some interesting side effects too." She moved toward the back of his chair, picking up a small book on the desk as she went. "Just sit still Mr. Nash."

Nash looked over his shoulder as much as the flab would permit and watched Janet squat beside his chair, revealing a long solid leg as the slit skirt separated. He grabbed the arms of his chair for security as she gripped the chair leg with the broken caster and lifted the entire chair, fat man included, two feet off of the floor. She placed the book down and gently replaced the chair with the broken leg resting on the book.

"I think that will help level your chair Mr. Nash," she breathed.

Nash pulled a handkerchief from his pocket and wiped his mouth. "You lifted me with one hand. I must weigh three forty and you picked me and the chair up like a feather." His voice had risen to near hysteria.

"It's just a positive side effects of the treatment Mr. Nash," Brad injected as Janet returned to the front of the desk. He thought that it would be just his luck if the old buzzard had a stroke right in the middle of the meeting.

"Then it's real. You've actually done it." He replaced the handkerchief and seemed to regain his composure. "This will absolutely be the biggest thing since . . . . since . . . . well, there's just nothing to compare it with."

"It's what we've been working towards for many years sir. And of course these two people are pretty excited about it."

Nash smiled and pressed his fingers together. "I have never been one at a loss for words but I frankly don't know what to say. I'm just flabbergasted."

"We have one small problem sir." Brad swallowed the lump in his throat. "We experimented on these people without permission from them or any government organization."

"I figured that out myself. All government activities come through me so it stands to reason you've broken some laws."

"What kind of problem does that give me?" Brad inquired.

Nash waved an indifferent hand. "Don't worry about any of that. We'll sit down later and talk about the law. I'll take care of it. Right now I want some details about these two."

"There isn't really much to tell. Both were pretty much on their death beds in a nursing home when I began their treatments. Janet seemed to respond more quickly than Leonard. The reason at this time is a little unclear."

"Are there any more on this program?" Nash interrupted.

"Not any longer. There were twelve. Two died and the rest were removed from the experiment."

Nash frowned. "Afraid they would die too?"

"Oh no," Brad quickly said. "I just felt that the fewer people we worked with gave us a better opportunity to avoid trouble with the authorities."

"Why didn't you come to me before any of this illegal activity," Nash continued.

"To protect you sir. If my experiment had failed I didn't want you implicated in my crimes."

"Very good Bradley. Now why don't we send these children out while you and I talk about the trouble you're in." He pressed his intercom without waiting for an answer. "Betty, get me fifty dollars from petty cash and give it to the young people leaving my office." He switched off the button and smiled. "You two go out to lunch while Brad and I discuss the best way to introduce you to the world."

"Thank you very much Mr. Nash," Leonard said, obviously pleased at the prospect. "You are most generous."

"Not at all. Enjoy yourselves." Nash smiled and waved to them as they went out the door. He remained pleasant until the door closed and turned to Brad with a snarl. "What the devil have you done?"

"I'm sure several people have died because of my research." Brad was amazed that his voice did not tremble. "One of my animals also escaped and killed one of my students. His father later took his own life because the authorities suspected him of murdering the boy."

"You're talking about that homosexual that was torn apart and dumped into a garbage can a few weeks ago."

"Yes. Robin Slane."

Nash shook his head. "Do the police suspect you?"

"Probably one snoopy detective thinks he has the answer but I don't see how anyone could ever prove it." Brad's armpits began to itch but he didn't move towards them. Sweat was running down his back and staining his shirt. "I paid off a nursing home administrator and a funeral home director. One let me experiment and the other disposed of the bodies."

"This is going to be a tough one Brad, but the thing that will save you is that your experiment works. For crying out loud it works," Nash exclaimed. "You'll be the Nobel Prize winner without even trying."

"If we can just get others to try it," he remarked. "The government might fight this one."

"Let them." Nash's fist slammed the desk. "When I'm done the world will demand this. Everyone over fifty will riot in the streets to get just one drop. No, don't worry about the Feds. By the time I'm done with this the whole thing will be swept under the rug and forgotten."

"Thank you sir."

"You realize of course that this will work only while your people stay young. Any problems and your backside goes into a noose."

Brad smiled, all fear having left him. "The one thing I'm sure of is my work. These people are perfectly, absolutely normal."

The Top Hat was famous in Columbus for its steaks. Lunch was just as big a business as dinner. Despite the packed dining area heads turned when Janet and Leonard entered. They carried an almost awesome air about them, a feeling that was practically physical and forced people to move out of their path.

"Are they movie stars?" a young girl whispered to her open mouthed friend as they passed.

"I don't know but look at his bod," she replied.

Leonard strolled to the reservation table and quietly brushed aside a man inquiring about his table. "I need a table for two my dear," he interrupted.

"Say," the man bristled. "Just who do you think you are pushing your way in front of me."

Leonard slowly turned to the man and smiled warmly. "I'm Leonard. What's your name?" He extended his hand and the other man automatically took it.

"Look pal I'm Bob Warner. Now maybe you didn't . . . ." His voice froze in pain as Leonard began to squeeze his hand. He immediately responded by bearing down in return, thinking how childish this show of strength was. "Come on man, I played football in college and you're not going to . . . ." a faint crack signified a tendon tearing away from the bone.

"My dear old friend Bob has offered me his table," Leonard informed the hostess. "Isn't that right Bob?" Another finger broke at the first joint.

"Sure, sure of course," he gasped. Sweat exploded on his upper lip and his face was white. Nausea twisted his stomach. "I insist you take my reservation. Please, please take it."

"Thanks Bob." Leonard released the damaged hand. "Say hello to the family for me." He waved to Janet and they followed a confused hostess past the white faced business man.

"What happened?" Janet inquired as he helped her with the chair at their newly acquired table.

"Oh nothing." He smiled warmly. "Just some fellow decided to cancel his reservation and they gave it to us."

"Gee what luck," she said with sarcastic humor. "I'm sure he insisted with no persuasion to cooperate."

"Of course not my dear. But then I'm a man of great persuasion."

"Would you folks like something from the bar?" A waiter had appeared at the table, order pad in hand.

They looked at him for a moment with quiet amusement. Most restaurant help seemed to be young people or older women. This fellow was in his fifties and nearly bald. He looked like he should be home baby-sitting his grandchildren or selling life insurance or something, anything but waiting tables. "No thank you," Leonard finally answered.

"We're alcoholics," Janet added somberly.

"Oh, oh I see," the obviously shaken grandfather waiter stammered. "Would you like to order now?"

"Yes." Leonard continued to take the lead. "Two New York Strip steaks with all the trimmings."

"And how would you like them done sir?"

"Rare as you're permitted to serve them," Janet hurriedly interjected. "Preferably room temperature and raw."

"Yes Ma'm." The waiter hesitated for a moment, as if waiting for Leonard to speak up and correct the order.

"Do you need something else Bozo?" Leonard snarled. "We'll tip you after the meal."

"Yes sir. Excuse me please." The waiter lowered his head and walked quickly away.

"Is that how you charmed the other guy out of this table?" Janet cocked one eyebrow.

His hand darted out and grasped her forearm. "If pain works I'll use it," he whispered and squeezed her arm like a vise.

Janet slowly put her hand over his and smiled with her mouth but not her eyes. "The thing you're forgetting darling is that I've had the same injections as you but I came along more quickly. That makes me stronger." Leonard's eyes flew open with pain and fear as she bent his middle finger back just shy of the breaking point. "Now do you know how that man felt when you shook his hand? I was watching you all the time you ignorant clod."

Leonard was struggling to regain his composure and at the same time rescue his finger. "Please let me go Janet. My finger is going to snap."

She slowly released the pressure and sat back in her chair. "I don't care what you do to all the dorks we meet Leonard, but don't you ever, ever try to strong arm me again. Do we understand each other?"

"Perfectly," he meekly replied, rubbing his throbbing finger. They both sat silently through their salads, Leonard angry and Janet sorry that she had spoiled the luncheon.

"Your steaks." The grandfather waiter appeared with two virtually raw pieces of meat, smiling inwardly that these two were getting precisely what they had asked for. He would lose his tip and have to take them back to the broiler for more cooking but he didn't care.

"Perfect!" Janet cried with delight, much to the waiter's surprise and disappointment. She began to attack the meat immediately, the waiter moving away from the table quickly to avoid being ill.

"Raw meat?" Leonard asked. He looked at his plate doubtfully.

"Just try it once," she answered with her mouth full. It will turn you on for an outsider so much that you'll want to scream."

This was the only mention either of them had ever made concerning the desire to destroy, simply because they didn't understand the feeling and could not comprehend that it was even wrong. When the feeling overcame Janet she felt like a dog in heat. Her entire body and mind screamed for a man, blocking out all other logical thoughts. She hadn't even realized that she had murdered that young man. She didn't even remember hurting anyone. Still, the craving was there.

Leonard had been slower in development and was just beginning to acquire the madness. He still had the ability to use reason and felt that raw meat was a bit much. "Janet. I can't eat this," he protested. "It's raw for crying out loud."

"Try it once," she insisted. "Come on Adam, listen to Eve." She smiled playfully.

"I'll try but it seems rather barbaric," he grumbled. The fork shook slightly as he watched the blood drip from the piece on his fork.

"Go on," she prompted. Her eyes were slightly wild with anticipation. She nodded with satisfaction as he gingerly placed the meat in his mouth and began to chew.

The effect was as sudden as a snort of drugs. Leonard's heart began to pound and the pure animal desire for death filled his entire being. Not the same feeling he had when they nearly tore each other to pieces shortly after their first meeting. His feeling now was to tear at flesh and drink blood. Their eyes met and Janet immediately knew he felt what she felt, needed what she needed.

"Shall we meet each other later?" she asked breathlessly.

"Yes," he said. "If you've finished go ahead. I'll take care of the check."

Janet had nearly inhaled her meat and rose immediately to go. She was trembling so severely with excitement that she nearly fell as she stood up. She winked and quickly walked toward the door, glancing back to see Leonard wolfing his steak as quickly as possible.

—

TWENTY

Steve Haines was standing just outside The Top Hat as Janet emerged. He would never have bothered trying to pick up a doll like this one. She was too totally great and he wouldn't have a chance. He nearly made a fool of himself when she walked by and smiled softly.

Steve felt his jaw start to drop and closed it with a snap. "Hello," he said in a voice that was too small. My heavens she was coming back!

"Hi," she said and struck a pose with one hand on her hip. "What's your name?"

"Uh, Steve. Steve Haines." He paused, his mind racing. Say something you idiot his head screamed at him. She's going to walk away and you're going to blow this.

But she didn't. Instead she said, "Come on Steve. You want to ask me something like will I go to your place. The answer is yes let's go." She hooked a finger into one of his belt loops. "Am I wrong Steve?"

He nearly had to hold on for support. "No, not wrong. This way." He was acting like a jerk and still could blow this opportunity. He was a quiet, lonely man who had been divorced for a short six months. His wife hadn't slept with him for over a year before the divorce and finally asked him to leave. Steve had actually been relieved because he didn't have the nerve to go on his own and couldn't bring himself to cheat while the marriage still existed, even if it was in name only.

A new job as a marketing rep for Elco Industries took him to seven states and over seventy cities, including Columbus, Ohio. The traveling helped ease the loneliness and frustration he had felt for months. Why he hadn't thought of trying to pick up girls before was a mystery, but he had been watching television at his motel and suddenly decided that he needed the companionship of a woman. Steve was nervous as he stood on that busy sidewalk and wondered how to approach this situation. The campus was a fifteen minute walk from the motel and it seemed logical that a free spirited college girl would be agreeable to an hour of sex between classes or something. He was just realizing how idiotic that logic was when Janet walked out of The Top Hat. She looked so good that he couldn't believe his eyes. His approach was going to be with an ugly girl in a good body. That seemed to be the safest path to take in avoiding rejection.

"Why are you so quiet," she asked.

Her voice pulled him back to the present and with surprise he found them walking up to his room. "I guess I just realized that I really am with a woman that looks like she just won a beauty contest," he admitted. The key stuck in the lock and he cursed himself. "I guess I'm just not very good at this." The key finally rolled the ancient tumblers and the door swung open.

"I think you're doing just fine," she soothed and walked into the shabby room.

Steve struggled for a moment with the key and shut the door. He turned toward the bed and his mouth went dry. Janet had removed her dress and was already stretched out under the covers. Magnificent was perhaps not a strong enough statement to describe her.

"Well, what are you waiting for?" She curled her finger in invitation.

They soon were resting quietly against each other, Steve enjoying the soft sturdiness of her body. She began to slowly slide from her embrace and kissed him on the chin and then the neck. Her lips touched the hollow of his throat and moved to the top of his chest. Steve totally relaxed and closed his eyes. A searing bolt of pain suddenly blasted the middle of his chest, causing every muscle in his body to tense and his head to jerk up in an attempt to see the reason for the sudden agony.

Janet was lifting her head in a grimace that was sort of a smile. About one ounce of Steve Haines' chest was hanging from her lips. Before he could react she swallowed it and buried her head again, striping an area down to a bare rib. He screamed in fear and pain and pushed her off the bed. Blood was rolling down both sides of the gaping wound and he looked at it for a moment, not believing what he saw. The moment's hesitation gave Janet the opportunity to leap from the floor and pin him to the bed. She straddled his legs and grabbed a wrist with each hand, instantly crushing the bones with the intense pressure.

Steve screamed and struggled to no avail, watching helplessly as she bit chunks from his chest and laughed hysterically. It took almost three minutes for him to die, the shock and loss of blood finally taking its toll. Janet finally drove her head into the hole she had created, bursting his heart and lungs. After several frenzied minutes of tearing his body apart she grew quiet, the inner pounding at the front of her forehead finally gone.

She showered as before, moving slowly to savor the experience. She took her towel into the bedroom, smiling as she dried her hair. Like the previous murder she was in a different world. Outsiders were to be used, she finally understood that now. They gave pleasure and stopped the often present ache that seemed to be ever present in her head. Everything seemed to have a price. Eternal youth meant living with headaches, but outsiders held the answer. Hundreds of years

—

would pass and not one of them would be missed. Who could possibly care about such inferior animals?

The sunshine hit her eyes as she left the apartment, making her sneeze violently several times. Some things never changed. Sudden bursts of sunlight always made her sneeze. Janet wondered with a smile if four or five hundred years from now someone would invent a cure for her sunshine sneezes.

Several young men smiled and spoke to her as she walked back to the lab. Janet considered lining them up for future headache cures but quickly dismissed the idea as too risky. People got to know you when a relationship was started, people that could lead police in her direction if someone died. Besides, pickups were available almost at any time. She arrived at the lab and went in to wait for Leonard, completely unaware of the automobile across the street with a lone figure watching the building.

Leonard left the restaurant soon after Janet, enjoying immensely the thought of the waiter's anger when he discovered there was no tip. He considered telling the little creep himself but decided he wasn't worth the effort. Besides, his head was starting to pound just above the bridge of his nose. Until he became young again Leonard hardly ever got headaches, now he seemed to live on aspirin.

His eyes wandered about the busy street full of young people, many of them girls in tube tops and shorts. Leonard felt his headache growing worse the longer he watched the parade of women. His pulse quickened and his mouth went dry with desire. Several girls eyed his solid muscle and rugged handsomeness openly as he watched their braless shirts. He smiled at an unusually pretty girl that was almost bursting through the fragile fabric of her tube top. She wore cutoff jeans that showed the white pocket liners extending below the ragged edges of the legs. Several hours of daily sunbathing had burned her to an almost perfect brown. Several years of picking up good looking men enabled her to shift gears in mid-stride without looking awkward. She smiled a perfect row of teeth and walked up to Leonard, standing so close that she touched the front of his shirt with her breasts.

Leonard's heart began to race, more with fear than lust. He struggled with an almost uncontrollable urge to split this magnificent creature's head open like an over ripe melon. He considered running away and even tried, but his legs seemed buried in concrete.

"My oh my, but look at you." The girl bent her head back to look at his face. Leonard was six inches taller. "My name's Veronica. What's yours?"

"Leonard." His head was pounding so fiercely that he could barely hear his own voice. Or was he whispering?

"How about a drink?" She slipped her arm through his and led him toward a nearby bar.

"I, uh, sure," he stammered, still confused by the suddenness of her approach and the steady pounding in his forehead.

Veronica proudly pulled him into the bar and put his arm around her so that Leonard's hand rested against the side of her left hip. "Hi gang," she shouted to a group of college age people sitting at a table near the front door. "Been waiting long?"

An immediate hush fell over the table as all eyes turned toward an enormously muscled young man with blond hair and the face of a model. His eyes flew open in surprise and then instantly narrowed in anger. His fair skin burned scarlet as he rose from his chair, towering four inches over Leonard and outweighing him by thirty pounds.

"Hi, I'm Leonard," he said with a smile.

"No you're not," the blonde growled. "What you are is dog meat."

Leonard instinctively backed up a foot as the big man advanced. Leonard held up a hand, palm out. "Now wait a minute. What's the problem here," he asked.

"The problem is, you slime, is that that's my girl you're paradin' around with. She drags a new one in every so often and I have to rearrange their bodies a bit. She loves it."

Leonard smiled and raised one eyebrow without making a comment. Finally he shook his head in disgust and turned his full attention to the enraged boyfriend. "Look, I don't want any trouble. I didn't know she was spoken for and I'll just walk out and leave her to you. Okay?"

"He was sure super in the sack," the girl giggled.

The young man reacted like a cannon blast. He drove a huge fist into Leonard's stomach, a small smile turning up the corners of his mouth. The smile turned to shock as Leonard didn't fold up like a cheap accordion as he was accustomed to seeing, in fact he didn't move an inch. The rage melted like snow in August, and his red flushed face was turning white with sudden fear.

Leonard calmly grasped the wrist of the closed fist that was attempting to retreat with haste with his thumb and forefinger and squeezed. The big man choked back a sob of pain and fell to one knee. Tears filled his perfect blue eyes and spilled down his cheeks.

"You hit me," Leonard said flatly. "I told you I didn't want to fight and still you hit me. Tisk tisk."

The entire room was sitting in stunned silence, waiting to see what would happen next. They didn't have long to wait. "You're breaking my wrist," the blonde man sobbed.

"Maybe that would stop you from beating up every poor slob that your girlfriend the tramp brings in here," Leonard snarled.

—

"Hey now just a minute." The girl came to life when she was called a tramp.

"Shut up!" Leonard barked. She covered her mouth with a shaking hand. Looking back at the sobbing man Leonard grated "Now, do you agree that your girlfriend is a tramp?" He squeezed just a little harder.

"Yes, yes she's a tramp," the blonde cried. He was on both knees now, tears dropping from his nose and splashing onto the bar room floor.

"Now I think proper restitution is in order," Leonard said with a smile. He loosened his grip slightly. "I think you should lick my shoes."

The whole room was still watching in stony silence and watched as their giant friend was being humiliated, but no one offered to help. Finally a girl said, "Don't make him do that man. He's had enough."

Leonard removed his fingers and the blonde fell back, rocking back and forth while he rubbed his painful wrist. "Now big boy," he said in contempt, "since your friends have decided they don't want you to have to do any boot licking that has made me decide. I would suggest you get busy."

"No." His voice still cracked but some of the confidence had returned.

"Okay," Leonard said and quickly stepped forward. He grabbed a handful of yellow hair and jerked the again terrified head back. Leonard placed his hand almost gently on the man's perfect nose and calmly pushed it flat. The young man screamed in pain and a gush of blood from ruptured vessels shot onto the front of his muscle shirt. Leonard then gave the crushed nose a twist, dooming its owner to several sessions of reconstructive surgery to correct the damage.

There was still no sound coming from the table, the quiet emphasizing the groans of the blonde. Leonard turned his attention to Veronica. She had become very pale and didn't look very pretty. "Maybe you and your boyfriend will stop playing this little game for a while. You're a real slut you know."

This time she didn't react to the insult. She seemed unable to take her eyes from the smashed nose. Leonard spat on the floor, turned on his heel and walked into the sunshine. He sneezed several times in reaction to the sudden change and smiled at the thought of lover boy trying to sneeze through that smashed pulp of a nose. He felt better now, at least the pounding in his head was reduced to a dull ache. He rubbed his forehead and turned in the direction of the lab.

TWENTY ONE

Sandy was too tired and hungry to wait outside the lab any longer. He wasn't really getting anywhere anyhow. The girl had returned by herself after the morning arrival of Dr. Richardson and then all three departed. Sandy was trying to piece together why people were living in a laboratory unless the experiments were now so technical that someone had to be there all of the time. Or were they to make sure no more animals escaped and killed someone.

He also wondered if the doctor knew his people were making it during working hours. Many, many questions, all of which may or may not mean a thing. Sandy yawned and drove away thirty seconds before Leonard returned. A stop at the White Castle took away his hunger; the small burgers were still his favorite.

Almost as an afterthought he switched on the radio in his car. His name was being called by an obviously exasperated operator. "Lieutenant Gibbs *please* call in at once."

He smiled at the dispatcher's plight and thumbed the microphone. "This is Gibbs."

The silence on the other end indicated a shock that he was actually there. Finally the radio responded. "You are to report to Captain Salinski's office immediately."

"It's too late," he replied. "I'm sure the Captain has gone home by now."

"He left instructions to be called at home when you reported in."

Sandy frowned and turned his car toward the downtown police headquarters. This had never happened before. When Cap went home he left the job behind him. Something awfully big must be in the air. "I'm on my way," he answered.

Traffic was light so Sandy arrived at the police station parking garage within fifteen minutes. He moved quickly through the complex and arrived at Cap's office less than twenty minutes after he received the radio call. The Captain was in his office reading a report. Sandy walked to a chair and fell into it heavily. "You must have been out the door before the phone hit the cradle, Cap. You're a good thirty minutes from here normally aren't you?"

Cap eyed Sandy carefully. A lot of years had passed between them and Cap felt a lot of friendship toward the veteran police officer. He wanted to choose his words carefully and yet had to make the point as clearly and painlessly as possible. He sighed and began. "We've known each other for a lot of years Sandy. I want you to know I think you're a great cop."

"You didn't call me in here and run yourself clear across town just to tell me you're in love with me Cap." Sandy's grin wasn't returned and he began to really worry.

"How long do you plan on going before retiring?"

Sandy felt the sweat break out on his upper lip. He fought the urge to wipe it off. "I kind of thought I'd stay five, maybe six more years," he said quietly. Fear began boiling in his stomach like a volcano.

"I've been given orders to convince you to pull the pin. I don't like it, in fact I hate it but that's the way it is sometimes."

"What if I refuse?"

"Don't."

"Stuff it Cap. I don't quit just because someone asks me to." Sandy stood and walked towards the door.

"Wait a minute Sandy. I think you should let me tell you what happened this afternoon before you make a decision."

Cap's voice was so intense that Sandy felt compelled to hear him out. "I'll give you five minutes" he said bitterly, returning to his chair.

"I got a visit today from the Secret Service. It seems they've got a special division that's even more hush hush than the CIA. The guy wouldn't even tell me the name of it."

Sandy ignored the attempt at humor. "What could the Secret Service have to do with me Cap? I'm the most boring person in the world."

"Let me put it to you this way. This guy, oh by the way, he said his name was Jones."

"Jones?" Sandy injected. "You've got to be kidding."

"No joke. The man said his name was Bob Jones. He told me to call the Chief of Police, which I did, and my instructions were to give Mr. Jones absolutely anything he wants. He only asked for two things, your retirement and Robin Slane's file."

Lightning didn't have to strike Sandy twice to make him wake up. Doctor Richardson had met with success and now the government was going to cover up a murder he was responsible for. Sandy was getting too close so he had to be quieted. "Cap, I know what this is all about. I can tell you who is responsible for that boy's death and some pretty convincing details."

"Hold it right there." Cap shook his head. "Frankly I don't want to know what this is all about. Sandy, this department can destroy us as easily as picking up the telephone. Your career has just ended and I don't want mine to end too for the sake of trying to make an uncaring world listen." He began pacing from wall to wall in the small office. "These people have power Sandy."

"Sit down Cap, you're making me dizzy." Cap gave him a wry grin and sat down. "I've given my entire working life to fighting things that were wrong. I just can't turn my back on that now."

Cap sighed and rubbed his face with both hands. "I was afraid you'd say that." He pushed an intercom button. "Mr. Jones are you there?"

Almost instantly the office door opened to reveal a young man that looked like a twelve year old in a grown up body. Sandy was struck by his smooth round face. The only feature that revealed his age and experience were his eyes which were gray and very, very cold. He was wearing a tailored suit and was slim but powerful looking. Sandy's trained eye measured his height at about six feet. His hand shake was firm and brief and the smile that curved his lips revealed even white teeth. The smile did not reach his eyes.

"Lieutenant Gibbs it is a pleasure. Your Captain speaks very highly of you." He nodded toward Cap. "He felt we would have to talk for a bit. Frankly I would have been sorry if you had given in too quickly." His smile broadened and almost, but not quite, reached his eyes. "Would you excuse us for a moment Captain Salinski? I think maybe the Lieutenant and I need to talk privately."

Cap left the room without comment. Jones sat down in the visitors chair nearest Sandy. "You know the whole story don't you Lieutenant." It was a statement not a question.

"Dr. Richardson had something to do with Robin Slane's death" Sandy replied flatly. "I was getting close to the answer when his experiment worked on people, probably illegally, but because nobody wants to flush away the fountain of youth you've decided to cover the whole thing up and let the good doctor be a hero. The question is has anyone else been murdered because of his work. I would presume you'll check that out."

Jones clapped his hands lightly. "Very good Lieutenant. You're surprisingly close. So close that to be honest with you the only reason you haven't been eliminated is your status as a police officer. The public outcry might be a bit uncomfortable."

Sandy felt the anger begin to boil in his chest. "Maybe I should give you reason to want to change your mind."

"Before you go too far Lieutenant let me talk a bit about a young lady named Cindy. I don't believe the dear child even has a last name, but usually she's somewhere around the bus station."

"Yea I know her. She's a hooker. Pretty decent sort really, I've given her a break a few times."

Jones raised an eyebrow and touched his fingers together under his chin. "Most interesting. It seems that Cindy is prepared to reward you by swearing that she's provided you with money and, shall we say, sexual favors for the past five years in return for your ignorance of her activities." Jones raised a hand to stop Sandy's comment. "And let's look at a certain piece of slime named Eddie Paxton. As you know he's been a pusher of drugs ever since he discovered he couldn't afford to buy enough for his own usage."

Sandy spoke through clenched teeth, "Let's hear what Eddie has to say about me."

Jones chuckled mirthlessly. "It would seem that you've been supplying Mr. Penton with drugs stolen from the police property room and replacing it with powdered sugar. Now aren't you a bad boy Lieutenant."

"How much did you have to pay them for these lies Mr. Jones?"

Jones shrugged. "It doesn't matter. The point is we can make you appear to be anything we desire. If these two aren't enough to get you fired and take away your pension we'll come up with more. Enough to send you to prison if necessary. Actually, that was my original suggestion. No one would care if a disgraced cop in prison was killed, then we wouldn't have had to worry about you at all."

"That's very good Jones," Sandy said with a certain amount of genuine admiration.

"Thank you," Jones responded with a reptilian smile. "I was rather proud of the idea if I say so myself."

Sandy stretched his back and winced at the slight pain. "I guess what you're saying is I dedicated my life to a system that's a lie because there is no justice."

"Alas, tis true" Jones crooned. "But don't take it so hard." His tone was sympathetic. "The system is geared for the general welfare of all the people. Endless youth is just more important than a few dead people, or for that matter one old cop. Surely you can see that."

Sandy fought to keep the disgust from his tone of voice. "I suppose you're right. Besides, I haven't much of a choice."

Jones leaped to his feet with a look of satisfaction on his face. "Wonderful. I knew you'd see it my way if I just explained the situation thoroughly. Captain Salinski has your paperwork drawn up and will see to it that your exit will be swift and painless." He walked over to Sandy and held out his hand. "You're a good cop you know. Most men would have let this die a long time ago."

Sandy grasped his hand, somewhat surprised at the power in his grip. He half smiled and said, "Thank you for that anyway."

Jones shrugged and exited without further comment. The silence in the room seemed like a tomb. Sandy wondered if he was to wait for Cap or just slink out of the building and go home. You'd think there would at least be a clock to tick in here. How the devil did Cap stand the silence?

He began to whistle softly to break the seal of noiselessness. Loss of hearing frightened him more than the thought of blindness. Death was quiet and he didn't like the thought of not existing. The best way to stop the hurt he was feeling would be a quick bullet in the head from his service revolver but he knew he wasn't enough of a coward for that.

Cap finally came back through the door and Sandy felt genuine pity for the man. This was really a tough thing for him to do. "I hope I don't look as bad as you right now," Sandy quipped. For crying out loud, he was trying to console the man who was throwing him out of the department. "Perk up a little," he added.

"Sandy, this is the dirtiest thing I've ever been asked to do. I feel like I ought to help you but I don't have the guts."

"Don't worry about it." Still trying to soothe his feelings. "We'd just lose anyway. These people have power that you and I could never dream about. Why throw our lives away for nothing?"

"Yea, of course." Cap sounded unconvinced. "Well, I'll have to take your weapon and badge."

"Already eh?" Sandy replied.

"No sense in putting off what has to happen."

"I suppose you're right." Sandy pulled the old police special from its holster and placed it gently on Cap's desk. "The holster is mine. I had it custom made."

"I know," Cap replied.

Sandy reached for the leather case that held his badge. Department regulations demanded that the badge be turned in at the time of separation from the force. Every cop schemed to find a way to keep the shield. They considered it a special test to beat the system. An old bullhead named Steve Bainbridge once kept his for a full year. The department refused to issue any retirement checks until he turned it in. Bainbridge swore that he had lost it but the brass decided to make an example of him. Bainbridge never knew they decided that one week after his fourth anniversary checks would be issued. The poor slob gave up one week too soon. Cap had told Sandy one night in a bar when the two of them were pretty well oiled up. Sandy never repeated the story to anyone. Let old Bainbridge be a folk hero. If the guys knew he had given up too soon he would be remembered as a jerk.

"Cap." Sandy paused to choose his words carefully. "I want to go out a legend. I lost my shield."

Cap grinned and shook his head in agreement. "I figured that. Not only is the shield yours but I'll go you one better. Brag it up to the other fellows all you want. Show them the blasted thing. Even if the department snitches squeal on you no action will be taken."

"Boy Cap, you must be feeling guilty, but I'll accept before you change your mind."

"What will you do with yourself?" Cap had become sorrowful again.

"I guess I don't know yet. I'm young enough to still be a good cop. Maybe I'll run for Sheriff somewhere. I'll have to think it out." Suddenly Sandy was tired. He just wanted to go home and rest.

"Do you want to go get drunk somewhere?"

"No thanks Cap, I'm tired. I think I'll just go home and get some sleep."

Cap felt a guilty pang at the feeling of relief he had. "Stay in touch, okay?"

"Sure," Sandy replied. "That's a promise."

TWENTY TWO

Many times Brad felt that he had lost control of his situation. Nash and the government people were directing all phases of security and housing for his subjects. He was being pressured to turn his research materials over to the Secret Service. He adamantly refused, knowing this was the one thing that made him irreplaceable to the project.

He stretched his arms in front of him and blinked the sleep from his eyes. Summer was here and it was unbearably hot. The digital clock on the night stand said ten thirteen A.M. He turned his head and looked at the one person who made life tolerable and worthwhile. Lois lay asleep looking, as usual, like sleeping beauty waiting to be kissed awake. Brad had abandoned his personal age retarding regimen. He felt that with his new schedule he could not devote the proper amount of time to walking, eating the right foods, and sleeping enough. Lois was somewhat upset at that decision, but he had reminded her that the youth serum could be used on himself.

The government had resisted adding any new people to the experiment until the long range effects on Janet and Leonard could be measured. They seemed to be pleased with this decision also. Brad guessed that they liked the status of being the only living human subjects. Brad did not totally disagree either as he was learning much about the serum himself. He was still a doctor and did not want anyone else to die due to his work. Lois had some guilt feelings concerning the deaths. He had been very open about what happened and she had become his sounding board for problems.

The Slane family was his only true regret. They had been destroyed by the unfortunate incident in the lab. Still, the boy had been where he did not belong and Brad could not help it that his father could not accept homosexuality. The man's weakness was also no one's fault but his own. Anyone who would take their own life was in Brad's opinion a coward.

He felt little regret that the old people at the nursing home had died as their lives were pretty much over before he began using them. He would never really know if their deaths were hastened by the serum to any degree of significance because of their poor condition. The overall gift to humanity made up for all of that anyway.

Brad was anxious to tell the world about his discovery but permission had not been granted. The government officials felt that too many unknowns still existed to risk global embarrassment. Brad determined that no one would know the secrets of his research until he received full credit for discovering eternal youth. Currently it was a standoff.

He swung his feet to the floor and moved slowly to the bathroom. Lois sighed and opened her eyes to watch him cross the room. "You're moving pretty slow this morning," she commented.

"And good morning to you my dear," he said dryly. He went to the bathroom and urinated without lifting the toilet seat, a habit Lois despised. "I think I'm getting a touch of arthritis," he said over his shoulder, "nothing serious."

"You never had these problems before," she complained.

"Old age catches up, even with a health regime." The last half of his sentence was garbled from the addition to his mouth of a toothbrush. "Sooner or later I'll have to start injections myself." He spat toothpaste into the sink.

"You can wait until the formula has been proven. Long range it could be bad to use."

"What could be worse than death?" He strolled from the bathroom naked, another habit Lois hated.

"I don't know," she reluctantly admitted. "I'd just rather you waited until you were sure. It's not like you were a doting old man."

"True. However, we don't know if this will prevent or even cure cancer or heart disease or anything else. Maybe you have to start treatments before a fatal disease is contacted. If that's true the whole world should take it immediately."

"Just wait till you're sure," she repeated.

"Okay. For you I'll wait." He returned to the bathroom to shave. "We should know a lot more in the next year or two. The real key of course is Leonard and Janet. They have to stay healthy."

"When will you announce this to the world? Can't you tell the Secret Service to butt out?"

Brad emerged from the bathroom, half his face covered with shaving cream. Lois fought an urge to laugh at him. "I'm afraid you don't tell these people anything," he said. "They tell you what to do. It's kind of frightening really. The one thing I absolutely will not do is give them my notes until this thing is out in the open. You know if no one knows I'm the discoverer they can cut me off."

"Surely they wouldn't do that," Lois said, not sounding very convinced.

"They've covered up deaths for me Lois. Not because they like me but because they want my formula. Some nobody with a political favor owed to him could be announced as the great genius of all time and I, no we, because they would have to take care of everyone who knows anything about this, would be quietly disposed of."

She was truly frightened now and jumped out of the bed to see him in the bathroom washing shaving cream from his face. "This is the United States Brad, not some Communist country. Our own government is not going to throw us to the wolves."

Brad pushed by her and went to his dresser drawer. He took out knee length black socks and drew them on. This was another habit she hated as he would parade around for the next ten minutes wearing nothing else, putting on deodorant and powdering himself from neck to knees. With fear pulling at her throat she wondered how she had ever fallen in love with someone filled with such idiotic habits.

He turned to her with talcum powder in hand and began to dust. "Even in the good old U.S. of A. our government will cut a throat or two if someone in power deems it necessary. We've become prisoners my dear. The only thing that keeps us safe is my knowledge. Some day they'll give up and release the discovery with my name on it and we'll be safe."

"As long as I keep my research from falling into their hands."

"Where do you keep your notes now? I might need to know if anything were to happen to you."

He was finally getting underwear from the drawer. "You're right of course. We both need protection. Several months ago I began to get a little worried about the safety of my records so I built a trap door in the floor of the lab. Remember the cage we kept Rama the chimpanzee in?"

"Yes. It's in the southwest corner isn't it?"

"That's it. If you slide that cage out and lift off four tiles there's a handle. Grab it and pull and a block of flooring lifts out. I had a kid build a metal box for his high school industrial arts project that fits in there like a glove. He really did a beautiful job."

"Aren't you afraid they'll find it?"

"They'd have to dismantle the building and I don't think they'll do that. These people don't like to draw attention, and besides I think they're convinced my records are here."

"Why would they believe that?"

"I take dummy files with me so they can see me carrying paperwork. Most of their searching has been done here also."

Lois stiffened. "What do you mean searching here. They've been in my house?" She looked around her with alarm, almost like she suspected someone was there now.

Brad was calmly selecting a necktie. "Of course they search here. Probably once a week I'd guess. I'm surprised you haven't noticed."

"What could I notice?" Lois was almost hysterical. She was looking around the room again in disbelief, trying to see something out of place. She ran to the closet and pushed clothes back and forth looking for a clue.

—

"Settle down will you." Brad was pulling on his black wing tip shoes. "They're very good at what they do. You'd never know they were here unless you're observant. I set little traps for them like memorizing certain things in a drawer. It's almost impossible to replace every item exactly as they found it. No one is that good."

Lois began to cry silently, her shoulders trembling. She turned away from Brad, hoping to compose herself before he noticed, but he knew immediately. She could tell by his silence and did not know if she should be relieved or hurt that he did not attempt to comfort her. She soon collected herself and turned to him with a slight redness in her eyes the only positive proof remaining.

"Look." He paused in obvious discomfort of the situation. "I've got to get going. I want to get the research to the point where they have to go public and eliminate our worries. That means a lot of extra hours work for me."

"What about fire," she persisted. "If the lab burned your records would go with it."

He tapped his forehead with a finger. "I've got the formula up here. I couldn't reconstruct all of the background research but that's okay. The formula itself is most important."

She grabbed his arm, stopping his hurried exit once again. "What about the serum. They could steal it and analyze the contents."

Brad sighed and walked her over to the bed. He sat on the edge and patted the mattress. She obediently sat beside him. "I produce enough to use on the spot just to prevent that from happening. That is a good thought however. Fortunately there's more to the secret than just throwing some chemicals together or they could figure it out by my supply orders. For extra precaution I order things I don't need, just to keep them guessing."

Lois felt somewhat better again with these self assurances and finally smiled. "I guess I just sometimes forget to trust you darling. You've always taken care of me and I should remember you can outsmart these people."

He put his arm around her shoulders and kissed her gently. "My plan sure isn't foolproof but I believe it's sound. Remember, they've got a lot more heads working on this than I do so they have a much better chance at tripping me up. But don't worry, a couple more months and I figure we'll go public." He released his hold and stood up. "Now I've got to get to work so I can push the issue as soon as possible. Are you okay now?"

"Yes. It'll be fine now." She looked up at him and pouted slightly. "I still don't like them coming in here and poking around in my things. That makes me feel, I don't know, raped I guess. It's just not fair."

"I know honey, but there's not a thing we can do about it so I'd suggest we just cope until our time comes. It won't be long, I promise."

TWENTY THREE

P. Osgood Nash pulled his huge bulk up the steps of the old federal building that held the Columbus office of the Secret Service. He paused just inside the door of the building and tried to catch his breath. His discomfort was intensified by the irritation he felt at having to come to Jones' office. That third rate small fry had nothing to do except wait for a President to show up once every three or four years and he was trying to play big shot with a university official.

The pounding in his chest lessened slightly so Nash moved toward the ancient row of elevators. Otis Elevator had done a great job fifty years ago but age was beginning to take its toll on the old system. Nash stepped into the car as the door clanked open and noted with mild concern that the ancient compartment sank several inches with the addition of his weight. Fortunately the cables held for the millionth time and Nash soon was gratefully stepping onto the third floor.

The hallway was dingy and poorly lit. Most office doors did not have a name on them as the entire floor was reserved for the Secret Service, despite the fact that the Columbus office was staffed by three people. A door at the farthest end of the hall stood open so Nash headed toward it in hopes of finding Jones.

A young girl was sitting behind an old manual Underwood typewriter, carefully polishing her nails. She glanced up at Nash as he waddled through the door and bent back to her task without speaking. Nash approached her desk breathing deep and hard, his heart and lungs struggling to keep up with the fat.

"Where's Jones" he wheezed.

"You got an appointment?" The girl stroked the nail on her little finger with purple polish.

"I'm P. Osgood Nash. I have an appointment at eleven o'clock." The girl could have been pretty without the wild clothes and tons of makeup. Her lips were full and stayed slightly open, a look that always aroused Nash. "Can I go in," he asked, a command more than a question.

"Nope. He's not here and no one can go in his office unless he's here. Top secret files and all that you know" she confided.

"But it's five past eleven now," he complained with his best official voice. "I'm a busy man and he called the meeting."

"Don't gripe to me pal." The nail on her ring finger turned purple. "I just do what I'm told. Talk to Mr. Jones when he comes back. In the meantime you can wait there if you want." She nodded toward a low couch and several chairs. "Take your pick."

Nash cursed to himself and went to the couch. The chairs had arms and he knew he would not have fit them. He tried to drop gently to the sofa but it was too low and he hit it very hard. A loud snap filled the air as a support brace broke in the sofa's back. He blushed deeply at the sound of the girl's giggle. He wasn't accustomed to this kind of humiliation and was ill equipped to handle it.

Jones came in at eleven twenty four. He walked to his office door without acknowledging his guest's presence. He pulled a key ring from his pocket and unlocked the door before speaking over his shoulder. "Come on in Nash."

He didn't even get an apology for being kept waiting and Nash was furious. His fury turned to rage when he discovered he could not raise his huge bulk from the sofa. "This blasted thing is too close to the floor," he mumbled after several unsuccessful attempts to stand. The young girl was obviously enjoying his plight as she watched him struggle. He finally had to roll from the sofa onto his hands and knees on the floor. With a mighty grunt he came to his feet and almost fell back onto the sofa.

Jones shouted from within his office "Nash, are you coming?"

The girl at this point openly guffawed, showing a mouthful of incredibly wide spaced teeth. Nash was so mortified that he almost laughed himself. For some reason at that moment an old high school joke flashed into his head. Girls with teeth like that were called corn women because they could eat corn through a picket fence. His return of humor took the joy of his embarrassment from the girl and she quickly closed her mouth, almost as if she knew he was thinking of the old corn woman joke.

He composed himself quickly and entered Jones' office. Fortunately the guest chair was wide and tall. He settled his enormous body into it with no further incident.

"Look Jones." Remember, the best defense is a strong offense. "You not only kept me waiting in this lousy rat trap office but your secretary made me feel like a fool. Do you realize who you are dealing with here?"

"Yea, a fat pig with a swelled head to match his overgrown body." Obviously Jones had read the same book on being in command. "Now shut up and listen or I'll call in a piano moving crew and have you thrown out of here."

Nash felt the color rush to his cheeks and his overburdened heart began to pound even harder than normal. "You can't talk to me like that," he blustered.

"I not only can talk to you any way I see fit, I can arrange you to be part of the sewage in the treatment plant this afternoon. Now shut up and let me tell you what you're going to do."

Nash's rage turned to fear as Jones wouldn't be talking like this if he couldn't back it up. Many years of working with people had taught him when to recognize a bluff, and this was definitely the real thing. Until he could find out what kind of clout this guy really had the prudent thing seemed to be cooperation. "What do you wish to tell me Mr. Jones?"

Jones smiled and relaxed. "That's better." His face then immediately returned to stone. "There's several things we've got to take care of. First, I want Richardson's notes."

"He refuses to turn them over until we give him open credit for his work."

"I know that. If necessary we will, but there are a few scientists that are owed important favors by people in very high positions. We'll both get a proverbial feather in our caps if we can turn the research over to these men."

"What about Dr. Richardson?" Nash questioned.

"He would of course be left out of the discovery." The words were spoken matter of factly with absolutely no emotion. "Time is of the utmost importance," Jones continued. "We're going to be forced to go public very soon and if Richardson's notes aren't in my hands and deciphered in the next couple of months we'll have to let him keep the credit."

"Why don't you lean on him," Nash questioned.

"We have to be careful. The last thing we want is Richardson screaming to the press. All moves to push him out must be strictly covert. We search his home and office at least once each week by the best team in the country. I'm sure he has no idea we're hunting for his notes. These guys are very good at what they do."

"What has his reaction been to your questions concerning giving up his notes," Nash interrupted. "He told me he would display his secrets to other scientists when we make his work public."

Jones nodded his head. "I got the same answer. I offered some of the best minds in the world as help to prepare for the unveiling but he won't buy it. I think he fears exactly what will happen if he gives us what we want." He chuckled mirthlessly. "I wonder how he knows."

"He knows because he's a smart man. How do you think he discovered the secret of youth?"

Jones produced a bottle of nasal spray from a desk drawer. He squirted and snuffed noisily. "I suppose you're right. I should ask him to come up with a cure for sinus blockage while he's at it."

Nash fought the urge to vomit as the Secret Service man relieved his other nostril. The liquid ran down his upper lip only to be wiped away with the back of his hand. Nash looked out of the dirty window to his left and swallowed hard. "I'll continue to try to convince Dr. Richardson to hand over his notes. Is that all you wanted?"

"Yea, that's it." Jones paused to sneeze into his bare hands. "We have some other loose ends to tie up but I'll take care of that myself."

Nash heaved his bulk from the chair. "Why didn't you just talk to me about this on the telephone."

Jones smiled like a snake ready to strike. "Never use phones. Too easy to tap. I check my office every morning for bugs but I can't count on you to do that." He extended his hand. "Let's work together Nash. Why fight each other and make life tougher?"

Nash automatically grasped the man's hand in return and blanched at the slimy wetness from the sneeze that lingered on Jones' palm. He pulled his hand away and held it uncomfortably at his side. "Sure. We'll work together." He hurried from the office and went to a men's room where he scrubbed his hands thoroughly. P. Osgood Nash had been violated. That just did not happen. The man responsible for that would have to pay.

Bob Jones sat in his office feeling the weight of responsibility, his meeting with Nash already forgotten as at this stage of the game it was not important. He leaned back in his chair and breathed deeply several times before picking up the telephone. He dialed a local number which was answered after the first ring. A quiet voice simply said "Yes."

"It's me."

"Yes," the voice repeated.

"Complete plan A."

After a pause the voice said, "Complete plan A."

"That is correct," Jones replied. The line promptly disconnected.

He walked out of his office and paused at his secretary's desk. "I'll be out for the rest of the day."

"Yes sir." She smiled with her lips together, hiding the picket fence teeth. She wondered for the thousandth time why he didn't make a pass at her. "Have a nice day" she added.

"Hmmm? Oh, thank you," he answered over his shoulder. Jones walked to the elevator and waited patiently as it clanked slowly toward his floor. He looked back toward his offices and wondered what his secretary would say if he asked her for a date.

A small, balding man hung up the telephone. He turned to his companion and pointed to a suitcase standing in the corner. "We've got a go on Plan A," he said.

His partner stood and stretched his lean, muscular body. "When do we do it?"

"Now."

Without another word the balding man picked up the suitcase and placed it gently on the bed. His partner stood behind him towering two feet above the top of the hairless head. They were known in the Secret Service as Mutt and Jeff. Other men and women did the same kind of work but these two men comprised the best death squad in the Service.

The smaller man opened the suitcase. He took two folders from the inside and closed and latched the lid. He was the brains of the team, plotting out the right moves and positions. His partner supplied the muscle. They were both familiar with the people in the folders as they had been in Columbus for three weeks preparing for the phone call that instructed them to kill.

"Who do we want to do first?" the big man asked.

"Both are so easy it doesn't make a whole lot of difference, but let's do Wilson first. The earlier we take him the more plausible it will be that he fell down the stairwell. The suicide can be done anytime."

The big man reopened the suitcase and took out a pistol. It was not registered anywhere and commonly is known as a Saturday night special. It was enclosed in a plastic bag and had been carefully wiped free of fingerprints. A suicide note sealed in a separate bag had been forged by the best people in the business. Every detail had been considered.

"Are we ready?" the small man asked.

"Let's do it," his hulking partner said without emotion.

The last family had left for the evening so Frank Wilson put out the lights outside of his funeral home. Business had been slow, only two bodies rested inside. He quickly checked the doors and started upstairs to his living quarters. Wilson's greatest weakness was television. He subscribed to the local cable company and delighted in all the options they made available to him. Movies were his favorite and the start time was at hand.

Someone who was expecting danger might have sensed the huge figure waiting in the shadows of the hallway at the top of the stairs. Wilson had no worries and noticed nothing. He never even felt the hands grasp his head and snap it quickly to the left. The vertebrae at the top of his spine broke in half, paralyzing him instantly. His windpipe collapsed and shut off his air supply. He was still alive when he was carried to the top of the stairs and actually died about halfway down. Both men checked the body for a pulse and sprawled him at the bottom of the stairs.

Thomas Maywood was quietly altering his books to squeeze a little more money out of the government. He delighted in his work as he enjoyed a dishonest dollar much more than honest labor. Two men calmly walked into his small office wearing black clothing and gloves.

"What the devil do you two want in here?" he protested.

Without comment or hesitation the big man moved behind the desk and wrapped his arms around his victim. The grip wasn't overpowering and increased only when Maywood began to struggle.

"Let me go. Do you guys want money? I haven't got much here but . . . ."

His words were abruptly ended by the smaller bald man. He had produced a plastic bag which he pulled over Maywood's head. The air was instantly exhausted and within two minutes the terrified man had died. He couldn't even thrash in the throws of death because of the huge man's grip on his body. The two men quickly released the limp body and produced six bullets, the big man placing each shell in Maywood's fingers to leave fingerprints. After loading the gun that they had brought along, his hand was fitted into the weapon. The big man placed the gun in Maywood's mouth and squeezed the dead man's finger around the trigger. The deafening blast of the pistol was contained in the small room, and the bullet blew a fifty cent size hole in the back of Thomas Maywood's head. Blood and brains sprayed across the headrest of the chair.

The note was carefully unwrapped and the victim's hands were placed on the paper to create the necessary prints. The big man lifted Maywood's head and dropped it face first onto the desk top. The two front teeth split and burst through the dead man's upper lip. The two men stepped back and surveyed their handiwork. Satisfied, they slipped out the door and left the nursing home undetected.

Neither man spoke as they returned to the spacious hotel room they had shared while on this assignment. Immediately upon return the big man turned on the television set and the smaller man opened the suitcase. The last part of the file was a package marked in bold print. OPEN ONLY UPON SUCCESSFUL COMPLETION OF PLAN A.

He quickly broke the seal and lifted the contents from the package. A picture of a man and woman met his gaze. The woman pulled his attention immediately. She was perhaps the most beautiful creature he had ever seen. How sad it would be to kill her. So beautiful. The method he would use he knew immediately. His partner would appreciate it also. This little lady, providing the call came to kill her, would die as a result of a brutal rape.

—

TWENTY FOUR

Leonard and Janet had never gone together to relieve the pounding headaches that came upon them. Neither really knew why the other kept their activities separate but both secretly wanted to share the experience. Perhaps part of the reason was that Janet felt the need to kill and destroy was lessening and wanted to control the urge. She felt that the killings would sooner or later get them caught and she questioned the value of the risk.

Many times Leonard almost gained the courage needed to ask Janet to join him but he had thus far remained silent. He felt the time had come one evening after a relaxing dinner and decided to ask her before the television was turned on. "I'd like to ask you something," he began. "Ever since we've been going out at night to be with the outsiders we've gone alone. Why don't we go out together sometime?"

She thought about her answer for a few moments before replying. He looked so nervous that she wanted to formulate her answer in a way that would put him at ease. "I've often wanted to go with you but never had the courage to ask. Thank you for taking the lead and mentioning it first."

Leonard was visibly pleased with the compliment and his confidence immediately grew. "I guess part of our problem is we've never talked about what we do."

"Or why," she added.

"Maybe that's the most important question of all," he agreed. "When you go out do you always," he paused again before actually saying it, "kill the person you're with?" Now that it was said he felt better and waited anxiously for her reply.

"Yes, I kill and then destroy the body. My whole being seems to be on fire and the outsider's blood is the only thing that eases the burn. My headaches go away too."

"That's almost exactly what happens to me," Leonard agreed. "I guess the two main differences for me is I don't always have to kill for satisfaction and my headache never completely goes away."

"There's one other difference," she added, "unless you just aren't saying it all."

"I guess I'm not sure what you mean," he said with a puzzled frown.

"I don't have a very strong need to do it anymore. At least I think I can control myself. Kind of like a reformed alcoholic."

"I don't know if I should be happy or sad for you," he answered.

"I know how much I enjoy doing it and how good it makes me feel when it's over."

"Leonard, I lived my life as a gentle, quiet person. I have now killed people because I can't control myself, or I should say couldn't control myself. I hate, at least deep inside, hurting people. Besides, we're going to eventually get caught. The newspapers are screaming for a solution to the whole thing."

"Obviously this urge is a side effect of Brad's shots," he said. "Maybe the intensity depends upon your first youth. I wasn't a very nice person Janet. Hurting people has never bothered me and now I like it. I'm not sure I can control it. Or even if I do want to control it," he added.

"I think we have to," she persisted. "Our future will depend on keeping a clean slate. The world will soon know about us and we must keep public viewpoint on our side."

"I understand and agree. The problem is I don't think I can stop."

She took his hands in hers and looked into his eyes. "I'll help you darling. We'll do it together."

He smiled and kissed her on the tip of her nose. "I'll do my best."

"We haven't mentioned one other possibility," she said, pulling away and crossing her arms under her breasts. "Should we tell Brad about our problem. Maybe he can change the formula and eliminate the whole thing."

"I think I didn't mention it for the same reason as you," he replied. "What if he can't stop that and decides we're too dangerous. I don't know about you dear but I've decided I like my new lease on life. No, I'm afraid we can't take the chance."

"You're right of course," she admitted. "Well, we just have to work out the answer ourselves."

"Agreed," he said.

"I started this conversation to talk you into going after outsiders together," Leonard said with a grin. "Why don't we still do it?"

She sighed and shook her head. "All this time I've wanted to go with you and now we've decided to control ourselves. No, I think we'll just need it even more if we start something new. Besides, like I said before, we're going to get caught. We've got to stop this Leonard."

"Well," he said with a heavy sigh, "like I said, I'll try."

—

126

TWENTY FIVE

Sandy sat in his small apartment wondering what suicide would feel like for several days following his retirement. His despair had reached as close to the bottom as possible when he suddenly thought of a reason for living. Several weeks of preparation passed while he filed the necessary paperwork and waited for the State to churn the establishment waters. His Monday morning mail held the reason for Sandy Gibbs to continue his existence. This bright sunny morning dawned officially on a new licensed private investigator.

The small diner that had been his opportunity for hot meals over the years once again looked inviting. He took his customary stool in the middle of the counter and winked at Ethyl, the ageless short order cook that had worked at the diner for as many years as Sandy could remember.

"Well, well, well," she boomed. Ethyl always talked louder than necessary. "I haven't seen you for weeks. Thought I was loosin' my shape or somethin'." She had probably been pretty once upon a time, maybe when she was in her early twenties, but life had been hard on this woman. Too many long hours at work and years of standing on the concrete floor of the diner had caused early wrinkles and lots of sagging. A few small scars on her face were the product of a drunken husband when she was thirty, her first and only try at marriage. Occasionally she used to get the itch for a man and would pick up one in a bar. None of them ever took the time to give her pleasure, so she finally gave up on sex and tried to ignore the occasional urges.

"Ethyl, I don't know how I could ever ignore you," Sandy teased. "I should be kicked for taking a chance of losing the only girl I'd ever consider marrying."

She blushed, knowing he was only fooling but somehow thinking he might be a little serious. This talk brought back some of the old desire too, which she kind of liked. "One of these days I'm going to take you up on that offer of marriage Sandy Gibbs, and you're going to fall right off that stool."

"Not fall off Ethyl, more like jump."

"Oh?" She felt her feelings being crushed.

"That's right. I'll jump right over that counter and grab you before you can change your mind."

She flushed and felt good again. "Why are you so frisky today?"

"Because, my dear, life kicked me in the head and now it's giving me some aspirin to ease the pain." He considered explaining the meaning of his statement but decided to let her be confused. "Don't try to figure it out Ethyl. Just let me enjoy feeling good today."

"Sure Sandy. Why a person isn't happy don't make no difference anyway. The important thing is just love life."

He winked and dropped a dollar tip on the counter. "That's the attitude." He enjoyed her surprised smile at his generosity for a moment before heading toward his car.

His mind raced ahead as Sandy's car moved toward the northwest part of the city. Continuing to push in the direction he had decided to go would very likely end in his own personal ruin and perhaps even death. Neither prospect bothered him very much but he felt one person had to agree with his decision because her life would be affected also.

The Slane residence was pretty much as he had remembered. He pulled into the long driveway and noted that Mrs. Slane must have plenty of money despite the loss of her husband. Homes take a certain amount of upkeep to remain show places and this one certainly looked like a model. The grass was smooth and weed free, with the edges of the lawn edged as with a razor. The blacktop had been recently resurfaced and topdressed, both a rather costly job for such a large area.

Not the slightest thing was out of place; no flaking paint or crumbling chimneys. A man couldn't keep this place up without professional help, let alone a woman. Sandy trudged up to the front door and pushed the bell. He heard a faint song playing on the door chimes inside the house.

He considered leaving when there was no response to the second ring but finally heard movement coming towards the door. A dim figure peered through the thin curtains extending the length of the door. Sandy debated whether to shout through the door, which would startle her, or wait until she acknowledged his presence. Only thirty or forty seconds clicked by but it seemed like forever as he was getting embarrassed at pretending that he couldn't see her.

The deadbolt finally slid back and the door was opened slightly. "May I help you?" Her voice was soft and almost sexy.

Sandy remembered her face clearly immediately upon hearing the voice. He had seen her worried and torn with grief but recalled that she was still quite pretty. "I'm Sandy Gibbs Mrs. Slane. I talked with you as a police officer when you suffered your tragedy."

She opened the door to expose herself completely. Black slacks and a fairly form fitting white blouse revealed a well proportioned and very lovely woman. Probably in her late forties she looked no older than thirty, a product of careful makeup and workouts at the health club. She eyed her visitor for a moment before speaking. "Have you found something about the death of my son?" There was a hint of hope in her voice.

"No Ma'm. Well, sort of no. You see, I'm not with the police department anymore and I think your son's death may be connected with my job ending."

"I'm sorry," she said with sincerity. "I hope my misfortune didn't lend itself to you."

"No, not at all" he hastened to say. "I just retired sooner than I had hoped. No real damage."

"I see. Well, I'm glad to hear that."

"May I come in for a moment Mrs. Slane? I would very much like to talk to you for a few minutes. If you don't like what you hear in the next fifteen minutes I'll go and never bother you again."

"How rude of me," she answered quickly. "Of course do come in ah . . . . is it Mr. Gibbs since you're retired?"

He smiled and stepped over the threshold. "Sandy Ma'm. Always was and still is."

"Fair enough Sandy. I'm Carolyn."

"Thanks Carolyn." He followed her through the spacious rooms to a too tidy family room. It was meant for children to have toys here and there and the overstuffed sofa should have been rumpled instead of fluffed and on display.

"Please sit down," she said, giving him her practiced hostess smile. "May I offer you coffee?"

"If you decide you want to hear all of my story I'll drink a cup," he replied. "First, I want to get started and give you every opportunity to stop me and tell me to leave, which I will immediately do upon your request" he added.

"My but this sounds serious," she smiled. "I'm so curious now I'll have to hear it all."

"Fine, but you stop me anytime you don't want to hear any more. I should warn you that we'll reach a point in our discussion where I'll have to tell you some things that could endanger your life if anyone thought you knew."

"How fascinating," she interrupted. "I think my woman's curiosity will demand that I hear every detail."

"Don't take this too lightly," Sandy gently chided. "This is absolutely deadly."

"I'm sorry," she answered, feeling the heat rise in her cheeks. "I don't suppose that you happened to consider that whoever would want to kill me for knowing this secret may think that you've told me anyway."

"You're a pretty good detective yourself to think of that angle Mrs. Slane," Sandy said with a sad smile.

"Carolyn," she reminded him.

"Oh yes. I'm sorry. You know I truly didn't think of that, but I don't believe they'll bother with me at this point. They think my fear for my pension will keep me in line, otherwise I think I'd be dead already."

"I don't know whether to be frightened or amused," she injected. "Why don't you just tell me your story and we'll speculate later."

"Fair enough. First of all, I think I know who killed your son, or I should say I know who is responsible for his death."

"I would like to clear my husband's name of that," she reflected.

"What makes you so sure I wasn't going to tell you it was him," Sandy wondered.

"I know, I knew my husband Mr. Gibbs."

"Sandy."

"Excuse me. I knew my husband Sandy. He wasn't capable of taking another person's life."

"There's a chance he didn't even take his own," Sandy added. "The people involved in this thing have a way of making things look like they want."

"Can you prove that?" She sounded hopeful.

"Not at this point and maybe never. Maybe he did kill himself Carolyn. All I'm saying is there are people that would eliminate him for knowing too much. I suppose that it's not likely he was able to learn anything but if he did any amateur sleuthing and asked the wrong people the wrong questions . . ." He paused to get her reaction.

"I don't really think so. About all my husband did between Robin's death and his own suicide was sit around the house and mope."

"Then you saw a lot of him during that time."

"He nearly drove me to distraction hanging around the house. It's not likely he was doing any investigating."

Sandy was disappointed because of the information he was hoping he could get from conversations Carolyn may have had with her husband. Often times a person involved found things the police would not, because the case loads kept them from giving an investigation the time needed. Carolyn was feeling the same emotion for a different reason. She had for a moment thought that her husband could be cleared of both deaths. She realized, perhaps at this very moment, that this would never happen. Tears began to push their way toward the surface. To hide this she stood up and walked toward the kitchen. "Let me get that coffee," she said. "I'm pretty sure I'll want to hear more."

Sandy remembered his manners and stood up to her retreating back. "Thank you," he said, hoping she would turn and see him standing, but she went into the kitchen without looking back. He wandered around the family room while he waited for his hostess to return, trying to learn something about her through the way her home was decorated. Women usually took the responsibility of picking

—

the colors and fabrics, simply because they tended to have good taste and men did not. The family room was plain and functional. Dark brown carpeting helped hide any spills from evening snacks or parties. A long sofa in a tan print would hide any mistakes too. Twin tilt back chairs matched the carpeting perfectly, so well that they almost gave the appearance of two humps of carpeting pushed up on each side of the bay window. An insert in the fireplace converted it to the efficiency of an air tight stove, an addition probably suggested by her husband. Original oil paintings were displayed on each wall as a quiet symbol of their wealth.

"The coffee will be ready in a few minutes." Her entry into the room brought with it the delicious aroma of fresh brewing coffee. "I won't have instant in the house, it's too artificial tasting to me."

"I can always tell the difference," Sandy lied.

"Well do go on with your story."

"There is research going on in this country to stop us from getting old. It sounds pretty much like science fiction to me but I've been told we may be pretty close to a breakthrough in some areas. I think a doctor may have done something very important the way he's being protected. Part of that protection is the cover-up of the death of your boy."

"Why would a doctor want to kill Robin?"

"I'm guessing the doctor himself didn't really do it. The whole thing was probably an accident. His lab has a lot of different animals and I think Robin went there and probably stumbled into one of them that had escaped. For some reason the thing killed him."

"And the doctor covered it up," she finished.

"Probably. Instead of admitting a tragedy he thought he would make it look like murder that no one would ever solve. Unfortunately, he didn't know the background of your son's problem."

"So my husband was destroyed in the bargain," she finished.

He nodded his head sympathetically. "That's about the size of it."

"What makes you think it's this doctor, and by the way who is it?"

"I don't want to tell you as yet. Wait until you're sure you want to hear the whole story."

"Very well, but I'm not going to miss any of this now."

Sandy scratched his chin thoughtfully and quickly made a decision. "Look, let me tell you this and if you really want to be involved then I'll quit talking in circles. The government is involved in this thing. Some special branch of the Secret Service. I believe they've killed and would not hesitate to kill again. Should I go on?"

"Please continue." There wasn't a moment of hesitation.

"The doctor's name is Brad Richardson. He's spent half of his life working on a theory that he says could reverse our age. Not long after Robin was killed he became a part time staff doctor at a nursing home. Pretty odd for a guy whose schedule is already packed tight. Next he makes a few trips to a funeral home, another odd thing to do when you figure no one in his family has died recently."

"What on earth is he doing?" she asked.

"I would guess he's been trying his experiments out on people in that nursing home. Those that die are shipped to the funeral home for quick disposal with his name on the death certificate." Sandy paused for a moment to let all of this register. "Now," he continued, "I think whatever he was doing to those people must have worked for a couple of reasons. One is the Secret Service. The other is a couple of people that lived at the lab for a while. They share an apartment now, but why do they spend most of their time at the lab."

"Maybe they work there," she offered.

"Not too likely. The Doc's wife works there and she has trouble staying busy. I think he's studying them."

She rolled her head around in a circle in an attempt to relieve some tension. They both had forgotten the coffee. "You said the government had killed people. Why do you think that?"

"This is where it really gets interesting. I'm not totally sure about this, but I've got some ideas. The funeral home and nursing home operator are both dead. One fell down his steps and broke his neck; the other swallowed the barrel of his gun and pulled the trigger. The press didn't connect them and the police say accident and suicide."

"And you think that's too coincidental."

"Wouldn't you?"

"I guess so," she agreed.

Sandy continued, "Anyway two people that could say something if any funny business was going on are dead. The only thing that baffles me about this whole thing is the other mutilation murders."

"You mean there have been others like Robin?"

"Don't you read the paper? There have been a rash of mutilation murders. I investigated a couple of them myself before I got pushed out of the department. All I can figure out is the government wants everyone to think a cult or some nut is killing people, including Robin."

She held up her hand and shook her head. "Now wait a minute. Why should they go to that trouble when everyone is convinced that Charles did it?"

"I don't know," Sandy admitted. "It's the one thing about this whole situation that has me stumped. I can't believe the Doc would be so careless as to let more animals out, unless of course there are still some loose. I just don't know at this point."

"I guess I have another question. Why did you come to me with this? How can I be of any help?"

Sandy smiled and winked at his host. "You are the key to the whole thing. State law will not permit me to work a case without a client. I want you to hire me for one dollar to solve your son's murder. Bear in mind that if you permit me to get involved in this, your life will probably be in danger."

She shifted in her chair and smoothed her skirt before answering. "I think I would like to know who really killed my boy. If my government has anything to do with it or is causing more people to die I want it stopped and those responsible should be punished." She paused to once again smooth the skirt that still lay perfectly across her legs. "Do we sign anything or do I just get you my dollar."

TWENTY SIX

The friendship that had been growing between Lois and Janet began reversing itself. Lois wanted to learn more about the woman's feelings not only to help advance her husbands' research, but she felt a genuine fondness toward her too. Janet fought her hatred toward this 'outsider' but the battle was rapidly being lost.

Brad and Lois socialized with the research couple mainly because the Secret Service people were concerned that the wrong people would discover their secret. Leonard had insisted on an apartment to share with Janet. Brad had at first refused, thinking they would be safer locked in the lab each night, but Leonard had become so insistent that all parties had finally agreed.

This particular evening found the four people about to leave the apartment for a Johnnie Mathis concert. The excitement of the evening at least temporarily had stilled the tension between the two women as Janet was feeling like a schoolgirl. "This is fantastic," she said. Her face was flushed in her delight. "I was in my fifties when I first heard Mathis and I've been mad about him ever since. The thing that amazes me is I've never seen him perform live before, and in all fairness never should because I ought to be dead."

"Well we certainly are grateful that you aren't," Brad commented. "We would have missed some very charming company without you two."

"Indeed," Lois agreed, and in an attempt to rekindle a friendship added, "I would have been cheated out of knowing a very special person." She gently squeezed Janet's arm.

Janet flashed back to the present moment and smiled coldly. "Well I guess I'm not too bad for a mere laboratory rat."

"Yes, well we'd better be going," Brad said, embarrassed for his wife. "They may not seat us if we're late."

"Oh my goodness, I don't want to miss one note." Janet came back to her girlish excitement as quickly as it had left. "Did you remember to put our tickets in your pocket?" she inquired of her companion.

"Yes dear," Leonard answered and rolled his eyes. "You'd think I was seventy eight years old and feeble minded."

They all laughed and hurried toward Brad's car, momentarily at least forgetting that they were anyone special.

Sandy pulled out behind them at a respectable distance, not really trying to be totally secretive and yet not being overly anxious. He smiled slightly as the Secret Service tail came in behind him. The stage was set now; they knew he was working on an answer. Sandy knew they would act quickly. Hopefully he could keep his guard up enough to survive, at least long enough to expose the truth.

Leonard had been strangely quiet throughout the evening. He was jumpy and nervous, obviously irritated about something. His table manners had never been the best but tonight he ate his rare steak almost like a dog. Brad and Lois had gotten used to Leonard and Janet eating their meat almost raw, but these table manners were extremely unpleasant. When the foursome ate together at home the meat was consumed raw by the two test subjects. Brad had given them extensive tests thinking that the treatments were robbing their systems of some needed nutriment, but no imbalance was visible. Both people claimed they just liked to eat their meat rare.

Janet seemed to understand Leonard's actions and was calmly ignoring him. Fortunately the restaurant was dark and nearly empty. The waitress was mildly shocked at each trip to their table, but she remained silent. The meat seemed to settle him somewhat, but Leonard remained quiet and brooding.

The ride to the historic Ohio Theatre put Brad and Lois back into the mood of the evening as Janet virtually bubbled over with excitement. "Can you believe it, Johnny Mathis. Can we stay after the show and try to get an autograph?" She looked like a teenager on her way to the prom.

"I don't see why not," Brad grinned. "In fact I know the manager of the Ohio and I'll bet he can get us backstage."

"Do you really think so," she squealed. "I'd just absolutely die if I met him."

Lois looked at them both with a puzzled expression; Leonard with his quiet sourness and Janet with her juvenile prattle. "Are you two feeling alright?" she quizzed.

"Feel all right," Janet giggled. "I'm about to pass out but it's from excitement." She grabbed Leonard's arm and looked to him for a response but he didn't answer.

Lois turned her attention to Brad but he just smiled and seemed totally relaxed. She found herself wishing this evening were already completed. The car pulled to a stop in a parking lot and her train of thought was temporarily interrupted as they began the short walk to the theatre. Janet was practically running back and forth like a small dog wanting to run while everybody else was walking. The general increase of people finally helped them to blend in.

—

They had seats in the third row and Brad excused himself to find the theatre manager. Janet was by that time so agitated she was trembling. Leonard in turn seemed to gain a darker depression. The light blinked to indicate the start of the show and Janet became quite upset.

"Where is Brad? He'll miss the show." She stood on her tiptoes and looked about. "Do you think he can get us backstage?"

"Easy now," Lois soothed, pulling her toward her seat. "Brad will be right back."

Brad reappeared a few moments later with a broad smile on his face. Janet looked at him with wide eyes, anticipation obvious in her manner. "We'll meet Mr. Mathis," he announced proudly.

"Oh, I can't believe it" Janet breathed, patting herself on the breast. "This is the most incredible night of my life. Leonard, isn't this magnificent?"

Leonard sank into his seat with his head lowered, chin resting on his fingertips. He rolled his eyes upward and without lifting his head mumbled, "I'm absolutely thrilled."

The concert began and ended without further incident. Lois did, however, watch her friend closely, noting that she trembled almost uncontrollably during most of the performance. Surprisingly enough she was quite calm when, following the performance, the four people were ushered to the singer's dressing room. Both Janet and Leonard were very controlled and polite during the few minutes that they talked to the very gracious star.

Very little was said on the way home so Lois finally asked, "Well, was it the thrill you expected?"

Janet smiled and slowly nodded her head. "It was marvelous. Thank you Brad very much."

"My pleasure," he assured. "Well, here we are. You're home again."

Pleasantries were exchanged and Brad and Lois were soon on their way home. Brad was whistling softly and drumming his fingers on the steering wheel as he drove. "I think we're almost out of the woods. Nash told me we've almost got approval to go public."

"You didn't see it did you Brad." He looked almost ghoulish with his wide smile showing up against the dashboard lights. Lois wondered at moments like this what she had ever seen in him.

"Didn't see what?"

She marveled sometimes at his lack of observation. "Those two people are having some serious problems. I would say they are almost perfect textbook cases of schizophrenia."

The ghoulish smile disappeared. "What the devil are you talking about?"

"Brad." She paused to gain control of her anger at his blindness, but sharp words were just likely to make him defensive. "My major in college is psychology.

Those two were so far off the beam tonight it was frightening. I thought Janet was going to run up on the stage like a star struck kid." She watched, in profile, his right eyebrow narrow. "Leonard was so depressed I thought he would do something desperate before the night was over."

Brad had reached the faculty parking lot. He dug out his pass card, lifted the gate, and parked the car before replying. He finally turned sideways in the car seat and faced his wife. "I'm sorry darling, but I think you're trying to be an amateur shrink. They don't act the least bit strange to me."

"Oh come on Brad." The anger was rising despite herself. "First of all I am not pretending to be a doctor. Besides it wouldn't take one to see how erratic their behavior is."

He shook his head and climbed out of the car with Lois following suit. "Look how calm and polite they were when they met Johnny," he said over the hood of the car. "They couldn't have been any politer."

"Exactly," she countered. "Janet was so excited she about shook her seat apart. Why did she suddenly become so calm?"

"A normal reaction." He walked around the car and took her arm in preparation for the short walk home. "She was so overwhelmed at meeting the man that she was just, what's the expression, blown away."

She saw the direction this was going. He was going to rationalize it away. "Brad, is it possible," she tightened her grip on his arm as they walked, "that you could be refusing to see the problem because you don't want them to be abnormal?" She waited for him to explode in anger.

"Perhaps." He smiled at the startled look on her face. "You didn't expect that answer did you. I don't honestly think they are having mental problems. Really I don't," he emphasized. "I think Janet was excited and Leonard was jealous."

"Jealous," she repeated.

"I think so. Watch him closely sometime. The man is crazy about her. When she got excited about seeing her idol he resented it. Her actual reaction when she met him was an overwhelmed feeling that came across as calmness. When Leonard saw that she wasn't going overboard he felt more secure and lightened up."

They arrived at their home and Lois continued as her husband struggled with the house key. "What about on the way home, that no big deal attitude."

"You mean Janet? Blast this lock. The Secret Service had picked it so often that the key doesn't work right." The lock finally yielded and they walked into the soft darkness of their home. "I think it was simply a letdown. The big event was over, and as nice as it was, the anticipation is always better than the real thing. No big secret really."

Lois sighed and inwardly gave in. Besides, perhaps he was right. After all he is the doctor, trained to read people's reactions. She at least had to hope he was right.

Sandy chose to stick with the young couple when he followed them home from the theatre. The doc somehow didn't seem to be the way to crack this puzzle. These two might not be the right way to go either, but he had to go in some direction, so why not this? He watched the light go on in their unit and waited until they went out again. Years of experience in stakeouts had taught him to wait at least two hours after the lights go out before giving up for the evening. Many subjects use the appearance of going to bed as a means of slipping out later. Two hours seemed to be a safe time to wait as Sandy had never known anyone to wait that long before making a move. His car was parked at a perfect angle to permit him to slouch down in his seat and watch comfortably.

Maybe he went to sleep. If so it was only for a moment. Surely there had to be some reason for his guard to slop. The unmistakable sound of a gun cocking startled Sandy to a full alert. He felt cold steel touch behind his ear and froze immediately, his side vision revealing a man leaning through his open window.

"Move an inch and you're dead," the man whispered. "And I mean one tiny little inch."

Sandy's mind raced as he sat very still. A dozen itches erupted at various places on his body that screamed to be scratched. He had heard stories about that happening but until now never believed them. His gun was under his left arm and a six inch knife was strapped to his right leg. Both hands were presently resting in his lap. He fought desperately the urge to scream as he waited for a bullet to smash into his skull. After what seemed like minutes but really was just a few seconds the intruder spoke again. "I'm going to open your door. Don't move now." The gun was moved away from his skull as the man leaned back through the window and opened the car door.

"I've got a terrible itch," Sandy complained. "Can I scratch it?" He squinted his eyes against the dome light as the door opened.

"You won't feel it if you're dead," was the reply. "Just follow orders. I want you to very, very slowly swing your legs out of the car." He paused after Sandy complied. "Now bend over and grab your ankles and roll onto the ground."

His heart leaped as Sandy bent over and grasped his legs just above the ankles. He could feel the knife's handle through his pants. Pushing slightly with his feet Sandy rolled from the car in mock slow motion, falling to the right to provide greater cover for the knife. As he fell Sandy pulled his pants leg up high enough to expose the knife handle in his hand, grasped it and pulled it free. He stayed very still and awaited instructions.

"Now, you just lay still while I check you for weapons," his captor said. "Just don't make me nervous."

Sandy forced himself to be very still as the man bent over him and began to pat him down. His gun was discovered quickly and his captor tossed it into Sandy's car with a satisfied grunt. As he hoped, Sandy noted that the gun pointed at his head wavered while the man shifted his concentration to the search. The perfect moment came when the gun moved several inches to the side of his face. Sandy jerked his left arm forward and grabbed the gunman's wrist. In the same movement he drove his knife into the man's stomach and pulled up hard. The force tore into his chest cavity and the sharp blade cut into the heart, killing his opponent almost instantly.

Sandy scrambled to his feet and looked around the street. The silence was total, not even the crickets were chirping at them. He pushed his car door closed and enclosed the scene in darkness once again. Several minutes were used to wipe the knife clean and making sure no evidence linking him to the scene was there. He removed the man's watch and rings and emptied his pockets to give the impression that a robbery had been the motive for the death. Satisfied that all precautions had been taken, Sandy once again surveyed the area for possible witnesses. Although several apartment buildings stood beside each other on each side of the street, they were in darkness. His watch indicated that it was two A.M. Fortunately the world seemed to be asleep.

Crawling through the open car window eliminated the concern of the overhead courtesy light. The old engine caught as soon as the key was turned and Sandy was quickly away from the area. He waited for several hundred yards to turn on the headlights and headed for the river, choosing a bridge that spanned a large width of water. No other cars were on the road and he saw no sign of approaching headlights. A small flashlight in his glove box provided enough light to see what he had taken from the dead man. Using a handkerchief, he wiped off the watch and ring and threw them out of the passengers side window into the still water below.

He wiped off the wallet and opened it with the handkerchief wrapped around his hand. Sandy cursed softly as he looked at the I.D. picture inside the wallet. The dead man was a Secret Service agent. They would be all over this one. Any slip up meant certain death. He carefully removed the money and tossed the wallet out also. His knife followed the other items into the bottom of the river.

Driving towards home Sandy detoured to St. Andrews church and placed the money taken from the dead man's wallet into the poor box. He knelt for a silent prayer concerning the wasting of human life and then slowly returned to his car. Guilt was not what he was feeling. If he had not defended himself surely he would be dead. The sorrow he felt was for the man's family. Were there

---

children at home waiting for their father's return? Perhaps an elderly mother needed her son for support. The purposelessness of life sometimes got to the very heart of his soul, and once again he wondered how long it would be before this madness ended.

TWENTY SEVEN

Leonard was still not satisfied after making love to his roommate as the need for fresh hot blood made his forehead pound in agony. He sat on the edge of the bed, quietly starring at Janet's sleeping face. She had been totally exhausted after their violent love making and had fallen immediately to sleep.

They had agreed to avoid outsiders as much as possible to prevent detection. Janet found that with great effort she could subdue her urges, but her counterpart found the desire too great to resist. He quietly slid into his clothes and crossed catlike to the door of the apartment. Janet snored lightly, completely oblivious to his exit.

Leonard went to the roof of their building where a swimming pool glistened in the moonlight, unused at this late hour. He walked across the darkened shuffleboard courts and peered over the edge of the building. Darkness prevented a thorough search of the ground but Leonard felt reasonably sure that no one was watching the building. Caution was necessary however so he climbed to the top of the head high chain link fence surrounding the building's edge. He deftly jumped to the next building's roof. A normal man could not have spanned the twenty foot space, but Leonard's increased strength carried him over with several feet to spare.

A quick look around found this apartment building's roof deserted also. A recreation area had been constructed here as well and he noted smugly that his building's facility was much more lavish. Leonard walked quickly to the exit door and soon emerged from the front door of the complex.

The campus area was about two miles from his home which made that area the most obvious place to hunt for victims, besides which there were plenty of young and beautiful girls to choose from. Free love and physical pleasure ruled the young.

Leonard ducked behind a tree as a police car rolled slowly past. He feared the authorities more for their ability to take away his youth injections than the possibility that they would catch him destroying an outsider. He continued toward High Street only after the cruiser rounded a nearby corner.

Most of the campus bars were closed at this late hour as even the students tended to give up to fatigue towards early morning. Leonard's heart pounded with anticipation as he prowled the near deserted street in search of a pickup.

—

A young girl that appeared to be no older than fifteen or sixteen stood by the entrance of a bar. The door stood open, emitting a soft light and contemporary music from within. He sized the girl up quickly and decided she would do nicely.

She noticed his approach and returned his smile. "Hi how ya doin'," she said.

"Just fine." He nodded toward the open door. "Can I buy you a drink?"

"Yea, that would be fine." She smiled and led the way into the dimly lit bar. "How about a stool here instead of a booth." She perched herself on a high stool without waiting for an answer. She wore a skirt split almost to the waist. It fell away, revealing a length of leg that made Leonard tremble slightly. "What are 'ya drinkin' honey?" She licked her lips and winked.

"Order whatever you like," he said. "I'll have a Coke."

"You mean with rum or somethin' in it don't you?" she commanded in an amazed tone of voice. "You don't drink just plain soda pop surely."

"Just pop" he repeated. The bartender came to their end of the bar and paused for instructions. "A Coke and . . . ." he waited for the girl to place her order.

"If yours is Coke mine is too lover," she answered with a short laugh.

"Two Cokes," Leonard said. The bartender moved off without comment. "How old are you" he asked the girl.

"Old enough," she answered with a wink. "What you got in mind."

The bartender brought the Cokes and Leonard gave him two dollars. "Keep the change."

"What change," the man growled and moved away.

"I'd like to go to your place," Leonard said as he returned his attention to the girl. He reached out and stroked her bare leg.

"Yea and then what," she prompted.

"Take you to bed of course," he growled, getting tired of playing this stupid game.

"How about the entertainment tax" she purred.

He looked at her with a puzzled expression, not understanding what she meant. Suddenly he realized that he was talking to a prostitute. "For crying out loud a hooker," he laughed. "Honey, I can either look till dawn for another girl or pay you and be done with it. You're cute and I like your style so let's go."

"How much will you pay me," she asked, her lower lip sticking out slightly.

"What do you charge?" he returned.

"Now come on honey," she chided. "If you're a cop and I name the price you can pinch me. You've got to tell me."

He clapped a hand to his forehead. "Oh I'm sorry. You see, I'm not used to this. In fact you're my first."

She wiggled with glee. "Really? That's really neat. We'll have some great fun."

He slid his hand to the inside of her thigh. "How about a hundred bucks?"

She reached for her purse with a smile. "Let me take a look and see if that will fill my wallet." She opened the clasp and removed a shiny pair of handcuffs. Clasping one half to her wrist she quickly reached between her knees and closed the other cuff on Leonard's wrist.

He lifted their manacled arms as it they were Siamese twins and gave her a puzzled look. "What is this and are you into weird things or something? If you want kinky I think you'll be happy."

The girl was rummaging through her purse with her free hand and finally produced a small leather case. She flipped it open on the bar to reveal a badge. "Police officer lover, you're under arrest for soliciting."

"You can't do this," Leonard stammered. "You asked me to go with you. You tricked me."

She pulled a small card from her purse that contained the Miranda warning. "You told me what you wanted and gave me a price honey. You have the right to remain silent. You have the right to have an attorney present during questioning."

"Forget it lady." Leonard reached over and deftly broke the handcuff from his wrist, stood up and walked toward the door. "Go arrest someone else," he said over his shoulder, "I've got things to do."

The police officer sat dumbfounded for a moment, looking at the broken handcuff hanging from her wrist. She was trying to figure out how anyone could break metal that heavy and as a result reacted rather slowly. Suddenly she burst to life and came off the barstool. "Wait a minute. You're under arrest. Don't you just walk out of here."

Leonard only smiled and walked onto the sidewalk. He moved quickly toward home with a shouting police woman following. She had a small walkie talkie in her hand and was making a call for assistance.

"Stop or I'll have to shoot you," she screamed at him.

He glanced over his shoulder and saw the flash of a gun in her left hand. Hesitating for only an instant, Leonard began to run, his neck tickling as the hair there rose in anticipation of a bullet entering his back. His powerful legs churned as he began to put distance between himself and the girl. No shots rang out as he rounded a corner onto a darkened street.

Looking over his shoulder once again he saw nothing following him. Crossing an alley at top speed without looking for cars, he saw a police cruiser swing across his path, too close to stop his forward motion. Leonard hit the cruiser at about half speed with the incredible strength of his body, crumpling

—

the car's front fender, which in turn sliced into the front tire. The startled officers inside were thrown to the side of the front seat and cracked their heads together. Leonard flew over the hood of the cruiser and bounced to a stop on his back.

The two officers fell out of their disabled cruiser holding their heads in pain. Leonard leaped to his feet and continued to run. The female officer rounded the corner and stopped at the disabled cruiser in fatigue and amazement.

"What the devil did you call us in on Josie," one of the officers inquired. He was still rubbing his head while checking himself for other injuries.

"How did you wreck your uni," she gasped, fighting to catch her breath.

"Your subject did it," he shouted unnecessarily and pointed down the street. "He ran into us like a freight train and instead of killing his stupid self caved in our right front, flew over the hood like a sack of rocks, bounced like a blasted basketball and jumped up like he was never touched. I never saw a human run that fast."

"Look what he did to my cuffs," she said, holding up her arm that still was locked to half the handcuffs.

The other officer joined into the conversation. "I've seen guys on dope have superhuman strength but this one went beyond normal human limits. He must have been going twenty miles per hour on foot when he hit us. That and the damage he did to our cruiser just isn't possible."

"Well it is because it happened," she challenged. "Besides I don't think he was on drugs, he was just trying to rent a hooker." She lifted her hands in a hopeless gesture. "We'll not get him now unless the helicopter gets in and spots him."

"I called as soon as my head quit ringing. The chopper is tied up with a north side burglary."

"Then all we can do," she concluded, "is file our report."

Leonard hid in some bushes several blocks from his apartment and tried to examine his injuries. A long scrape on his arm was already completely healed thanks to that by-product of the injections. Several large bruises on his legs were lighter than a few minutes before and would soon be gone. His clothes took the worst punishment. The pavement had almost torn his shirt off his back and dirt had ground deeply into his tan pants. He left his shirt in the bushes and walked to the rear of the building three down the line from his apartment. A quick run up the inside steps gained him entrance to the roof. There was not a recreation area here so there was no concern of discovery. After a quick calculation he took a short running start and leaped to the adjoining roof. Repeating that action took him to the roof of his own building.

Fatigue had set in and drowned the desire for killing as Leonard wearily trudged back to his apartment and entered quietly. He took off his clothes and put them in a paper grocery sack. After rolling the sack into a tight ball he threw it into a wastebasket.

The shower woke Janet and she went to the bathroom to check on her roommate. "Leonard," she called over the noise of the water, It's five o'clock. What are you doing up already."

He stuck his head out of the shower curtains and smiled. "I've had trouble sleeping and thought a hot shower might help. Sorry if I woke you."

"That's all right," she lied with a yawn. She returned to the bedroom and sat in a chair to wait for him. The farm report was the only offering on television so she turned it off in favor of the radio.

Leonard came in wearing a thick robe and toweling his wet head. "I've been up almost all night. Wouldn't you know I'm finally getting sleepy."

"Well, why don't you go back to bed and sleep till nine or ten. I'll call Brad around eight and tell him we'll be late today. We deserve a little time off anyway."

"Sounds good to me Babe. Three or four hours is all I need."

"I'll just lie down with you. I'm still tired too." They settled into the king size bed and within minutes both were asleep.

TWENTY EIGHT

Captain Salinski was getting very weary of Mr. Jones from the Secret Service. He felt that his only purpose in life had become the government's slave to this campaign. Cap realized he knew too much and feared of what could happen when this whole mess was settled. Jones was pacing about in Cap's office when he arrived, a full two hours earlier than normal. Neither man was very pleased with the hour but Jones had the advantage as basically Cap was scared to death of him.

"We've got a situation here that has to be solved and quick. I don't care if you have to put twenty men on it I want results."

Cap sank wearily into his chair. "What seems to be the problem?"

"The problem is someone has killed one of my agents who was assigned to Richardson's lab subjects." Jones was turning a deep crimson as he renewed his fury. "I want to know who did it and why."

"Of course we'll investigate it," Cap assured. "Let me check the report and I'll have a better idea of which direction to go."

"I can save you the trouble. I've already been briefed. He was knifed and robbed while on a stakeout outside of their apartment building. I've got to know if it was a legitimate robbery or somehow related to our project."

Cap picked up a pencil and tapped it lightly on the desktop. "I would think men in your department could have some enemies from other cases you might have worked on."

Jones reached across the desk and took the pencil from Cap's hand. He broke it in half with a sneer and threw it onto the desk top. "We keep a very low profile. Most of our enemies no longer exist and those that do generally don't know our line people."

Cap picked up a second pencil and began to tap it on the desk. "Then it could have been a burglary."

"Not likely." Jones glared at the pencil but made no move toward removing it from Cap's hand. "These guys are very, very good at what they do. People don't even know they are there let alone get the drop on them. Most likely my man was talking with the murderer for some reason. He made a mistake and got killed."

"If this was done by a pro it's not likely that there will be any evidence," Cap guessed. "Surely you've seen it before, you just have no physical evidence to go from." He put the pencil back into his desk drawer. "We'll know more when the lab boys get finished."

"Just turn the scene upside down," Jones grated. "I want the answer." He stormed out before Cap could reply.

Cap picked up the telephone and dialed his aide. "I want extra men on that last night stabbing case and I want Sandy Gibbs in my office this afternoon." He paused while the other man replied. "I don't really care where he is. Find him and get him in here." Cap slammed the phone down for effect. His instinct told him that Sandy had some answers to this. Maybe if he leaned hard enough he would get results.

There was a soft rap on his door. Cap looked up at the glass, which revealed Lieutenant Ted Mentel. Cap couldn't decide if his dislike for the man was a result of his youth, the fact that he was Sandy's replacement, or both. Mentel was sharp enough. He had scored in the upper ten percent of his Lieutenant's exam and performed his duties expertly. Well, he supposed it wasn't the kid's fault. Someone had to replace Sandy. He waved the young man into his office and tried to act civil. "Hi Ned, what's up today."

The kid was nervous and tried not to show it. The irritating thing was he was fine around anyone other than this Captain. He mentally braced himself and plunged ahead. "You might want to hear about this one sir. Some guy with a superhuman act had a run in with a vice cop and a cruiser about six blocks from one of our murder scenes. They said he almost totaled the cruiser with his body and broke a pair of cuffs like they were string." He waited for a moment for a response and when he didn't get one continued, "Could there be a connection?"

"Maybe," Cap answered thoughtfully. Could this be connected with the two lab workers? "Get me all you can on it Ned. And put a tail on the man and woman in this apartment." He wrote Leonard and Janet's address on a slip of paper and handed it to the Lieutenant. "Make it a twenty four hour surveillance."

"Yes sir." Mentel left without further comment.

Cap's telephone rang and he answered it on the first ring. After a short pause he smiled. "You've found him already? Get him in here." He had not expected to see Sandy this soon.

Sandy burned his clothes and even the shoes in his building's incinerator. A speck of blood or a piece of hair could be missed even after the laundry. Burning eliminated any possible concern. He remembered the murder that was solved back in sixty two when their only clue was a footprint with an X cut into the sole of the shoe. That one could have never been solved without that shoe.

—

He took a long bath, taking great care to scrub his fingernails and washing his hair four times. Convinced that no trace of the dead man could be found connected to him Sandy went to bed and fell into an exhausted sleep. His apartment door sounded like a football team was pounding it and woke him up. He groaned and checked his bedside clock. He had slept for about three hours.

The pounding increased and he rolled out of bed, automatically reaching for his gun in the nightstand. He pulled on a robe to cover his nakedness and walked to the door's peephole. He slid the gun into his robe pocket and opened the door to two uniformed police officers. "Hey guys, what's happening. Come on in." He stepped back and admitted the two grinning policemen.

"How's it going Lieutenant," Patrolman Ron Harris inquired. He stuck out his hand and Sandy shook it vigorously. The other man followed suit but Sandy did not recognize him.

"Ron, it's going good," he replied. "You guys taking a break from the mines or is this official."

Harris grinned even broader. "You must be the new public enemy one for them to send in a couple of champions like us Lieutenant. I was telling Sam here that maybe we'd better call in a backup to bring you in."

Sandy returned the wryness with his own humor. "I flushed the dope down the toilet when I heard you knocking so you won't have much to go on anyhow."

"Yea, well Captain Salinski asked us to bring you in for a visit anyhow," Harris replied. "Seriously Lieutenant, he's pretty anxious to talk to you." The smile had been replaced with a very official sounding tone. "We'll give you a ride as soon as you're dressed," he added.

"Okay fellows, whatever you say. Give me a few minutes in the bathroom." His heart was pounding with concern. Had he somehow missed a minor detail last night? The argument of self defense would do no good with these people. If he was implicated in the death of a G man Sandy Gibbs was history. He put his gun in a bathroom drawer and cleaned up before emerging. He dressed quickly and rode downtown with scarcely another word being spoken.

He saw Cap sitting quietly behind his desk, obviously putting off all other business while waiting for his old comrade. Using his best attempt at calmness Sandy strolled into Cap's office without knocking. The two uniforms waited just outside the door for orders.

"Thank you men, that will be all," Cap said over Sandy's shoulder. The door was closed and the two officers walked away with obvious relief. "Sit down Sandy." His attention reverted to his guest and Cap noted that Sandy looked a bit too relaxed, as if he were faking his calm attitude.

—

"If you wanted to see me, a phone call would have done it Cap." Sandy settled into the chair across from his ex boss' desk. "I must admit though, I like your style. How many people get a police escort when they visit an old friend. Or did you call me in here to offer my old job back." He hoped his grin wasn't too strained.

"I wanted to see you to make sure there wasn't any chance of you working again. Retirement becomes you Sandy."

"It doesn't feel too good though Cap," he answered dryly.

"I'll bet it beats prison denim though," Cap shot back, "or a box in the ground."

"Life isn't really worth living without a purpose," Sandy countered, "even if it means taking some risk."

Cap sighed, tired of the verbal game. "A Secret Service agent was murdered last night outside an apartment building he was assigned to watch. You wouldn't know anything about it I don't suppose." Cap was looking for even the slightest reaction but didn't get it. That bothered him even more as a complete lack of emotion usually indicated a facade.

"Why would you even think I might?" Sandy shifted slightly in his seat and hoped he wasn't giving anything away.

"I see you've gotten a private investigator's license." Cap had played his trump card. "You aren't getting involved with that Slane thing are you Sandy?"

"I only want to still be known as a cop, even if it is private," he answered. "I probably won't even do anything with it unless someone offers me a really interesting case."

"Just so it isn't Mrs. Slane that comes up with any ideas. I understand you've been out to her home."

"Wow, I'm important enough to warrant a tail," he said in an impressed tone. "You really do care."

"Don't be a smart mouth," Cap shot back. "You know darned well you've been tailed because you've slipped every one that's been laid on you. I don't think you realize how close the Secret Service came to having you put away. Jones pushed awfully hard to outright murder you. Someone, I don't even know who, said frame him and send him to prison. I told them if anything drastic happened without giving you the opportunity to agree to back off I'd blow the whistle on them myself."

"Gee Cap, that's really nice but . . . ."

"Now you just shut up a minute and let me finish." Cap was shouting now, the veins in his neck standing out like clothesline. "If you so much as make these people *think* you're messing around with this case you're probably not going to jail, you'll just become part of the freeway system. Now am I getting through?" Cap paused to suck in a breath of air and almost blacked out from hyperventilation.

"Cap, can you sit back and watch this happen?" Sandy spoke softly and made it a statement rather than a question. "How many people have to be murdered before we take a stance for what is right."

"Look, you don't know people are being murdered. The Slane kid was an accident and his old man couldn't handle the shame." Cap was almost pleading. "Just let it go Sandy. You're a friend I don't want to lose. Just let it go."

Sandy felt tears stinging his eyes. He wiped across his nose with his thumb and forefinger and fought for control. "I've discovered something through all of this Cap. All those years as a police officer never worried me once about getting killed. I guess it just never came close enough though, because I want to tell you I've never been so frightened. I'm not willing to die yet Cap."

"Well then . . . ."

"Now wait," Sandy interrupted. "It's your turn to hear me out." He paused and when Cap didn't speak Sandy continued. "As frightened as I am I am even angrier. Someone has taken from me a job I loved much sooner than it was necessary. That same someone has covered up at least one murder and maybe more in the name of research. I want to tell you something, there is no sign of science in what is happening here. All I see is a bunch of self serving big shots destroying lives and it makes me sick to my stomach."

"Sick enough to die for?" Cap inquired.

"I think so. No, I know so."

"Sandy, did you kill that agent?"

He choose his words carefully, realizing that Salinski might turn on him at any time. "If I would have killed that man, which I'm not saying I did, it would have been in self defense."

"Come on Sandy. You can't resist an official of the law and call it self defense."

"Let me tell you something. If someone put a gun to your head and didn't identify himself would you kill him if you could?"

Cap's voice was shaking as he asked, "Is that what happened?"

"Remember Cap, we're just pretending. I didn't kill anyone."

"Are you investigating Robin Slane's death?"

Sandy gave him a wry grin. "I'm not doing anything except some fishing."

"I'll come to your funeral Sandy."

"No you won't," he answered. "You'll be too frightened that Big Brother won't like your involvement so you'll stay home. Guilt by association you know."

Cap stood up to indicate the end of their interview. "I think I once told you you're a darn good cop Sandy Gibbs. Unfortunately I think you're too good. And I will attend your funeral."

Sandy got up and walked toward the door without offering to shake hands. "From you that's a compliment. Thanks Cap."

"Sandy." Cap's eyes were brimmed with tears and his voice was breaking. "I've got to report this."

Sandy paused at the door and smiled at his former friend. "No you don't and thanks for the warning. Will you give me enough time to get to Carolyn Slane?"

"I don't think they'll bother her."

Sandy chuckled mirthlessly. "Come on man, use your police sense. They can't have loose ends with a cover-up." He pointed his finger and thumb like they were a gun. "Remember, you're a loose end too Cap. And by the way, I changed my mind. I don't want you at my funeral."

TWENTY NINE

Sandy left the station house and walked to the nearest pay telephone. Carolyn Slane answered the first ring. "It's Sandy. How soon can you have a bag packed?"

"Oh, in say thirty minutes, but what . . ."

"Make it fifteen. I'll pick you up." He hung up the telephone and trotted to his car. The midsize sedan that pulled out behind him had government all over it. Sandy marveled at their stupidity.

Three blocks away from the police station he jumped out of his car at a red light and ran back to the Secret Service vehicle. The man was obviously surprised but made no move as his quarry approached. Sandy pulled a knife from his pocket and snapped open the blade. He knelt at the left front tire and sliced off the valve stem.

He ran back to his car with the sound of escaping air rushing to his ears. The government man was so completely taken by surprise that he sat in shocked silence behind the sinking front end of his car. Sandy sped away with the green light and followed a direct route to the Slane home.

She was waiting at the front door with three heavy bags. Sandy grunted with mock agony at their weight and carried them to his car. Not a word was spoken until he pulled out of the drive and headed west.

"You're an incredible woman did you know that?" he asked.

"Why thank you, and although I may be smart enough to know it I would never be vain enough to openly admit to it. What gives you such a high opinion of me?"

He chuckled and shook his head in amazement. "Do you realize a man you hardly know calls and said pack your bags and let's go. With no questions asked you pack half the world in ten minutes and calmly drive away with me without as much as a hello. That my dear makes you, in my book anyway, a class act."

She blushed, lowering her eyes like a schoolgirl. "Maybe I was hoping your intentions were not honorable."

"Don't tempt me lady," he chided. "Life gets pretty lonely sometimes."

"I know, that's why I'm tempting you," she answered shamelessly.

"If only we had more time," he murmured. "Look, I was stupid and played my cards to my old boss. Maybe I was hoping he would change his mind and help us. Anyhow he's going to fill in Big Brother any minute now."

"I thought you were going to keep this under wraps as long as possible." She betrayed her outward calm with a slight break in her voice.

"I can't believe how incredibly dumb the whole thing went," he chided himself. "I about had a stroke when two uniforms picked me up this morning. I figured they knew and I'm about to be sent to prison on a bum wrap or killed. It turned out they were on a fishing expedition and didn't know anything. Then, like an idiot, I spilled my guts to Cap. Maybe it was guilt."

"What do you have to feel guilty about?" She felt a need to defend him. "You're just trying to get things straight concerning Robin."

"Well, there is another problem," he admitted. "Last night I killed a Secret Service agent."

She recoiled in the car seat and looked for a moment as if she were considering jumping out of the moving automobile. Her lips turned white and the pupils of her eyes dilated in an animal like fear that Sandy was used to seeing in victims and criminals alike. "I didn't count on being a part of murder when we started this," she said. "I don't want to live with that every day of my life."

"Maybe you should let me explain what happened first," he suggested. "You might not feel guilty when you know all the facts." She calmed down slightly so he continued. "I was sitting outside an apartment building in my car when a gun was put behind my left ear. I was not given any indication of who he was or what he wanted. I frankly thought he was robbing me. I got the opportunity to get the drop on him and did so. Frankly I think it was him or me."

"Would you have killed him had you known he was a Secret Service agent?" she questioned him in almost a whisper.

He thought long and hard for a few moments before attempting to answer. Should he be completely honest or would a small white lie be in order. He disregarded the lie in short order because this woman was too intelligent to swallow half truths. "I think that no matter what, I had to kill him. When he discovered who I was he would have either been ordered to dispose of me or his superiors would have taken some kind of drastic action. I'm sorry if you feel responsible but I would not be here if that man had lived."

"Very well Sandy Gibbs. If you've made a murderer out of my immortal soul I'm damned anyway, so be prepared to do it up right," she said.

"What do you mean," he asked, genuinely puzzled.

"You didn't murder anyone in my estimation is what I mean," she said. "You were defending your life from forces that in this case are wrong. But what I really mean is that when we reach a hideaway you're going to make love to me. I've wanted you since the day you came back with your offer to investigate the death of Robin and Charles. I guess that's why I agreed to cooperate." She looked at his profile, waiting for an answer.

"I'm not the man you think I am Carolyn." He waited to speak again until he was stopped for a red light and could turn to look her in the eyes. "You're a society woman with obvious breeding. "I'm just an old flat foot cop with no class or breeding. What appeal could I have to you?"

"Maybe that is the basis of your appeal," she answered honestly. "Charles was always so socially perfect, even in our private lives. Maybe I just need to find out what a real down to earth man is like." She blushed again. "Am I being too presumptuous? Perhaps I don't appeal to you."

A car honking its horn brought Sandy's attention back to his driving, which was a welcome opportunity to again avoid her eyes. The truth was he was becoming embarrassed. "You appeal to me very much Carolyn. In fact that's why I've hesitated so much; I guess I'm insecure around you."

"Isn't that amazing," she smiled. "We're like two school kids with complexes, each feeling they're not good enough for the other." An awkward silence followed as she tried to think of what else to say and sensed he had the same problem. "Pull into this ATM she said, breaking the silence and the mood they had been in.

Sandy obediently followed her instructions and asked as they parked, "What are we doing here?"

"I'm going to empty my checking and saving accounts. If we're going to be on the run we'll need money and they're likely to put a freeze on my account when the heat gets put on."

"You should have been the cop," Sandy replied with genuine admiration. "I didn't think of that."

"I've got your mind clouded with passion," she teased as she climbed out of the car.

He watched intently as she walked through the double glass doors into the bank branch and once again admired the cut of this woman. She was well preserved for someone who was probably in her mid fifties and was very sexy indeed. Several younger women entered the bank as he waited so Sandy compared them to Carolyn as he waited. Maybe Mother Nature built in an appeal that matched ages because Sandy would have chosen Carolyn Slane over any of these younger girls. Maturity did have its values.

Too much time went by and he began to worry about her. Perhaps Cap had not given him any time and the Feds were after them already. They could be stalling this transaction to have agents here to pick them up. Sandy started to get out of the car to investigate. He hesitated for a moment and then unlocked the glove compartment, taking from it a 357 Magnum revolver. After checking the loads, he stuck it in the waistband of his pants.

—

He buttoned his coat over the large revolver and hoped the bank did not employ a guard at this small Southside branch. The weapon was so large that a trained eye could tell it was there and the last thing he wanted was a nervous guard thinking he was trying to rob the bank. He saw Carolyn sitting at a bank officer's desk and noted that there was no guard in sight.

He walked to the desk and smiled at the man taking care of the transaction. "Is everything all right Mrs. Slane?"

She was slightly startled at his entrance but quickly recovered. "Yes Mr. Gibbs, thank you. This gentleman was just pointing out the disadvantages of removing such a large amount of cash at one time while we are waiting for the downtown office to clear the transaction."

He pulled his private investigator credentials from his pocket and showed them to the bank officer. "That's why Mrs. Slane hired me to escort her. In fact she was taking so long in returning to the car that I felt I should check her whereabouts."

The man smiled and nodded in agreement. "A wise precaution I'm sure Mrs. Slane. And as for you," he turned his smile towards Sandy, "Mr., ah, Gibbs wasn't it, I assure you your employer is in capable hands. In fact here is Mrs. Zerkle now with your money."

Sandy had to struggle to control his own amazement as a woman approached, carrying two large cardboard boxes full of money. "Now Mrs. Slane," the officer was saying, "we'll take a few minutes to count it for you and then we'll have you sign this receipt."

"I really don't want to wait while you recount the money," she said. "Your bank has been dependable for many years and I see no reason to doubt that now."

"You're too kind," the man crooned as she signed the receipt. "Please be careful as you transport this large sum, and we thank you for your patronage."

"You'd better carry the boxes Mrs. Slane," Sandy advised, "so I can keep my hands free."

The banker suddenly took notice of the large bulge in Sandy's coat and turned slightly white around the eyes. "Let me get the door for you," he said and hurried to the front door, which he held open for them to walk through.

"I began to think you were having a problem," Sandy whispered as they rushed to his car. "Did that guy try to stall you?"

She waited for him to close her door and go around to the driver's side before answering. "I don't think he did anything out of the ordinary if that's what you mean. After all they're bound to be careful when this much cash is being withdrawn."

Sandy pulled onto Livingston Avenue and headed toward Route 33. He glanced at the boxes sitting between them and asked, "How much is here anyhow?"

"Three hundred and fifty thousand dollars, rounded off," she answered calmly.

Fortunately there was no oncoming traffic as Sandy swerved into the other lane. He quickly regained control and pulled to the side of the road. He looked from his client to the boxes and back again in rapid fire order. She had a puzzled look on her face that Sandy mistook for amusement. "Come on Carolyn, don't do that to me. My gosh, I'm jumpy enough without pulling my leg at a time like this. We've got to be really serious about this thing."

"What are you talking about," she shot back. "You asked me how much I withdrew and I told you." She pulled down on her blouse to smooth out the wrinkles. "When you told me we'd have to be on the run I figured I'd better get as much as I could because it may not be safe later."

"You are totally incredible," Sandy declared. "What makes you think I won't just blow your head off with this oversize cannon?" He pulled the pistol from his belt, brandished it for a moment and then returned it to the glove box. "I could be out of the country before anyone even knew you were dead."

She scratched her chin thoughtfully before answering. "I don't know it it's because I'm so sure I would appeal to you or if I'm so sure you're not the type to kill for any reason except necessity. Realistically it's probably a combination of both but at any rate it never occurred to me."

"I guess I'm really just angry that a newcomer to this cloak and dagger business is better at it than I," Sandy admitted. "When these guys get on our trail any trips to the bank would mean instant capture. You were absolutely right and I wasn't smart enough to come up with the answer. And by the way," he said as an afterthought, "you do appeal to me a lot." He pulled back into traffic and missed her girlish blush of pleasure.

"Where are we going," she asked after several minutes of silence.

"There's a nice hotel in Lancaster that is a pretty unlikely place for anyone to look too soon. Most of the searching will be done in Columbus and I'll only have a thirty minute trip to do my snooping."

"What are you going to do," she asked with real concern in her voice.

"I'm going to keep looking for answers," he said. "Just because my stupidity let the cat out of the bag there's no reason to quit now. Someone has to answer to justice."

"You're not Captain Marvel," she reminded him softly. "Marvelous maybe but you didn't make Captain."

"Sorry about the speech," he answered with a wry smile, "but I'm going to do my best."

"Sandy." She bit her lower lip and gave him her best innocent look, "why don't we take this money and go to Brazil or some place and let the Secret Service murder half of Columbus if they want to, but let's fade out of this."

He sighed heavily as he reached the motel and pulled up to the front door. "You'll never know how tempting that is. Right now I'm so tired of all this that I'm half sick, but I don't guess I'm ready to give up yet."

She touched his arm as he prepared to leave the car and said, "You get our room and maybe in a few minutes I can change your mind."

THIRTY

Bob Jones exited the commercial jet carrier and was met by a Washington staff member who rushed him to the Capitol building. Jones tried to small talk his driver to no avail and finally gave up to return to his worrying.

Things were not going well in Columbus, Ohio. Several people, including one of his men, were dead, and that ex-cop Gibbs had taken the Slane woman and lots of her money to parts unknown. The greatest discovery of the history of science was being kept under wraps so that they could steal it from the poor jerk that developed it and Jones had failed to produce the formula.

Assistant agency chief Floyd Devoe had called him personally and requested an audience in D.C. for this morning. Jones knew he had to be in trouble and simply hoped that he could talk his way into more time. Sooner or later things would smooth out. Devoe's office was totally incredible. The taxpayers had given this man surroundings that bordered on unrealism. White carpeting almost too thick to walk through was always spotless and never showed a wear pattern. An oak captain's desk custom made for the immense room sat in front of a solid wall of bookshelves. Even the trim molding around the ceiling was hand carved. Jones knew from past visits that one entire wall hid a liquor cabinet that folded open at a touch of a button. A complete bathroom with a shower was included behind one door.

Guests were always ushered in by the magnificent looking redhead that had been a receptionist for three assistant chiefs. She knew this one's routine quite well by now. He demanded hot black coffee at nine sharp each morning and sex at precisely four o'clock on Wednesdays. Fortunately he wasn't kinky like her last boss. She had almost decided to quit when he was finally transferred. She kept herself in top shape and figured she could sleep her way through about ten more years worth of chiefs before age claimed her beauty. A transfer would then be made by someone who liked younger women but she would have a secure civil service job with that many years. That was the way it was done in this land of the politically correct, and she had learned to live with it.

Devoe liked to make an entrance, so he was never in the office when someone arrived. The redhead would escort the visitor to a chair across from the huge desk and simply state that Mr. Devoe would be in momentarily. She walked slowly from the room if the visitor was male to provide him with a long look. Jones was so nervous today that he failed to appreciate the show.

Ten minutes was the normal waiting period before the grand entrance occurred. This gave the guest ample time to admire the surroundings. Jones checked his watch when he entered and glanced at it again when the outer door opened. Eight minutes. Well, he had seen the office several times before and supposed he thought he would save some time.

"Robert, Robert, Robert. How are you doing this glorious day." The man was short and round like a snowman. Fat was probably not a fair description, he was just built round. Most of his hair had been lost on top years before and he clung to three small strands that ran from back to front like they were the last possible touch with youth. One strand was sticking up like an antenna searching for more hair to keep it company.

Jones stood up to greet his superior and gave his best attempt at looking humbled before his master. "I'm fine sir and you?"

"Marvelous, simply marvelous. Sit down Robert and let's talk."

The two men eased into their respective chairs with Jones wondering why the man did seem to be in such good humor. He had no way of knowing that Devoe was always happy on Wednesdays. "And how is the family sir." Get all of the social graces out of the way before one is forgotten.

"Fine my boy thank you. Would you join me in a drink?" The rear wall was already opening.

"Thank you sir. I'll have whatever you're having."

"Good," Devoe thundered. "I'll mix them up and you sit still." He walked toward the bar and Jones soon heard the tinkling of ice on glass behind him. "We've got some problems to talk about don't we" he said at the bar.

"Yes sir." Jones turned in his chair to help his voice carry to the back of the room. "I was counting on some advice sir." Play all the cards, what harm could it do.

Devoe came over carrying two large glasses of orange juice. Jones braced himself for the taste of vodka but instead tasted only juice. "Great stuff isn't it. I have the oranges flown in from California fresh each week. No booze, it just dulls the senses." He winked at his uncomfortable underling. "Guys in our business have to stay sharp right Robert?"

"Absolutely sir." The acid in the juice was eating at his already nervous stomach. He swallowed hard to force down the rising bile and smiled rather sickly.

"Do you know Stanley Forth? He graduated in the class right after yours."

Jones felt like he was going to pass out. "I've only heard of agent Forth sir. Wasn't he responsible for saving the President's life last year?"

—

"That's the one." Devoe slapped his desk with the palm of his hand, the loud crack making his nervous subordinate seem to raise out of the chair. "I've come to a decision Robert. I think you could use some help on this one. After all this is possibly the biggest assignment we've ever had."

Did he dare ask? But yes, it was necessary. "Sir, uh, who will be in charge?"

Devoe took a drink from his glass and kept it pressed to his lower lip. Looking over the rim of the glass he said, "Why Robert my boy, do you really have to ask?" He pressed a button and the redhead appeared. "Would you ask Mr. Forth to come in please?"

"Yes sir," she answered obediently, thinking more about how she hated Wednesdays than wondering why Jones looked ready to die.

She ducked out of the door and returned almost instantly with a tall blonde man that looked like he belonged on the cover of *Gentlemen's Quarterly*. Incredibly broad shoulders tapered to a trim waist. A finely tailored suit accented his weight lifter body, giving him an almost artificial perfection. Confidence was so obviously a part of this man that all of them, including Devoe, hesitated as if waiting for him to take charge.

Devoe finally shook off the trance and smiled the grin of a man who was successful thanks to lady luck. "Robert, meet the new agent in charge of Columbus, Stan Forth."

Jones was able to stand and greet his new boss only through a tremendous effort of inner strength. His whole life was crashing around his ears but he decided on the spot not to give up. He would knuckle under for now and wait for the current opportunity to destroy this pretty boy if necessary. No one was going to crush the boyhood dream of Bob Jones.

"Jones," even his voice was deep and rich, "do you feel that you can work on my team after once being in charge?"

"Mr. Forth, my life is dedicated to the service of my Country. If she asks me to be in charge I do my best to be a great leader. If she asks me to be a subordinate I follow to the utmost of my abilities. I will attempt to follow your every instruction." He hoped that was enough to set the jerk at ease and yet not leave a phony impression.

"That's all I can ask for. Welcome aboard."

"Thank you sir." Apparently it had worked. "Do you need me to brief you as to our current situation?"

"You've done an excellent job with your written reports Bob" Forth said with a condescending smile. "I think we have a pretty good feel for what has happened." He turned his attention to their superior. "Floyd, if I may, I'll immediately begin my recommended solution to this entire problem."

"Fire away my boy." Devoe suppressed a chuckle at that idiot Jones' open mouthed stare at the use of his first name. A man of Forth's caliber would go far in the Service, perhaps farther than himself. Friends in high places were a must, especially young ones that were obviously moving fast.

Forth walked to the office door, opened it, and motioned to someone in the reception area. Jones wondered how many people were hanging around out there. His flesh crawled as Mutt and Jeff came into the office. These two had a cloud of death hanging around them, almost a physical odor. Maybe the Secret Service wasn't the best job after all.

"These men are an integral part of my plan," Forth was saying. "May we gather around your desk Floyd? I would like to lay out my paperwork."

"Of course," Devoe agreed. "Just take charge here and show us what you've got."

He opened his briefcase and took out several folders, which he lay side by side like a row of targets on the desk. "Now as I see it we have a multisided problem on our hands. We've got a brilliant doctor who has discovered a way to make us young. Someone much higher in our government than any of us has decided that the discoverer of this technique should not get credit for his own work. Why is not really for us to speculate I suppose, but most likely there's a doctor in the President's family or something. Our job would be a lot easier if this part of our assignment were forgotten, but we must do as we are asked." He paused for comments and got none.

"Then of course," he continued, "we have what I would call our loose ends. Thanks to an unfortunate accident and a suicide," he paused again to smile at Mutt and Jeff who made no change of expression, "we have tied off a couple. We still have," he opened a folder, "Mr. Nash. From what we have learned from his background studies the man cannot be trusted. We must have his death appear as if from natural causes. The former police Lieutenant and his new wealthy lady friend must be located and disappear permanently. That should not pose too great a problem, they'll just disappear with all that money." He opened another folder with Sandy and Carolyn's file.

The next folder Forth laid his hands on gently, almost reverently. "This is our dear Captain Salinski. His is a greater problem than the lieutenant originally was. We're dealing with a higher rank so our public outcry could be intensified. I haven't decided what to do with him as yet." He sighed and seemed to be gathering his strength to go on.

"This is our last folder." He didn't even touch it, a highly polished nail on his index finger hovering precariously close to the stiff manila. "We shan't open this one or even discuss its contents at this point because it's my catch all file. We mustn't leave any doubt in our minds as to the completion of this project. Anyone with knowledge of our activities, including ourselves gentlemen," he paused for effect, "must be looked at with great consideration as to loyalty and, of course, silence. Our two friends here," a nod went toward Mutt and Jeff, "insure a permanent silence in some cases, drastic though these measures may be."

"There's one folder you didn't remove from your case," injected Devoe. "Is that one even more secret than this last one?" There was a strong hint of irritation in his voice at being a superior officer but still included in the possible disloyal file.

"That file contains our good doctor and his wife. We want to keep them carefully out of this conversation until we have the formula. I understand that it is so complex that despite the collection of a small amount of the liquid, without Dr. Richards' our best scientists have been unable to duplicate the formula. I suspect that if we continue to fail we will ultimately have to give him credit for his discovery."

"What about torture," Devoe asked.

"I've highly considered that. As you well know we have some experts in that field. Even though their success rate is over ninety percent we cannot risk the discovery of modern man to a slip-up like the subject withstanding the torture or dying before we get the notes. We must either find them through searches or ultimately give Dr. Richards his credit."

"What is your next step," Devoe asked.

"I will give Mutt and Jeff these folders." He stacked and handed them, with the exception of the last folder. "Now I must head for Columbus." He smiled and dusted off his hands triumphantly. "Shall we go Bob?"

"Yes sir." Jones leaped to his feat and started toward the door, a show of blind loyalty.

"And you gentlemen will study the folders and prepare for our next move?" Forth nodded his head toward Mutt and Jeff and raised his eyebrows for effect. Jeff nodded slightly in return. "Good, then all is prepared. Floyd, keep in touch."

"Certainly," Devoe answered, totally removed from control of the meeting. "You too" he added at the closing office door. He looked around the office, almost disoriented for a moment, and noted that Mutt and Jeff were sitting in the office. "Oh, did you men want something else?" he asked.

The smaller man looked up at his large partner who whispered something. He nodded and turned his attention to Devoe. "Do you want us to start a file on Mr. Forth?"

Devoe looked blankly at the man for a moment and then smiled. "Yes, I believe that would be wise."

—

THIRTY ONE

Love was an emotion that Sandy thought had long ago escaped his being. Such a dangerous emotion it was. People have killed and felt no shame because of it, others live their lives in horror and sadness as a result of a feeling that can't even be physically touched.

She lay in the double bed with three pillows behind her back and head permitting a view of the hotel room with no effort involved. The covers were piled up to her chin, leaving only her head and arms exposed to Sandy's vision. She watched him as he carefully strapped a knife and small gun to each leg and put on his large shoulder holster to carry the magnum.

He looked at her when the small ritual was completed and saw the worried frown creasing her brow. "You're going to start showing your age with that wrinkling forehead," he said fondly. How had he fallen so deeply in love in so short a time?

"What?" she asked, surprised.

"Oh, I guess I was thinking and then thought out loud. It's a habit living alone gives you. There's no one to talk to and the silence gets pretty bad so you end up speaking some of your thoughts. Since no one is there you don't have people thinking you're nuts."

"So what's this about being too old," she demanded. "Am I too far over the hill for a youngster like you?"

"Oh my," he said hastily, "you're more than I would dare dream about. I was just thinking that worry would make you seem older than you are."

"Oh, I like that." The wrinkles left her forehead and tiny crows feet appeared at the corner of her eyes as a smile sprang to life. "All I've got to say is learn to stop talking to yourself because from now on I'll be asking what you're driving at."

"I like that," he echoed. "Do you still want to take the money and run?"

"More than you'll ever know" she said without hesitation, "especially now."

"I can hardly resist the temptation myself," he admitted. "We could go to, oh, Australia let's say and never worry again. Maybe open a little gift shop somewhere."

She sat up in the bed, clutching the covers to her chest. "Why don't we do it? We could drive to another state, cross country to Arizona if you want, surely they won't be watching for us there. We'll just drop off the face of the earth via a charter plane to Australia and go under assumed names. It happens all the time doesn't it?"

"Whoa, slow down a bit," he chuckled. She looked like a small child anticipating Christmas and he loved her all the more for her hope. "Let me see if I can do any good for a few days sneaking around like an escaped convict. Realistically I've pretty much ruined my effectiveness by opening my big mouth. You know, it's interesting too how brave you can be when life is bleak and meaningless." He went to the bed and kissed her warmly. "Now you've changed all of that. I really don't want to get killed over this whole mess any more."

"I know," she agreed. "How soon I've forgotten my anger over Robin and Charles. I should feel ashamed about it but heaven help me I don't." She hugged him tight. "Charles and I didn't have much of a marriage you know." She shrugged. "I don't know when it changed, but we drifted apart as time went on." She looked at Sandy and blushed. "I only know that now I want to spend the rest of my life with you."

He returned her hug, enjoying the sweet morning fragrance of her hair. "I don't think we have anything to be ashamed of. There's nothing wrong with wanting to live."

"Then let's do it," she urged. "Don't wait one more minute Sandy. Let's go now. Let someone else take some chances."

"Give me today and tonight," he decided. "If I don't get anywhere we'll leave before dawn tomorrow."

"And if you make some progress?"

"Then we'll have to stay longer."

"I'll pray for your safe failure then." There were tears in her eyes.

"I hope it's answered." He smiled and then kissed her and left without another word.

"Sir." The picket fence toothed secretary was trying to get the feel of her new boss. Mr. Jones had been fairly informal but this good looking specimen seemed very businesslike.

"Yes." Forth looked up from the stacks of paperwork he was trying to catch up with and didn't particularly like the interruption.

"There's an agent on line two and he says it's urgent that he speak to you."

"Very well I'll take it." He wondered as he lifted the receiver why such a fantastic woman never got her teeth fixed. "This is Forth," he barked into the phone.

The voice on the other end of the line was slightly static, usually an indication of a mobile field phone being sent in wireless. Forth also noticed a tightness in the voice that usually accompanied a hunter on the track of game. Hunting people was the most exciting sport in the world. "We've spotted Gibbs. This is unit fifteen."

No formalities in field situations, probably a carryover from the military. Enemy snipers looked for salutes to officers. Get rid of the leaders and the followers will be lost. Probably a sound concept. "Where is he now?"

"Route thirty three heading north into the city. We spotted him around the outer belt area."

"Forth felt his own adrenaline pump into his heart, getting excited just talking about the hunt. "Did you see him inside or outside the outer belt?"

"Inside."

That was unfortunate. A spot outside the freeway system surrounding the city would have indicated he came from outside the city. Now they couldn't be sure, as he may have just exited the freeway. "Is he alone?"

"Yes, at least as far as we can tell. If the woman is with him she's either laying on the seat or the floor."

"Okay, I would presume he's alone. Can he be taken?"

"Not yet," the voice crackled in return. "Too many other vehicles in the area. We've got nine units converging on the area and should have no trouble keeping him in sight. Shall we take him if possible?"

"Yes, but I don't want him killed. The man that kills the subject can resign on the spot and then answers to me personally. Is that clear?"

"Clear as crystal."

Forth was shaking with excitement. "I'll be sending agent Jones out to take command on site. You will instruct all units to take his orders unless they are overridden by me. Understood?"

"Perfectly. We're set up at the vacant restaurant at Fourth and Main Street."

Forth wrote down the location on a scratch pad. "Got it. He'll be there in thirty minutes." He threw the phone onto its cradle and shouted "Jones, I need to see you."

Jones sprang from his smaller office in an instant and waited at the doorway of his old office for permission to enter. Forth waved him into the room. "Get to this address and take over the operation. Call me every fifteen minutes with updates. Gibbs has been spotted and it's up to you to get him in and uninjured. If our interrogators don't get a shot at him we may never find the woman. Don't come back here with the news that he didn't talk before he died." Forth looked ugly as he screwed his face into a look that seemed painful. "Don't let me down," he whispered.

"Consider the job as good as done sir," Jones answered, hoping his boss could not see that his legs were trembling.

"I'll count on you. Now go."

Jones ran from the office and took the stairs instead of waiting for the elevator. Forth had done to him what he had never done to his agents. Failure was now the direct responsibility of Bob Jones instead of where it belonged, in the lap of the agency commander. How could he assure the man could be taken alive. Gibbs was probably armed and would not likely give up without a fight. Anytime an agent is instructed to take a dangerous subject without using deadly force you have simply increased the chance of injury or death to the agent.

The command post was fairly quiet when he arrived. Everyone was waiting for his instructions. Jones had been furiously thinking as he drove the short distance and hoped for an answer to his problem. He stood on a small entrance landing and surveyed his base of operations. The place had been a bar and grill in a pretty seedy section of town. He guessed by the dust that it had been closed for at least a year. Twenty two people were crowded around portable equipment that had been set up on the bar. The first approach of a new field commander was important. Jones had no desire to put down any man who had been running the show, in fact he would need his help. "Who is in charge here," he asked as he walked toward his people.

"I am sir. You must be agent Jones."

Jones looked at the middle aged man and envied him. He looked the classic G Man part, slender and hard bodied in his dark blue Brooks Brothers suit and Florsheim shoes. He was a man who had not risen to the top, but he was secure. The guy could retire right now if he wanted to, and Jones wanted to tell him to wise up and get out while he could. Instead he simply said "Come on, I'll just observe for a short time." He made a mental note that although the man had survived he was probably marginal, as no one had even asked to see his identification. Jones spent the next few minutes watching the people perform their duties and attempting to work out a plan. All phases of the operation were being followed by the book which was bothering him. Gibbs would not be caught by the book, he was too smart for conventional methods.

Suddenly the answer came to him, so incredibly simple that he couldn't believe he hadn't already thought of the solution. "Do we have a dog and cat team out there?" That was the popular agency term for a man and woman partnership.

"Yes sir." A young girl with very pale green eyes had spoken. "They're about ten minutes from our subject."

"Bring them up on the radio." He waited impatiently as the girl called to them several times before receiving an answer.

"I've got them sir," she said at last.

166

He grabbed the microphone and pushed the send button. "This is Jones. Have you been briefed as to how this man is to be handled?"

"Yes, no injuries," the woman's voice crackled over the speaker.

"Good. Now here's how we're going to take him."

Sandy was heading towards the campus area. He wasn't really too sure what to do with his last day of investigation, in fact he was tempted to just turn around and go back to the hotel. They could be three states away by tomorrow at this time and in a couple of days they would be in Mexico. From there they could buy some forged papers and fly anywhere in the world, maybe even Australia. Eventually the government people would give up on them, especially when several months went by and neither of them attempted to expose the program.

He made a sudden decision to forget all of this Dick Tracy stuff and pulled onto a side street to turn around. Thirty minutes from now he would have the woman who fulfilled all of his dreams close by his side and the rest of the world could flush itself down the toilet for all he cared. Traffic was fairly heavy as he waited for an opening in the steady string of vehicles. Usually impatient when he had to wait for an extensive length of time, Sandy found that today he was not concerned with the bottleneck. Love had a way of making everything work out.

A powder blue Impala pulled onto the side street he was on and Sandy realized at once that the woman driving the car had swung too wide and would hit him. He tried to get his car into reverse to back away from the crash but the sickening crunch of metal against metal grated into his ears. Since his car wasn't moving and the Impala was turning the corner very slowly the collision caused no injuries. Sandy got out and surveyed the damage, seeing that fortunately his car would be able to move. He planned to exchange insurance information and get away as fast as possible.

In the passenger seat of the Impala a man was yelling at the woman concerning her ability to handle a motor vehicle. Her reaction was to burst into tears. Sandy approached the vehicle with the hopes of acting as peacemaker. They both emerged from the car simultaneously, the man continuing to shout at his companion.

"Hey folks, why don't we calm down," Sandy began. "There really isn't that much damage and . . . ." Sandy froze in his tracks as the man and woman each drew a revolver and pointed them at his chest.

THIRTY TWO

P. Osgood Nash waddled into Brad's small laboratory and paused at the animal cages to catch his breath from the labor of walking the half mile from his office. He had always liked animals, dogs and cats especially, and objected to using them for experiments. Brad had insisted that he no longer used animals since he had human subjects to work with, but Nash still worried about the caged creatures. They were given the run of the lab at night which at least permitted exercise and all had become quite tame. Some were never caged anymore and seemed to sense that this freedom was a result of good behavior.

Nash could not decide whether to be on Brad's side of the youth formula issue or the Secret Service. Talking the doctor into releasing the formula could mean quite a feather in his own cap, maybe even a presidential appointment. Still, these Secret Service people kind of frightened him. No one had even called him since Jones was removed as agent in charge of Columbus. Dislike the man as he did, at least with Jones a person knew where he stood. The new man ignored him completely.

"Brad, are you here?" he called out. A tiger striped cat came running from across the room at the sound of his voice, mewing and rubbing against his legs. "Well hello little one," Nash said fondly. "Hop up on this table and I'll give you a treat." He reached into his coat pocket and produced a tuna fish sandwich. Always hungry as a boy, Nash had promised himself that someday he would never want for food again. He had been faithful to that promise for years.

"Come on little kitten I have more," he soothed as he unwrapped the tin foil from the sandwich. The feline's sensitive nose picked up the fish scent and it nimbly leaped onto the small table, eating the tuna greedily. Nash smiled and petted the cat's soft fur.

Brad was drawing blood from Janet's arm for testing when he heard Nash's voice, so it took him a few moments to respond. He walked out of the small operating area and saw the huge man entertaining the cat, surprised that he had any tenderness about him. He thought to himself that the fat slob should share the tenderness with humans. The cat had eaten its fill before Brad approached and ran away when it saw him. Too many experiments reminded the creature of pain associated with this man.

168

"Mr. Nash, so good of you to drop by," Brad began. "To what do we owe this rare honor?" He had begun to show much less respect for the man since his discovery. After all, Nash needed him now. "I don't think you've visited us more than a dozen times since we've been working on this program."

Nash ignored the insult more because he was too worried to notice it than anything. "Can we talk in private Brad?" His voice was almost pleading.

"Sure, just let me tell Leonard and Janet that we'll be in my office for a few minutes. Why don't you just go on in. I'll be right with you."

The outside door opened and Lois entered to feed the animals and clean cages. The animals were trained to use litter boxes which she also kept clean. "Hello Mr. Nash, how are you?" She greeted her husband's former benefactor with extreme politeness, more out of habit than current necessity. Brad had explained to her how his position had changed and Nash could no longer bully them with threats of cutting funding.

"Fine thank you," Nash mumbled and waddled toward Brad's office.

"Hello darling," Brad greeted his wife warmly. She reached him and he embraced her fondly. "Would you tell Leonard and Janet I'll be with them in a few minutes. Please set up for a blood workup through series four."

"Sure, no problem." She raised her eyebrows and nodded toward Nash who was trying to figure out how to ease his bulk into Brad's small office.

Brad shrugged his own confusion and went into his office. "Maybe we'd be more comfortable in the kitchen," he suggested to Nash.

"Yeah, I guess so," was the answer. Nash was sweating profusely and obviously was not himself. Walking into the small kitchen was an intense effort.

Brad busied himself with the coffee pot, pouring the hot water into cups containing herbal tea. He handed Nash a cup and saucer and leaned against the sink in surprise as the big man shook so badly he was forced to set the cup down. "Okay Mr. Nash. What seems to be the problem?"

"I think the time has come for us to protect ourselves Brad. There are some things going on with these Secret Service people that you're not aware of."

"I kind of doubt that," Brad said bluntly. "Look, you people seem to think that despite the fact that I found the secret of eternal youth and am a trained medical doctor I'm an idiot. My home and office have been repeatedly searched and the public release of my findings have been held up while you try to get my notes. Coverups are in progress for that Slane boy's death, but then we knew that already. Look Osgood, I'm not going to share my discovery with anyone. I did it, I worked hard on it, and you and your friends are not going to steal my life's work. Now do we finally have this whole thing cleared up?"

Nash had become a very pasty white and was struggling to keep himself in control. He attempted to speak but was forced to stop because tears were threatening to burst forth. Finally he gasped, "Brad, I'm sorry." He pulled an initialed handkerchief from his pocket and covered his eyes for a moment. He took a deep, shuddering breath and blew his nose before continuing. "Without your help I'm afraid I'm a dead man."

"Don't you think that's being a bit melodramatic?" Brad asked.

"I admit that personally I underestimated you Brad. No one realized that you were aware of the searches, but if you're that smart think a minute. How do you account for your funeral and nursing home contacts somehow picking the same time to die?"

"Wait a minute," Brad protested. "Those deaths were investigated by the police."

"Oh come on. Do you honestly think the police aren't involved too? Even on the outside chance that they weren't these people are very good at what they're doing. These guys are capable of killing in front of an audience and making it look like an accident."

"Well, I suppose that's true," Brad admitted, "but I'm safe as long as I have my research papers hidden."

"What if they find your notes?" Nash realized he had to sell hard now. His survival depended on this meeting.

"No way. They will not find my notes."

"But if they were to find it," Nash persisted. "Wouldn't you be safer if the material were in two different locations so if they find you out they're likely to not have all the answers."

"I shouldn't admit this but the whole thing is incredibly simple if you have all of the pieces, in fact that is probably why no one has ever cracked this thing. I could break my notes into a dozen pieces and any one of them would probably make it easy to see the answer if it was put into the hands of a trained professional. Besides, why would I give it to anyone else when I could just hide the pieces myself?"

"Perhaps honesty would be the best way to go at this point," Nash said.

"I would have agreed with that a long time ago," Brad interjected dryly.

"I didn't mean it that way." Nash began crying again. "I think I'm on the death list and I want you to help me. I've been so frightened I'm surprised I haven't had a heart attack already."

"Now just a minute," Brad said. He paused a moment to think about what he had been hearing. Finally he continued, "I guess I can't believe you're asking me to trust you after we've spent all these weeks arguing about disclosure to the government. No, I'm afraid my notes will stay right where they are."

"Brad, I'm fighting for my life here. I admit Jones had me convinced that I should help him get your notes, and they do want to steal them, but now I'm sure that we're all on a death list."

Brad rinsed his cup and left it in the sink. He then took a damp cloth and wiped up the spilled tea that Nash had left on the counter. Only after these minor housekeeping chores did he speak again. "The frightening thing is you're probably right. The sad thing is I can't trust you because I could be putting my wife's life in danger and, maybe this is the most selfish part of all, I could lose the credit for my discovery." He shook his head. "Osgood, the bottom line is you have nothing to sell."

Nash was seeing black spots before his eyes and wondered if he was going to pass out. "I'll tell you what, let's go public with this thing. Let me get some friends together from the news media and we'll splash it all over the world. That would eliminate the pressure. There would be no need to kill anyone."

"I don't think you're capable of approaching this thing properly," Brad countered. "Why do you think I haven't done that already? The government is not only essential to our backing but I could go to prison for murder and be disgraced as a physician. I have no choice but to wait them out. They are not going to find my notes, I'm sure of that, and sooner or later they're going to release it. It's too big to suppress much longer."

"Will you do this for me." Nash was grasping at his last hope now. "Let me tell them that I have a copy of the notes. That may keep the wolves away for a while."

"I'll do this," Brad agreed, "I won't tell anyone you don't have a copy."

"Good. Good. That may help." Nash pushed away from the counter and winced as his feet voiced their opinion to the shift in weight. "I don't know how to thank you for this Brad."

"The best thank you is one for yourself," Brad answered. "Go on a diet before you end up dead without the help of the Secret Service."

"Right, right of course," Nash mumbled and shuffled out of the office.

Brad waited until he heard the outer door close before going back to his work. Lois and the two subjects were having a friendly chat, the sight of which lifted his spirits. "Well, shall we get back to work?" he asked.

"Blah," said Janet in mock disgust. "All we do is work, work, work. Senior citizens like ourselves should be resting."

"Poor little you," Brad retorted. "Just like two galley slaves."

"What did Nash want," Lois inquired.

"Oh, nothing," he lied. "Just some bureaucratic junk."

Nash felt a bit more relaxed after meeting with Brad but still decided to go home and rest for the day. His heart pounded so hard that his head began to ache and a solid knot was building in his stomach.

Home for P. Osgood Nash was a fashionable condominium on the Northwest side of town. Maintenance free was a necessity for a man of his size. The exterior was kept in perfect condition for a fixed monthly fee. A maid service cleaned for him once a week. Dishes were a rare problem as generally restaurants provided him with food.

Except for his weight problem life had been kind to him. Hard work and brains had elevated him to the position at the university that he wanted. Until this research project came along it seemed trouble could not find a path to his door. Unfortunately that was now changed.

Nash unlocked the front door and trudged into his kitchen. He had stopped at the grocery store for beer and materials to make lunchmeat sandwiches, possibly his favorite combination. He drank two of the beers while constructing a huge pile of meats and cheeses on French bread. Finally the masterpiece was finished and he went to his T.V. room to relax. There were no windows in this room which made artificial lighting necessary for comfort. He switched on a light beside his favorite easy chair and his heart jumped into his throat. Sitting on the sofa were two men. One was short and almost twerpy looking. The other was a bulk of a man; in fact at that first glance Nash thought he was some kind of animal dressed in clothes. He stepped back in a reflex of shock and stumbled, falling backward and landing with great force into the middle of his chair.

"You look almost comfortable," the small man said with a pleasant smile. "Why don't you just stay right where you are while we have a little visit."

"Who are you," Nash demanded, "and what are you doing in my home." He didn't know what to do. His bulk prevented any sudden moves and besides there was no weapon in the house so he quickly decided to just sit still and cooperate.

"Isn't it awful," the small man was saying, "that the locks they put on these expensive places pop like corks out of a bottle. We got in here faster than if we would have had a key."

"Yea, I keep meaning to add a security system," he said. "I guess after today I'd better call someone." Nash attempted a smile that came out more like a grimace.

"That won't be necessary Mr. Nash," the small man said quietly. "After today you'll have all the security you'll ever need. You see, we're here to kill you." A short nod to his burly companion brought him to his feet. His hand went into a coat pocket and produced a large caliber gun.

"Oh no please don't," Nash began to blubber. "You can have anything. I've got ten thousand dollars in my safe and we can go to the bank and get more. Oh please, oh *please*." His chest pounded so hard that pain was etching its way through his throat and into his lower jaw. Nash looked at the gun and seemed unable to comprehend its size. The round hole in the end to permit the exit of the bullet looked like a cave waiting to swallow its victim into blackness.

The big man pulled back on the hammer of the pistol and locked a chamber into position. Nash saw the finger tighten on the trigger and screamed as he saw it pulled. The pain crashing into his body was not from a bullet. The firing pin clicked harmlessly into an empty chamber. The pain was caused by the fear the fat man had of his own death. His heart, enlarged from overwork and crowded by useless flesh, simply would not take the additional strain and P. Osgood Nash died from a heart attack.

The small man checked for a pulse and smiled when he found none. The electric shock treatments he had planned would no longer be necessary, thus eliminating any possible chance of foul play detection. The big man placed the empty gun into his pocket and the best death team in the business left quietly and without a trace by the front door.

THIRTY THREE

Sandy had been taken to a small cement block building in the country. The woman drove the car while her companion forced Sandy to lie on the floor in the back. A gun was pushed against his lower back for the entire trip.

Six men came out of the building when they arrived and bustled him into the building. There was a single bed in one corner of the room with four manacles attached to chains cemented into the concrete block. He was placed on his back in the bed and each wrist and ankle were locked to restrict any movement. He could lower his hands to the top of his head and pull his feet up about three inches.

No one had spoken a word as he was being restrained and he guessed it would have to be up to him to begin a conversation. "Well, now what happens. You've got me so when do I see my lawyer." Silence greeted his questions. The two men walked to a small table across the room and one of them produced a deck of cards. "Hey," Sandy tried again, "free up my hands and I'll play too. What do you say fellows? I'm good at all of 'em, poker, go fish, old maid." Still a total silence.

"When will I find out what happens next," he continued. He felt compelled to get a conversation started, hopefully to determine a way out of this. His captors total refusal to talk indicated strict orders from probably a very high source. Sandy was getting very worried and wondered if he would ever see Carolyn again.

The men played cards without speaking above a whisper for what seemed to be about an hour. One of them jumped up at the sound of an approaching car and peered out a small window. He nodded to the other men who had paused to watch their companion. They quickly gathered up the cards and slid them into a drawer in the table. Without a word or a backward glance at Sandy they left the building.

Sandy quickly checked the strength of his bounds and pulled frantically in a futile attempt to release himself. The room contained the bed, a table, and six chairs. There was nothing that could help him in the next few moments. A single naked light bulb lightened the room.

The door opened and Sandy forced himself to relax and cease the escape attempt. He looked at the figure standing in the doorway and was momentarily blinded by bright sunlight streaming in behind the man. He entered and closed the door before Sandy recognized his captor. "Well if it isn't my old buddy Bob Jones," he said with contempt. "Where's my lawyer?"

"Where is Mrs. Slane," Jones asked matter of factly.

"None of your stinking business," Sandy spat back. "Where's my lawyer."

"There's a gentleman outside trained to make people talk. If I must send him in I will, distasteful as that would be for both of us. I'm sure you will tell him sooner or later so why not save yourself the pain and me the distress of hearing your screams."

His throat was dry and the tremble in his voice could not be masked out when Sandy replied, "Where's my lawyer?"

Jones shook his head a little sadly and walked to the door. He waved his hand and a very average looking man in his late forties walked into the small building. He carried a small black bag that was similar to a doctor's bag. Without comment he opened it and looked at Jones.

"We wish to know the location of Mrs. Slane," Jones told him. He turned to Sandy and said, "When you tell us we will verify your story and then put a painless bullet into your skull. Until we have her your every living moment will be agony. Please, tell me before this begins, where is she hiding."

"I just want my lawyer," Sandy answered.

The man with the black bag took a nod from Jones and waited until the agent had left. He then removed the left shoe and sock from Sandy's foot. He pulled from the bag a small pair of sheers and quickly clipped off his toe.

Sandy felt the pain blossom upward clear to his crotch. He stiffened his body and fought the scream rising in his throat. The torturer was busy lighting a small propane torch produced from the bag and he held the flame to the bleeding stump. Sandy's scream could be heard by the farthest government outpost over a mile away.

Jones was standing by his car trying to control his stomach. He kept a look of stone on his face as the screams came again and again from the small building. One young agent was sitting in his car with his hands clasped over his ears in a futile attempt to blot out the noise. Nearly an hour passed before the door opened and the torturer emerged, wiping blood from his hands. He walked up to Jones and quietly gave him an address.

"Give him morphine and keep him as comfortable as possible until we check this out. I'll give you a radio message to terminate him as soon as we know."

"Wouldn't it be safer to do it face to face?" the man asked. "Radio calls sometimes result in foulups."

Jones shook his head. "I don't want to keep him in that condition any longer than necessary. If I call you and say 'end it', that will be your key words."

—

"End it," the torturer repeated. "You're the boss. I'll be curious to know if this is a legitimate address."

"Why's that," Jones wondered.

"I cut off one toe at a time and then burned each stump to intensify the pain and stop him from bleeding to death. I took off all his fingers the same way and he still didn't talk until I went for his ears. I've never had one hold out that long."

Jones fought off the shudder and looked at the man like he was something less than human. "How do you do this job anyway? What makes you able to sleep at night and look at yourself in the mirror each morning."

The man smiled slightly and pointed his index finger at Jones. "Who ordered me to do it," he said and cackled dryly.

"I know," Jones countered. "That's why I asked. I haven't had a decent night's sleep in years."

Carolyn was beginning to worry. Sandy had told her he wouldn't give up until evening but she expected either a call or an early return. She began packing away the few things they had with them and found a gun between two of her blouses. She supposed Sandy had put it there, intending to pick it up before they left the motel. He certainly hadn't needed it when he left, because he had been armed like a guard at Fort Knox.

She put the gun on the bed and finished her packing. With nothing left to do she turned on the television set and sat in the room's one small chair. The show went on practically unnoticed as her attention remained glued to the door. Perhaps wishing would bring her man home sooner. Tension brought with it fatigue and Carolyn began to drift into sleep. She was awake just enough to feel the need to lie down but couldn't make the move out of the chair. Her half sleep was suddenly violently interrupted by a wood splintering slam against the motel door. A large piece of wood flew into her lap and immediately another hard blow was delivered against the door.

She sat upright and stared for a moment as a hand reached through a large hole in the door and fumbled for the lock. Her hand went to the gun on the bed and she pulled it into her hands just as the door flew open. Three men burst into the room as one, each carrying shotguns at waist level. Carolyn put both hands around the smooth grip of the gun and started to pull back the trigger when the first shotgun exploded. Her right chest took the load which collapsed her lung instantly. The second and third guns roared in unison and caught her face. The flesh dissolved down to almost pure bone and the pistol flew from her lifeless hands.

Fearing for their own personal safety each man fired twice more and almost literally tore her in half. They all froze in place for several moments as smoke from the gunpowder surrounded her body like a scene from a horror movie. The mood was broken when a fourth man, Bob Jones, burst into the room. He turned his head quickly and walked to the suitcases and money. He checked for identification and, finally satisfied that they had killed the right woman, went to the radio in his car.

"This is Jones," he said when the voice at the other end acknowledged him, "the two words are end it."

"Would you confirm sir, that your message is 'end it'," the voice replied.

"That is confirmed. Carry out your assignment immediately."

"Yes sir," said the voice and the radio went dead.

THIRTY FOUR

Brad called Stan Forth and requested an immediate appointment when he received news of P. Osgood Nash's death. Forth readily agreed and asked to come to the laboratory. Brad sent Leonard and Janet to the movies and asked Lois to join him.

They waited in the cage room of the lab, playing with some of the animals. Lois was her usual beautiful self while Brad suddenly realized he was feeling his age. Perhaps the time had come to begin the injections on himself.

"Darling, do you think the Secret Service killed Mr. Nash?" she asked.

He studied the back of her head for a moment before answering. She was bending down and scratching the ears of a calico cat. "I guess I really don't know what to think," he said. "It does seem odd that all these people are dead; Maywood, Wilson' and now Nash."

"What do you plan to tell this new agent, what's his name?" She stood up and the cat strolled away indifferently.

"Forth. Stan Forth. First of all I plan to demand to do an autopsy on Nash to see if he really died from a heart attack. I may be out of practice but I'm still a darn good doctor. If there was any drugs or funny business I intend to find it."

"What about going public with your research," she said. "Maybe you can pressure them into turning it loose."

"I think you're right," Brad agreed. "We know the government can blackmail me with Robin Slane and my human experiments but maybe the time has come to bluff a little bit. After all, they need me too."

"And we have a certain obligation to Leonard and Janet," she reminded him. "They have the right to our protection."

"I'm not sure what you mean," he replied. "I think they both know that they're likely to be exploited, but I don't believe there's a thing we can do about that."

"Oh I know, I guess I don't really know what I mean either. Maybe I just feel bad about it. They're nice people Brad. Is it fair to display them like freaks?"

"They are freaks in a way," he said. "They should be dead and here they are, youngsters. I think they both agree that's it's a fair trade."

"Hello."

They both jumped slightly and turned toward the front door of the lab. An extremely good looking man with a broad smile was walking toward them. Brad recovered quickly and held out his hand. "I'm Brad Richardson and this is my wife Lois. You must be Mr. Forth."

"You're almost right. It's Stan." He took Brad's hand and returned a firm grasp. "And Mrs. Richardson I'm also pleased to meet you." He nodded slightly at Lois.

"Please call us Brad and Lois," Brad said, still taken aback but charmed in spite of himself.

"Agreed," Forth said with an even broader smile. "Can we sit somewhere and chat for a while?"

"We're kind of cramped for space but let's go back to my office," Brad offered.

"Good. Please, after you," he said amicably and waved with a flourish.

The trio was soon settled in the small office with Brad in his customary seat behind his desk. "Stan, there are a few things we need to get out into the open."

"That's why I'm here," Forth answered with a smile. "I'm at your disposal."

"I'm going to be very blunt with you," Brad began. "Several people have died that knew the details of my research. I don't know if there was any foul play involved, but we're getting a little, no, a lot, worried."

"There have indeed been some tragedies," Forth agreed, "but truly just a matter of chance." He shook his head sadly. "Life is, as you are well aware Brad, very fragile. Even the promise of eternal youth doesn't preclude accidents."

"Would you be willing to let me do a detailed autopsy on Nash?"

"Absolutely, Forth agreed with no hesitation. "In fact we still have to learn the exact cause of his death. Shall we deliver the body here or would you prefer to use the University Hospital facility."

"Have him brought here," Brad decided.

"When shall I ask them to bring him in?" Forth inquired.

"How about tomorrow?" Brad said, his nerves singing like high tension wires. How far could this man be pushed?

"May I use your telephone?" Forth reached for the instrument in anticipation of approval.

"Of course."

The Secret Service man punched the buttons quickly and waited for a moment before saying, "This is Forth. Please transport Mr. Nash to Dr. Richardson's lab tomorrow morning." He paused a moment and then added, "Thank you." He hung the phone up and said to Brad, "The body will be here at nine A.M. tomorrow morning."

"Well, thank you very much," Brad replied with surprise. Perhaps he had been wrong about the government's motives.

"As I told you I am here to serve." Forth gave him a large smile that he hoped seemed genuine. "Obviously Uncle Sam has given you the impression that we're out to get you and that just isn't true. Certain security must be observed in a project of this magnitude."

"What about the searching of our home," Lois demanded. "Who gave you the right to do that?"

Forth leaned forward, the smile dissolving into a thin lipped scowl. "Someone has been in your home?"

"Several times," Brad injected. "I set subtle traps after I suspected it was happening and there is no question about it, someone had been looking for something in my home."

"That is totally inexcusable," Forth almost shouted, hitting the top of Brad's desk for emphasis, "and I intend to get some answers. You know, the thing that scares me is I can't believe Bob Jones would have ordered that."

"Who else could it have been," Lois asked, her tone betraying her suspicion.

"Do you folks realize the value of this research to a foreign government?" He leaned forward and raised his eyebrows for added effect. "The Soviets would do anything for your notes Brad."

Lois obviously did a complete about face as the logic struck home. "Of course, how blind could we have been." She looked at Brad in horror. "Why didn't we see that from the beginning?"

"I don't know," he admitted. "How would the Russians know about this when nobody else does?"

Forth gave him his best puzzled look. "If we had the answer to that maybe we'd know how they end up with half the top secret information our government creates. When I was a Marine serving at the El Salvador embassy a courier would bring a sealed pouch marked Top Secret about once a week. The local paper printed the contents of the pouch the same day it was delivered. We never did find the leak."

"Then you're saying the U.S. Government has not been searching my home or laboratory for several months," Brad asked.

"I will verify that we have not but I can say I truly believe we are not entering your premises without permission. Why would we be searching and what would we be looking for?"

"My research notes of course," Brad said, amazed that Forth was failing to see the obvious. "Why else do you think we were suspicious?"

"You know, I guess we're so innocent I missed the whole point," Forth said with a wry grin. "The last thing your government would want to do is the very

—

thing we're saying the enemies of our way of life would. Why steal your formula when you're going to make it available? The only reason we would want to do that is if you were trying to sell it to another government."

"Wait a minute." Brad shook his head as if trying to clear the confusion. "The government has been insisting that I turn my notes over before we make the project public. I presumed that the Secret Service took things into their own hands and decided to take my project."

"Doctor, you have discovered the single most important discovery in the history of modern medicine. Surely we're not going to jeopardize such a project by not being honest with you. We can give you some brilliant minds to help with the research, but by all means handle this in a way that's comfortable for you."

"P. Osgood Nash told me you were trying to steal it," Brad countered without much conviction.

"Mr. Nash was somewhat upset because he didn't feel we were keeping him involved, but frankly our interest is toward you Brad." Forth raised his index finger to his temple and added, "Maybe Mr. Nash was our leak to whoever has been searching your home."

"Perhaps you're right," Brad agreed. "Well, I'll feel better about all this after my autopsy."

"Fine, you take all the time you need."

"I also am still not willing to give up my notes until we have a public announcement of my discovery."

"No problem," Forth said, the broad smile returning to his handsome face. "I'll check with Washington and see if we can't give you a date for when that will happen. Is there anything else I can do for you?"

"One more thing," Brad said. "I've added a refinement to my formula that uses some chemicals that by themselves are harmless, but when they are mixed they're as dangerous as gasoline in the house. Unless I'm very cautious when I'm doing the mixing I could start a very serious fire."

"That does sound dangerous," Forth agreed. "How can I help?"

"You can get me a sprinkler system installed," Brad answered.

"How about a larger, more modern lab," Forth suggested. "We could move you in a matter of days."

"I appreciate that offer but I'm really comfortable here." Brad waved a hand at his surroundings. "This is kind of like home. Oh, I realize that when we go public we'll probably have to move into better quarters and maybe even go to a different city, but until that happens I want to stay here."

"Well, as the old saying goes, you're the doctor," Forth said with a chuckle. He accepted their laughter in return before standing to leave. "I hope we have a

—

better understanding of where we're going. The Secret Service is on your side. In fact, we'll assign some agents to watch your home and the lab for intruders."

"Should we have protection for ourselves and Leonard and Janet?" Lois inquired. "Maybe someone will try to kidnap us."

"I wasn't going to mention that because I didn't want to cause you any undue concern," Forth said consolingly, "but I've already decided to have a very quiet tail on each of you. Hopefully you'll never even notice that anyone's there."

"That's an excellent idea," Brad agreed, "and I think we do feel better about our whole situation now that we've talked." He stood and held his hand out to Forth who grasped it firmly. "Thank you for coming in to see us."

"Thank you Brad. You're an incredible man and your discovery will change the world." He turned to Lois and said, "It was a pleasure meeting you. May I say your husband is a most fortunate man."

She blushed and dropped her head slightly. "Thank you for the lovely compliment," she said.

"Well, I'll be on my way. I should think we could have a sprinkler system installed within two or three weeks if we get right on this."

"Good, the sooner the better," Brad said. "The mixture I'm using is downright scary it's so dangerous."

"We'll get right on it," Forth reinforced. He backed out of the office and waved. "Call me if I can be of any help."

"We will," Brad promised. "And thank you." He waited until he heard the front door close before turning to Lois. "What do you think?"

She shook her head and shrugged. "I guess I really don't know. I was so sure before. Maybe we could have been wrong."

"Well, my examination of Nash should help answer some questions. If he really died from a heart attack I guess I'd be inclined to believe Forth. Let's save our judgment until then."

"Fair enough," she agreed, willing to stop thinking about this whole mess for a while. "I just wish this whole thing were over."

He pulled her to him and kissed her warmly. "It won't be much longer I'm sure. We'll just stick to our guns about keeping my formula secret until we go public. Maybe it's just as well that we're waiting, because I've come up with another major breakthrough."

Lois pushed away from his embrace to enable her to look at her husband's face. "You mean there's even more to this?"

He took her hands and squeezed tightly in his excitement of sharing his discovery. "I've been giving Janet injections of distilled water for over a month."

"I don't understand," Lois admitted. "Are you saying there's something about water that affects her?"

182

"No, no" he said, shaking his head enthusiastically. "What I'm saying is that Janet no longer seems to need the formula. She has become physically a woman in her twenties and it's holding."

"Do you think it's permanent?" Lois couldn't believe what she was hearing.

"I don't know. That's the trouble with research, there's so many unanswered questions. She could age normally and become old in another fifty years. She could get old overnight, or she may stay young permanently. I truly don't know what will happen."

"What about Leonard?" Lois asked.

"He has still needed the injections," he answered. "I think, however, that I may have the answer for him too. That's why I ordered these chemicals. They're dangerous to work with but I think I have worked out the formula to make him young without future injections too."

"Then when you finish mixing this batch of formula the next injection will take care of Leonard."

"Permanently," he assured her.

"Listen," Lois said, holding up her hand for silence. "Did you hear something?"

Brad walked toward the hallway that led to the front door of the laboratory. The door was closed and he saw no one. He went into the kitchen and turned on the light, taking a quick visual survey of the room. Everything seemed to be in its proper place so he turned out the light and went to the outside door. He hesitated for a moment and then quickly pulled the door open. It flew open so forcefully that he almost fell backward, cursing softly at his constant forgetfulness that the sticking door had long ago been replaced. He looked outside and saw nothing.

"Did you see anything?"

He jumped and barely managed to avoid a yelp of surprise. Lois was two steps behind him. "For crying out loud Lois you nearly gave me a heart attack," he complained. "Here I am looking for Jack the Ripper and you sneak up behind me."

"Well, I was scared in there by myself," she whined. "I didn't mean to startle you."

He closed the door with a slightly trembling hand and blew out a deep breath of air. "Oh well, it doesn't make any difference because you must have been hearing things. I didn't see a thing."

"I could have sworn," she began.

"Well just forget it because no one was there," he interrupted. "Now, let's get to work. You can help me get Leonard's serum prepared."

—

183

THIRTY FIVE

Leonard's head was threatening to explode. He had promised Janet that he would control the urge to destroy 'outsiders' until their position was more secure. She still had the urge but had been able to keep it under control, and this somehow made him even angrier. He wanted to taste death so badly that he felt like a heroin addict needing a fix. The need became so unbearable that he decided to ask Brad for help. Perhaps some change in the formula could take away the horrible pain between his eyes. Janet had gone shopping and he felt totally alone with the problem.

The laboratory was a short distance from their apartment and he had waited until he could stand no more. Several people passed him as he walked toward the lab and Leonard could practically smell the warm blood in their bodies. He hurried his pace and arrived at the lab within minutes.

He walked into the small entry way and heard voices in the cage room. Leonard closed the door and began to move toward the voices when something he heard caused him to stop abruptly.

"Then when you finish mixing this batch of formula the next injection will take care of Leonard," he heard Janet say.

"Permanently," Brad said.

Incredible as it was, Leonard heard them plotting to kill him. Perhaps they had found out about their thirst for blood, but if that were true why weren't they talking about Janet too? He considered walking into the room and killing them both. He wanted blood so badly he could have bathed in it, but perhaps he should talk to Janet before he acted. His head hurt so bad and it was so hard to think . . . He moved closer to the sound of their voices and bumped into a stack of empty cages in the hallway. His lightning reflexes stopped them from crashing to the floor but there was some noise.

"Listen, did you hear something?"

Leonard hastily tiptoed to the door and quietly let himself out. He ran around to the side of the building and hid for several minutes before heading back toward his apartment.

The pounding did not lessen as he waited for Janet and he finally realized something had to be done to give him release. He left the apartment and walked across the street to the late model car that had taken up fairly constant residence at the curb. A man was sitting behind the wheel, surrounded by magazines and junk food. He obviously was planning a lengthy stay.

Leonard tapped on the window and the man rolled it down with a puzzled look on his face. "You're the Secret Service guy that's watching out for my welfare aren't you?" he demanded.

"Yes sir I am," the agent agreed. "You really shouldn't be talking to me you know because I don't want to blow my cover."

"That won't make any difference," Leonard replied with a smile.

"I'm afraid my boss wouldn't agree with you," the agent reasoned. "He'd be pretty upset if he knew this was happening."

"Well, I guess you just don't understand what I'm getting at here," Leonard said, "because you aren't going to care when you're dead."

The man frowned and looked warily at this strange fellow with a foolish grin on his face. "What are you talking abo . . . ."

Leonard's hand moved so fast it appeared as a blur to the agent's eyes. The blink reflex didn't even shut his eyelids before an index and middle finger thrust into them and buried themselves into his brain. Leonard paused for a moment with his fingers in the agent's eye sockets as far as they could go and watched the dead man's body twitch. He finally curved his fingers down and easily pulled off the front of the man's face. It came off with a cracking, tearing sound like glue pulling away from a piece of cardboard.

The pain in his forehead eased immediately to a tolerable ache as he wiped his gory hand on the sleeve of the dead man's shirt and then pushed the body over on the car seat. He knew Janet would be furious and didn't particularly want to face her right now. The decision concerning Brad and Lois had to be his.

He felt good, almost high on himself, as he walked back to the lab. The decisions had been made, the proverbial die had been cast, and Leonard was content with the world. The doctor and his wife must die, their punishment for plotting to destroy him. After it was over he would pick up Janet and they would go away, just leave this whole disgusting bunch of 'outsiders'. He would make Brad give him the formula and he would make the formula for them. His ravaged mind told him that it couldn't be that hard to do if he just had the formula. As his head began to pound again, harder and harder, he began to see how clear it all was.

Leonard took his time reaching the lab. He wanted to think it through, decide how to approach this. He probably would have to hurt them first to make Brad give up the formula; at least he hoped that was the way it would be. He walked into the coolness of the building and stopped to scratch behind the ears of a laboratory dog that met him at the door. The animal followed him as he moved on, hunting Brad and Lois. They were working intently in the small operating room that housed a gas fed burner system commonly used by chemists.

A large container stood over four burners which were keeping the contents just under the boiling point.

Leonard watched them work for a few moments, their interest so tightly drawn toward the liquid that his presence went undetected. Brad was monitoring the temperature on a large thermometer and kept adjusting the flame on the burners. Lois recorded statistics as he reported them to her.

"My but you two look busy," Leonard began.

Brad jumped slightly as he was pulled from his concentration and glanced up at his test subject. He smiled and said "Hi Leonard. I'm glad you're here. You can help us for a few minutes."

"Oh yea? What are you doing?" he asked.

"Preparing an injection for you. I think this one will do things the others haven't" Brad said almost absently.

"I'll bet," Leonard agreed sarcastically with a sideways smile. His head screamed in pain as the pounding intensified. "What can I do to help?"

Brad adjusted the flame on the burners again before answering. "Lois, tell me when exactly two minutes pass, then we have to elevate the heat again. Leonard, I'd like you to look outside and make sure no one is coming, then come back in and lock the door."

"Why don't you want anyone coming in," Leonard asked. He knew he was talking too loudly, but his head was thundering so hard he could hardly hear himself speak.

"I'm going to get my notes to check some formulas and we've got to make sure no one sees where they are hidden. You know, security and all that."

"Sure," Leonard agreed. "I'll be glad to help." He left the room with an odd smile. This was going to be too easy. He was going to be handed the formula on a silver platter.

"Brad," Lois whispered as soon as Leonard was out of earshot, "do you want him to know where your notes are kept?"

"He won't," Brad whispered back. "I'll have them in a few seconds and he won't even see me get them. Besides, he'll be good protection if someone tries to take them." He hurried to the cage room and returned with his notebook before Leonard had come back inside.

"Did you close the floor again?" Lois asked.

"Yes, and I pulled the cages back in place. Leonard hasn't even come back in the building."

Leonard walked around the lab, looking for anyone who did not appear to belong. Fortunately Brad had mentioned this precaution, as Leonard had not thought of it. Even better was the fact that he could take the notes after disposing of them and duplicate the formula at his leisure. Janet would surely be proud of him.

He went back inside and locked the door, checking it to insure that the latch was secure. Brad and Lois were almost as he had left them except that Brad was now holding a thick leather notebook. He was turning the burners back up and glancing from the book to the temperature gauge monitoring the liquid.

Lois noticed him first and smiled. "Did you see anything suspicious?" she asked.

"No, not a thing, and I locked the door when I came back in," Leonard said.

"Good, thank you," Brad added. "Give me a few minutes here and I'll have your injection ready. We have to make three gallons of the stuff to get the proper mix for one shot but that's the way it works. When we go public with the research I won't have to pour it down the drain to help protect my formula."

He referred to a page in his notebook and poured a small container of powder into the liquid. "Now Lois, this is where we get critical. Help me watch the temperature as we don't dare let this stuff start to boil."

She nodded and lay down the clipboard to watch the temperature even more closely. "You're two degrees from boil now."

"Okay," he answered. "We have come awfully close for the heat to set it properly. It's tricky but right now the only thing that works."

"Why are you going to all this trouble," Leonard asked. "Are you killing me on your own and have to tell the government people it was an accident? That must be it or you'd just use a poison."

Brad looked up with a puzzled expression. "What in heavens sake are you talking about Leonard?"

"I came in earlier when you two were talking about killing me," he shouted. The pounding in his forehead was erupting like a volcano. "You must have found out about the others, is that it?"

"Leonard, I don't understand," Brad began. He took a step toward his test subject, intending to place his hand on Leonard's shoulder.

Leonard grabbed Brad's arm with both hands and twisted hard. A large snapping and tearing sound occurred as bone, muscle, and tendons tore and splintered like hollow reeds. The fabric of Brad's shirt gave away and his arm fell to the floor, torn completely away from his body. He looked at it dumbly, as if he couldn't believe the separated limb could be his.

Lois screamed and Brad gave her a puzzled look as shock refused to let his brain register pain or accept the knowledge of what had just happened. Blood began pumping out of the arteries in his shoulder as his heart kept doing its assigned task of moving blood. He tried to ask Lois why her blouse was turning red as his blood squirted at her, but somehow he couldn't speak. The room was spinning crazily and his world was turning black.

—

Brad's head turned toward his murderer as Leonard grabbed a handful of his hair and forced Brad to look into his eyes. "Bye bye Doc," he sneered and smashed his fist into Brad's face, cracking his skull in several places and knocking out three teeth. Brad's system, long pampered and cared for to prolong his life, shut down and he plunged into death.

Leonard pushed the lifeless body to the floor and turned toward Lois, who continued to scream at the top of her lungs. He grasped her throat, instantly eliminating the noise from her mouth. Her windpipe collapsed from the pressure and Lois' eyes began to bulge. Her tongue distended and pushed its way past her lips, blood dripping from the tip as her teeth punctured the soft flesh. Tears flowed from her bugged eyes and her body began to involuntarily twitch.

Laughing with glee, Leonard made sure he looked into her eyes until they were completely lifeless. He wanted her to take his face with her to the other side. So involved was he with the killing, he failed to notice that the formula was boiling. He shook the lifeless body like a rag doll and then quickly flung her across the room.

Lois' body hit the boiling formula almost dead center, knocking the container over onto the laboratory table. One of the burners was snuffed out when the container landed over the opening, momentarily shutting off the air supply. The other three burners were splashed with the liquid and the entire room promptly exploded.

Leonard didn't even have the chance to be surprised as the flames engulfed his body. He attempted to scream, but when he inhaled to accomplish this he took flames deep into his lungs. Within seconds the flesh was falling from his body in great chunks. He was dead before he hit the floor.

The fire spread quickly to the rest of the laboratory, burning screeching laboratory animals who were helplessly trapped. The binder with Brad's notes curled as it burned, the pages turning a charred black and crumbling to dust. Within fifteen minutes the only thing left standing was the cement block walls.

THIRTY SIX

A startled Secret Service agent assigned to watch the facility called for the fire department. He broke down the door in an attempt to get inside but was driven back by the smoke and flames. Actually, he inadvertently helped feed the inferno with oxygen by opening the door. The swiftness of the fire surprised even the fire department as they found there was little to do by the time they arrived. The fire had simply consumed all combustible materials.

Forth arrived with a crew of experts to sift the ashes for signs of the notebook. The only remains of the formula for the answer to the elimination of old age was a small scrap of burned leather notebook. Hurried tests and the observation of the agent who had been on lookout determined that the remains of the three bodies were Brad, Lois and Leonard. He was beside himself at the loss, and did not even react when he received the news that a car held the remains of another Secret Service agent.

Forth put all available personnel on the streets looking for Janet, she being the only key remaining for study. He wasn't too worried about finding her, because she would simply go home soon. The thing he dreaded most was his next duty, which was notifying Floyd Devoe in Washington.

Janet decided to go to the laboratory after her appointment. She had been careful to leave without being noticed by the constant watchful eyes of the Secret Service. She hoped that her news wouldn't be too upsetting to Brad and, maybe even more importantly, Leonard.

She noticed that something must have happened on Campus as the whole area was swarming with police, fire and rescue units. She saw the smoke billowing up and her stomach began to sink. Hopefully her sense of direction was wrong, but that had to be very close to the laboratory.

Circling around to permit herself an approach to the rear, she finally was able to see the lab. Her immediate reaction was to run toward the building to check on possible injuries to her friends if, in fact, they had even been there. Something caused her to pause for a moment and, call it intuition if you will, she turned and walked quickly away.

—

THIRTY SEVEN

Forth and Jones spent several frantic days trying to locate Janet. In the months that followed no clues were found to bring them any closer to the answer. Forth finally accepted the burning of the notes, as no other explanation seemed to make sense. They had literally torn the inside of Brad's house apart searching for another copy but nothing had turned up.

Strangely enough the two men became friends, perhaps because they shared the same fear of Washington. Many late night sessions were spent trying to determine what to do. During one such session both men were drinking heavily. Forth looked at his new friend with bleary eyes and raised his glass before drinking.

"What was that for," Jones wondered.

"That was a toast to the end of two great careers," Forth replied. "I figure it's just a matter of time."

"Until what," Jones asked with real concern in his voice.

"We'll be reassigned to the North Pole or some such place. We blew it Buddy, messed up. Screwed up. Our old boss Devoe can't ignore that too long."

"Well, I guess it could be worse," Jones said with relief. "Look at how some of the people involved in this thing turned out."

"Yea, like that cop."

"I don't think I'll ever forget the screams." Jones shuddered, sloshing some of his drink on the floor. He turned a tortured look to his companion. "Stan, is this what our service is all about? Reaching the objective no matter what the cost?"

"Of course it is," Forth answered. "We're just soldiers without uniforms. If a hill needs taken we take it. No failure or exception is acceptable."

The men were quiet for some time, lost in their individual thoughts and alcohol haze. Jones finally broke the silence. "Did you hear about that police captain?"

"You mean Salinski."

"Yea. The only other person outside the Secret Service left alive that knew about this project. Do you think Devoe had anything to do with that?"

Forth shook his head. "No, I don't think so. The guy just had an automobile accident, that's all. It happens every day."

"I suppose you're right," Jones agreed reluctantly. "Sure are a lot of dead people though."

"And basically for nothing," Forth said morosely. "I suppose we'll be cellmates in hell for this one."

"Probably. We sure deserve it you know."

"That we do," Forth agreed. "Look, I don't know about you but I'm too drunk and tired to go home. I'm just going to sleep right here in my desk chair."

"I'm with you," Jones replied. "I don't think I can even move."

They didn't speak after that, even though neither man slept for a long time. Dawn, conscience, and noise in the receptionist area awoke them, stiff from spending too many hours in a chair and hung over.

"Is it nine already?" Forth asked himself more than Jones who was trying to get his aching body to move from the chair.

"No, it's only about six, unless my watch has stopped," he replied.

"Then let's see who's here," Forth suggested, still a little bit drunk.

The office door opened before the two men could react and in strolled Mutt and Jeff. They stood by the door quietly and starred at the squinting, miserable looking pair.

"What do you guys want," Forth demanded, trying to keep his stomach from rejecting its contents.

Jones turned a stark white. He knew the purpose of their visit. "Devoe sent you didn't he." It was a statement, not a question.

The small man nodded his head in agreement. "No one above Devoe knows about this whole project," he explained. "Mr. Devoe thought that to protect his secret it would be better this way."

"Wait a minute," Forth objected. "If we're dead how about you two? Won't Devoe have to get rid of you too?"

The small man smiled thinly. "We've killed so many people our silence is guaranteed. Goodness, Mr. Devoe could hang us a hundred different ways. Besides, he may need our services at other times in the future."

Jones started to cry but Forth chose to react. He pulled open a desk drawer and grabbed for his gun. The big man placed three bullets into Forth's chest before his hand touched the gun. A silencer permitted a small pop as each shell burst in its chamber. Three more well placed shots took the life of Bob Jones. The small man checked for a pulse in each man and, satisfied with the result, motioned his partner to the door.

THIRTY EIGHT

Janet sat outside the small apartment building and enjoyed the Sunday morning sunshine. Life could have been better in Calgary, Canada where she had settled, but safety had its price. She worked as a waitress in a small restaurant and tips were usually good, especially when she smiled and kidded with the patrons.

The headaches never came now, and along with this relief was the loss of desire to kill 'outsiders'. She worried that her youth would dissolve over night without the injections, but thus far her fears were unfounded.

Fortunately Canadians were a friendly and yet not a curious people. She had never been asked for identification or any proof of who she was. Some day, however, she would want to obtain identity cards in her new name, Jane Seymour.

She heard faint crying from within her apartment and reluctantly pushed herself out of the spot in the sun. Opening the front door she heard the tiny voice more clearly and hurried to the bedroom. A baby in its crib was crying, red faced and angry from the discomfort of a soiled diaper.

Janet had never told anyone that she suspected being pregnant. That awful day when the laboratory had burned she had not been shopping but instead visited a clinic for the results of a pregnancy test. Excited and a little frightened by the news, she was hurrying to tell Brad, wondering if she or the baby would be affected by the injections she had been taking. The building was destroyed and something told her to stay out of sight until details were known.

News stories that evening told of three bodies discovered in the rubble, giving her the answer she had hoped would not be true. Janet knew she was all that was left and researchers would want to study her and the baby. That could not happen. No one must be able to make a freak of her child.

The baby stopped crying and reached out to his mother. Janet discarded the soiled diaper and drew her child to her bosom. Already he showed signs of being different. Not in looks but in actions. He stood up at three weeks of age and routinely broke slats from his crib when he became angry. Janet had tested his strength with pieces of metal, which he bent with little effort.

Some day he would have to face the world. Some day when he was a little older, but not now. Let him be a child for a while. She took the baby outside with her to enjoy the sun. They sat quietly in the warmth, each enjoying the sleepy feeling that overcame them. Janet turned her small son in her lap so she could look into his eyes. Their gaze locked in a special understanding way that only mothers and their children share. "You already know how special you are don't you little one," she cooed. "What will happen with your life? I'll bet you're going to be a great man. Maybe even change the course of history."

The baby just smiled.

THE END

.